ELIJAH

A NOVEL

FRANK REDMAN

INSPIRE PUBLISHING

ARLINGTON

Praise

"If your destiny ever requires a walk through hell, make sure to take Elijah Raven with you. Both lighthearted and horrifying, Redman's debut novel stares down evil through the eyes of the best kind of hero: one who has survived it and won't leave anyone to suffer the same. ELIJAH is a thrilling page-turner that won't let you down."
> — Erin Healy, author of THE BAKER'S WIFE and STRANGER THINGS

"Captivating, funny, suspenseful, heart-wrenching, believable, simply wow! Redman straps you into a front row seat of the protag's mind and sends you on a non-stop ride guaranteed to entertain."
> — Claude Bouchard, USA Today Bestselling Author of the Vigilante Series

"I'm in awe of Frank's voice. It's captivating."
> — Lynn Rush, New York Times & USA Today bestselling author of the Violet Night Trilogy

"Frank Redman is an author of startling insight and wonderful expression who brings to life his characters in such a way as to make you forget you are reading. They are living and breathing alongside you, a startling achievement for a new novelist. I highly anticipate reading more of Redman's work in the future. His is a voice that will shine on for many years to come."
> — Luke Romyn, USA Today and Amazon #1 bestselling author

"A strong first outing from Frank Redman who introduces us to Elijah Raven, a winsome Everyman who just happens to communicate with animals and has an uncanny knack for getting into trouble. Humor, romance, and supernatural intrigue follow in this fun, fast-paced novel. Looking forward to more from Frank Redman!"
> — Mike Duran, author of THE GHOST BOX and SAINT DEATH

"A tech-savvy hero with the ability to hear animals, a dog obsessed with Cheetos, and a cat with a British accent... what's not to love? Filled with action, sardonic wit and a lovable cast of furry characters, you'll cheer for ELIJAH--a story of redemption in the midst of darkness, of saving those who can't save themselves."
> — Tosca Lee, New York Times bestselling author of THE PROGENY

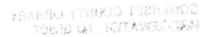

"ELIJAH gives us a memorable main character, a cause to cheer for, and one of the best dogs I've found in fiction. What a pleasure to read this first novel, and here's to much success for Elijah and his creator."

— Joe Finder, New York Times bestselling author of GUILTY MINDS

.

Copyright

Dedication

For God,

Thank you for keeping me around to write ELIJAH

For Sheri,

Thank you for saying yes

For Dad,

Thank you for believing in me,

Even when I didn't believe in myself

Chapter One

After finishing a late dinner, I stood and stretched and welcomed thoughts of going to bed.

But then I heard, or *perceived*, a voice that froze me. I glanced around my apartment and noticed a small, dark form outside the glass door to the balcony.

I turned on the light and slid open the door.

The voice hit me again, this time more clearly.

Danger. Girl. Hurry.

I looked down and saw the yellow eye-shine of a solid black cat reflecting at me. Some animals are wordier than others, but this cat's quiet anxiety was compelling.

The cat turned and darted down the steps, assuming I'd follow.

I'd give anything to trade my strange gift for musical genius or an eye for art. Or even to exist with no gifts at all. I *hate* being drawn into trouble that is not my own, risking my minding-my-own-business safety to go chasing animals out in the night and straight into danger.

But that's exactly what I did.

I ran down the steps, two-three at a time, and jumped the last several to try to keep up with the speedy feline. I lost the cat in darkness between streetlights, but kept running anyway as he emerged into light under the next lamp. I ran blind in those same patches of darkness.

A girl screamed.

I dared to run faster.

We crested a small hill and I saw a car in the middle of the street with the driver door open, the interior light splashing onto the pavement. Two shadows moved frantically by the sedan, muffled screams could be heard.

As I got closer, the rear door opened.

A large man was trying to force a smaller figure into the backseat.

Lyndsey Grant. An eighteen year-old senior at my old high school. She was a freshman when I graduated. Cute and petite. She wore yellow running shorts and a matching sports bra. Although small she put up a fight, trying to use whatever leverage she could muster.

The black cat was nowhere to be seen.

The sounds of the commotion and the perp's loud grunts masked my footfalls. He had managed to get a bandana around Lyndsey's mouth, using it like a dog leash to pull her to the car.

I came up quickly, undetected.

Four feet away, I launched myself at the kidnapper, knowing it would cause Lyndsey to fall hard to the ground, but expecting the man to reflexively let go of her to break *his* fall.

I'm 6'0" and wiry. Although the man was bigger than me, you'd have to be a mountain to stay on your feet when 190 lbs. hits you at full speed unexpectedly.

He wasn't a mountain.

He yelled, let go of Lyndsey, and tried to turn and stick his arms out.

But when I dove for him, I wrapped his arms up. He crashed hard, face-first against the pavement with my full weight landing on top of him. His head bounced off the street and my

1

nose bounced off his head. Blood flowed. Having experienced the pain of a broken nose before, I knew it wasn't broken.

Lyndsey tumbled to the street, but then got to her feet, grabbing at the cloth in her mouth. The perp didn't move. Not dead. Just unconscious.

I pushed up roughly from the man and wiped the blood from my face.

Lyndsey ran to me and squeezed hard, sobbing heavily.

Between gasps she managed to say, "Thank…you…Elijah." She repeated her thanks a few more times, gaining more control of herself with each repetition, and then let go.

My nose had stopped bleeding.

She tried to wipe her face with her hands but had little success. She didn't have anything else practical to use. Even though my shirt was bloody and sweaty, I handed it over.

She smiled meekly. "Thank you. You're bleeding."

I waved it off. "It's nothing. Already stopped."

She looked at the man on the ground with disdain, then walked over and kicked him hard four times in the ribs.

In semi-consciousness, he managed to curl a little.

"Feel better?"

She thought about it for a moment and shook her head, then kicked him three more times, grunting, "Now… I…do," with each kick.

"When he wakes up, he's going to hate breathing." I ran out of my apartment so quickly I forgot my cell. "You have a cell phone?"

She looked down at herself. "These shorts have no pockets."

"You might—"

She raised a hand to stop me. "Save it. I learned my lesson, don't worry."

I looked at the perp, loathing the thought of having to dig through his clothes for a phone. I instead went to the car, hoping to find a prize. "Nice." A cellphone. I called 911, gave them the scoop, wiped my prints off the phone, and tossed it back into the still-running car. I didn't care if it ran out of gas.

I looked at Lyndsey. "On the way."

"You know you probably saved my life. Is there anything I can do?"

I shook my head. "You don't owe me anything." I smiled. "What were you doing over here anyway?"

My uncle and I live at the far end of the neighborhood. The only things behind our street are trees.

"Trying a new running route. I got bored."

"Privacy."

She furrowed her brow. "What?"

"You can give me privacy. I'd really like not to be interrogated by the police or anyone else. So, I'll go hide over beside that house and watch until the police arrive in case Mr. Bunghole decides to wake up."

She smiled. "Okay, I can do that."

"You can claim a stranger helped and took off. Or, hell, just tell them it was all you." I gave her a hug. She squeezed painfully tight. "You okay?"

She nodded. "I'll be fine. Thank you. I'll never forget this."

2

She handed me my shirt and I took off just as flashing red and blue lights reflected on the trees.

Chapter Two

I was ten when I ran away from home. Twelve years later, I realize how crazy that was. I mean, what did I expect to accomplish with all the wisdom gained in ten years of life? Where was I going to go? I didn't have a clue.

I wasn't even smart enough to *ask* those questions.

I ran away because my best friend, Billy, told me to. Right before he was killed.

He saved my life.

Those are painful memories, even now, but I'm sure they'll come out as I get used to putting my thoughts on paper.

I was with my parents until then, but they weren't really people. At least not in the sense of emotionally stable individuals. Especially my father. A demon straight out of Hell. Beelzebub taking a spin on Earth in the form of a human.

Sounds harsh. You may think I'm exaggerating. Trust me, I'm not. I know I'll have to earn trust with only these written words, but I am confident that before this is finished, I will have done so.

He's dead now. May Satan have mercy on him.

As for my poor mother, she was powerless to save herself from the man, let alone save me or either of my two siblings. Her husband corrupted even her mothering instinct. My Uncle Joe told me she actually tried to be a good mother. Mom, as I remember her, was always strung out on crack, though then I didn't know the difference between being strung out and being in a coma. Now she's just dead.

I'll make sure these writings won't be all grim and heavy. In fact, Uncle Joe advised that I make a point to *not* be heavy-handed, but instead to tell the story in a lighthearted style. "People like fluffy waffles," he told me. "Not manhole covers."

Bad things have happened, yes. Strange things. That said, much of life is what you make of it. I choose to be happy. Not because I have to, but because I can.

Happiness is a choice, not a circumstance.

My name is Elijah Raven. Growing up, kids called me "The Bird," usually followed quickly with a gesture involving the middle finger and peals of laughter.

I live in Fort City, a medium-size town in northeast Texas. Triple-digit temperatures are common most of the year. It is hot outside. I don't like heat. I stay inside. Self-awareness and problem-solving are a great combo.

My hair is black, and looks even darker compared to my very *un*tanned skin. That whole staying-inside thing plays a factor. I have bright hazel eyes, which I'm told change from blue to green to grey depending on what I'm wearing.

There's a Bible story about an Old Testament prophet named Elijah. God told him to hide and He'd have ravens feed him. The birds brought Elijah meat and bread in the morning and evening. Now think about that for a moment: I can see how the birds got meat. Ravens feed on carrion, small mammals, lizards... But I don't understand how they baked the bread.

Uncle Joe said my mother named me Elijah. There wasn't a choice in the Raven part, my born surname. But there are multiple ironies in being named Elijah Raven. I sometimes think my name came from a Higher Source, for three reasons. First, I didn't know people could come up with names while in a crack comma—I mean coma. Second, I didn't think Mom knew what a

Bible was. Third, when taking into consideration my gift, the name bestowed on me before my birth seems to be prophecy itself.

My gift? First, I ask that you clear your mind of what you've seen in movies where people move things by thinking about it, bend spoons, start fires with their minds, and other such psychic phenomenon.

Animals talk to me. I don't mean they suddenly master the English language, develop vocal cords and a mouth capable of synthesizing human speech, and then tell me what they had for dinner. Well, I guess sometimes they *do* tell me what they had for dinner, but that's beside the point.

The best way I can describe it is to call it telepathy. Dogs don't actually talk. But I *hear* their thoughts. Animals seem to know that I can understand them. They *project* words, and in the case of more intelligent animals, such as dogs, even phrases.

For most of my life it's something I've avoided with all of my heart.

One might think it would be cool to communicate with animals. At times it is. But many times, the things I hear are bad. Real bad.

I'm not saying your neighbor's poodle drops f-bombs. I'm saying animals *see* things. They *know* what's going on, even when they are typically powerless to convey that awareness to humans. They see horrible things like murder, rape, abuse…

I'm still struggling with the "gift." It's more like a curse. That's why I'm writing this. Uncle Joe said if I write it all out, it will help me come to terms with it. I'm not so sure, but we made a deal.

Believe it or not, there's already a documented precedent for this kind of thing, a case even more bizarre. In the Bible, a donkey talked out loud to its master in the Book of Numbers, chapter 22. That donkey actually *did* use human speech, though I doubt it was English. Verse 28.

So, does this mean that God is making animals project their thoughts to me? Hell if I know (no offense, God). But it does require faith in something unknown, something unbelievable. Since God, who created animals and humans, with some of those animals—and humans—being pretty freaky (no offense, God), isn't it even slightly possible to suppose He could make other weirdness happen?

I fully recognize that I have an amazing gift, even if it feels more like a curse. I'm still trying to figure out why me. I suppose I'm expected to do something good with it, to help people. Sometimes I succeed.

Yet other than this odd talent, there are many people with backgrounds similar to mine. Kids abused by their parents, taken away by authorities, placed in children's homes, abused, bounced around foster homes, abused. I've known a few of these kids while they were alive. Sadly, I've known some who are now dead. My brother and sister among them.

Not all foster homes are bad. Some are wonderful and save children. I've just been unlucky at a few places.

So the math is a family of five, four gone, one left. Both parents and two siblings. How is that possible? Here's a spoiler: it has to do with my demon-father.

The very idea that a man possessed by such pure, concentrated evil could be the same man that brought me into this world makes me want to revolt against the slightest recognition, not to mention the acceptance, that there is a God. To believe a person could be so completely devoid of moral character, be a black hole that destroyed all goodness around it, is further proof against the existence of God.

Yet, despite the damning evidence that was my father, evidence that has played a major role in my life, I believe the contrary.

Faith is a funny thing.

This is the last time I will refer to him with a term as intimate as *father*. I only do so now as the word is an immediate definition of my genealogy. Going forward, he will be referenced by his first name, Allister.

As for what happened to my mother, she died after Allister gave her some bad drugs.

And Allister? I killed him.

Chapter Three

Thursday is the first day of my weekly shift at Buy City, the cleverly named department store in our fine town of Fort City.

I woke up in my apartment above Uncle Joe's garage, originally designed to be servants' quarters.

Uncle Joe is a famous psychologist who's written several self-help books. Believing that writing my experiences would be therapeutic, he made a deal with me: If I'd write, he'd give me a place to live.

Deal.

I love books. The children's homes I lived in had great libraries. People do a wonderful job of donating books to orphanages and the like. Books were my flight to grand adventure, mystery, and escape. Old books, new books, it didn't make a difference. Suspense, thrillers, scifi, fantasy… I even read scary stories. But no graphic violence. I've seen enough in real life. I had no need—or desire—to feed my imagination with images conjured by violence-addicted novelists. And no romance. Bleh.

I didn't know I had a famous uncle until recently because he and my mother despised each other. Uncle Joe said each year he would send money for Christmas. On one of those occasions when talking to Mom, who was probably high, she told him he didn't send enough. He discovered Mom and Allister were using the cash for drugs. He stopped funding their habit. She cut him off.

After that, my parents were poor by choice, spending everything they had on drugs.

Drugs will make you do anything. I mean anything. Even selling your kids. Or killing them.

I've seen it.

When no longer a "child of the state" and instead on my own, I stumbled upon a book written by Uncle Joe and that lead to me finding him after searching on the Internet. He didn't know I was the only one in my family still alive.

Now I live in the aforementioned apartment. He has a very nice house. I could live in one of the rooms in the main house, but we both recognize I need space.

I also don't have a free ride, nor would I want it. I've seen what money does to people. To some, money itself is an addiction. To others, it's a means to fulfill addictions. I don't want the temptation of having everything given to me and to never have to work for anything.

So, I work as a computer repair technician at Buy City, which enables me to pay rent and buy Heinz ketchup, among other life-sustaining necessities. I also do some IT stuff on the side, like ethical hacker stuff.

Don't laugh, ethical hacking is big business. I'm not at the level where it's big business for me, mind you, but there are some consultants and consulting firms who have major influence with, *minor* entities like the New York Stock Exchange or the Pentagon.

An ethical hacker is employed by the US government, for example, to attempt to hack into a sector of the government's network environment. If the hacker succeeds, he or she can then assist the government's IT personnel to secure the vulnerability. It's the good guys trying to rob the bank before the bad guys get the cash. Only, the good guys leave all the money behind if they successfully break in.

At my level, I'm mostly hired to do things like hack into residential wireless networks and then close security holes, so that cheap neighbors can't piggyback on my clients' Internet connectivity.

The tech job is fun because it gives me an opportunity to fix people's computer problems. I can't fix people, so this is an outlet. Plus, I don't have to talk much to them. Customers engage the customer-service reps at the counter, who then get a rundown of the technical difficulties the computer, or customer, is experiencing. But don't call them reps. At Buy City, they are called hostesses, or hosts, as the case may be. Said hostess (my preferred gender) then enlightens me on what I, the PC butler, must service.

At least I don't have to wear a tux. Just a business-casual uniform, which consists of black slacks, a long-sleeved bright-blue dress shirt, and a matching black-and-blue diagonally-striped tie.

The computer job also keeps me away from animals. I've yet to see a Doberman bring in his Macbook.

Being December, the store was decked out in holiday cheer. Boughs of holly were all over the place, not just the halls. Garland wrapped the columns, giant wreaths hung from the ceiling, Christmas lights danced everywhere. Every department had its own tree. Items offered by that department were displayed as unwrapped gifts underneath. Christmas cheer was in the air! Buy, buy, buy!

Though the decorations were excessive, the place did look festive, and there was an excitement that only Christmas could bring. Some of the hosts and hostesses wore elf hats, with lots of smiles to go around.

And, excellent music danced in our ears. Frank Sinatra sang "Silver Bells," Dean Martin crooned "I've Got My Love to Keep Me Warm," even some slightly off-key Sammy Jr.

I'm a Rat Pack devotee.

On this particular Thursday, decked out in my business casualesqueness (sans elf hat), Jenny, my favorite hostess of the preferred gender, approached me stating, "Nicholas Broxton wants to speak with you."

I don't talk to customers unless there is a need to get clarification on a specific issue. The hosts/hostesses are all computer savvy, so the need seldom occurs. We don't wear nametags nor do we provide our names to customers, even when asked. There are many reasons for this. So if someone knows one of our names, it's because he or she knows us.

Mr. Broxton was one of my clients.

The man was rich, a multi-millionaire, rich, and intimidating, though unintentionally— the intimidating part, that is. I'm sure the rich part was intentional. He had a very strong presence and commanded attention just by walking into a room. Deep bass voice, square-ish face, exquisitely cropped salt-and-heavy pepper-hair. (I'd never seen even a single hair out of place, whereas my hair does a decent impression of a feather duster). His vivid green eyes were the color of a ten thousand dollar bill. I know. I'd seen one. Mr. Broxton showed me. Salmon P. Chase is on the front. The George Washington variety is a faded green. I've actually seen a few of those.

I was shocked to hear Mr. Broxton entered the store. Even with the name Buy City, the establishment's target customers were upscale. We joked the store should instead be called *Extravagant* City, EC for short. But I guess that really doesn't mesh well with buyer psychology.

"Oh, I simply *love* those shoes! Where did you get them?" "Aren't they just divine? I got them on clearance at Extravagant City!"

But despite the upscale image, Buy City resided far below Mr. Broxton's tastes. We may be fancy for a department store, but the Avenue des Champs-Élysées we were not.

"Thanks, Jenny. Um, you look nice today."

She looked down at her clothes, or uniform, which consisted of a pleated black skirt and a blouse the same color blue as my dress shirt. "Ellie, I look like this every day at EC."

"Uh, then you look nice every day."

She laughed. "Your pickup lines need work."

Jenny was right, she's premiumware whereas I'm shareware. That's geekspeak for I didn't have a chance.

Her eyes looked like chocolate. Her silky hair owned a reddish brown color and flowed to the middle of her back. When she turned, the reddish strands glistened in the light, creating a shimmering reflection as if the strands were from some exotic waterfall on an alien planet.

Let's just say she was beautiful. Breathtaking. And I was infatuated. Yet, despite her beauty, that singular characteristic was not the cause of my infatuation. Oh, it helped, certainly. But her *inner* beauty pinched my heart. I'm being serious. Her grace, her vitality, her musical laugh… She could have easily shunned me, ridiculed my existence. But she always treated me with kindness, treated me like I was somebody.

Other people might not give me the time of day. But Jenny would say, "Three o'clock." Assuming it was three o'clock when I asked.

"You'd better not keep that man waiting. He's important."

I found myself staring at her and quickly averted my eyes just as I noticed a perceptive smile flash across her face, felt my cheeks heat up, and started to walk away when her last sentence finally registered. "You know him?"

She shook her head. "Not really, no. But I know who he is. He and my dad sometimes collaborate on derivative financial products for the stock market."

Huh?

And right after that singular thought of profound ignorance, I realized, as I marveled at her chocolate eyes, inner beauty, and timekeeping skills, I was ignorant about much of Jenny's life outside the walls of the Big EC. I mean, we talked about life and stuff, but not about *her* life. Nor mine, for that matter.

I studied the ceiling for a beat, then looked back at Jenny. "Let's pretend like I don't know what that means."

A different version of a perceptive smile flashed. She has a lot of these perceptive smiles, at least when talking to me. About seventeen. I've catalogued them. But new versions appear weekly.

She said, "I'll explain it to you sometime."

I walked through the thick purple drapes that created both a physical and visible barrier from customers behind the u-shaped counter. Yes, purple drapes. Not plastic strip curtains. We weren't the Geek Squad (no offense to my geek brethren).

To protect customer privacy, we never worked on a computer in view of other customers. Plus, every once in a while someone was stupid enough to drop off a computer with child porn on it. Always because of a virus, they say. Go figure. We couldn't let other customers see that, obviously. Or ourselves. When discovered, we stopped work immediately and notified the police. These offending customers didn't get the privilege of protected privacy. After the police investigated the material on the computer, we called the customer saying the computer work was complete and ready for pick up. The officer then greeted the customer in one of the manager's offices and the perp got to wear shiny bracelets on the way to the backseat of a police cruiser. I think these perverts should also get the opportunity of a brain massage provided by a 2000-watt microwave. I'll let imagination take over from there.

Customers were never allowed behind the scenes in what we named the Room of Sovereignty. Sadly, I'm not a king and I didn't have a chair resembling a throne. I had a barstool. Twenty-four-hour surveillance ensured we kept customers out and that we also didn't do anything that would be frowned upon, like stealing or looking at pics on computers.

Mr. Broxton wore a silver Brioni suit that matched his hair and a blue dress shirt. I wouldn't have known to call it a Brioni, except he once told me that's all he wore. It's supposed to be fancier than Giorgio Armani. Target is fancy for me. At least our similarly colored shirts made me feel honored.

"Nice shirt," he said as I walked up to the counter.

I nodded *thanks*.

He said, "Please visit with me over here," as he motioned to a spot a few yards beyond the counter where no customers mingled.

He was visibly upset. Though, to the untrained eye, he might have looked as if he had just gained a paltry million in financial trading, instead of a million-two. But to me, since I'd never seen him upset, period… I swallowed. And followed.

Panic struck me as I first thought something bad must have happened to my uncle. Mr. Broxton and Uncle Joe were close friends. He liked my uncle's books and was kind enough to buy several to hand out to friends and associates. Maybe I overreacted, but my uncle was *it*—all I had left. No other family.

"My apologies for interrupting you at work. I went to your apartment. Your uncle said you were here."

Whew. "It's all right, sir, you don't have to apologize. But you could have just called my cell." I wanted to add something like, 'I can't believe you'd be caught dead in here,' but I refrained. Sometimes I do actually possess a little tact.

"I need to discuss a situation with you that is too sensitive for a cellphone. It is also too sensitive to discuss here," he said, swinging his left arm out slightly and glancing around.

I knew something big was up, obviously, or Mr. Broxton wouldn't have been standing in front of me. But what could be such a big deal that made him scared to talk on the phone? And what the heck could *I* do about it?

I swallowed again as my mouth went dry, again.

"Will your schedule permit you to assist me tonight after your workday is complete?"

I almost laughed as I quickly counted my after-work social commitments and got all the way up to zero. "Yes, sir, of course. What time would you like me to be at your house?"

"Is eight o'clock agreeable?"

My shift ended at 6:00. That would give me plenty of time to eat and attempt to calm my nerves, so that I wouldn't make a fool of myself in front of Mr. Broxton. "I'll be there at eight o'clock, sir."

"I will make sure Tyler is in the backyard."

"Thank you, sir."

Mr. Broxton nodded. "He's a good dog, you know. He won't hurt you."

I smiled faintly.

"Thank you, Elijah." He looked at his Patek Philippe watch (I once asked about the brand) and said, "I have an important appointment to keep. Have a good day." He nodded, pierced my eyes with his, then turned and walked briskly to the store's front doors, glancing furtively left and right as he went.

I turned and walked slowly to the Room of Sovereignty. And wondered what I was getting myself into.

Chapter Four

At a pace fit for a turtle, I drove my '78 cobalt blue Chevy Nova, the *Beast*, to my apartment.

It has a Holley Double Pumper four-barrel carburetor, distributor curve kit, high energy electronic ignition, a Level 10 Bulletproof performance transmission, high-nickel content racing block with bored heads, and wide tires. I didn't know what any of that meant except the wide tires. A friend who's a hotrod nut helped me pick out the car. He said it had go-fast parts. I like go-fast parts.

Acquiring the *Beast* was also the first significant purchase I had ever made, and I worked for every dollar it cost. I love that car.

I drove slowly because mammoth grey-black storm clouds advanced across the sky like aircraft carriers heading for battle. Cannons fired huge bolts of lightning. Thunder cracked so loud that I tried to cover my ears each time it fractured the sky, but I was always a split second too late. The clouds brought a premature nightfall. Waves of rain beat down on the car, which was manufactured before the dawn of intermittent wipers.

Allister often sat in the living room while sharpening a large knife with a leather strop so we could all hear it. He tried to intimidate us, and it worked. The sound of wiper blades vibrating on the windshield reminds me of that fear, so in light rains, I manually move the wiper switch: *On, Off, On, Off.* During this storm, however, they weren't fast enough to keep up.

With the wipers on *High*, the rapid *swoosh-swoosh-swoosh-swoosh* of the blades sounded as if I had journeyed inside the heart of a giant chasing his tormented prey.

The longer I drove, the more anxious I got.

The heartbeat wipers seemed to take on a sinister sound, a *dead-dead-dead-dead* omen of doom.

I parked the *Beast* in the cold garage next to my uncle's Range Rover. The heavy dampness made it feel even colder than the 38° it was supposed to be. I shivered as I stepped out of the car.

Before going to my apartment, I walked through the main house, calling for my uncle. I'm embarrassed to admit it, but I wanted to give him a hug. I needed that brief moment of security, knowing he was all right.

From the garage I went through the kitchen to the dining room, living room, library, and then the media room. I went to the master bedroom, and peeked into some other rooms along the way. He wasn't home. Yet a part of me wanted to keep exploring. I envisioned my dead uncle chopped up into four-inch sections, neatly placed in rows like dominos.

I have a vivid imagination. Good for a writer, bad for peace of mind.

After fighting the urge to run from room-to-room, I manned up and went back out to the garage to climb the stairs to my apartment. I chose the interior stairs over the exterior. If I had to go outside to get to my place, my feather-duster hair would look more like a used mop.

For dinner, I decided on grilled cheese sandwiches with Campbell's tomato soup. I make a mean grilled cheese that I'm sure would win any Iron Chef competition if they could entice me enough to share my talent on the show.

I stretched out on my bed for a minute and stared at the ceiling.

My cave isn't much, but it's home. My home.

12

Unlike my rejection of Uncle Joe's invitation to stay in the main house, I did accept furniture donations. I'm not proud of this; it wasn't a petition from the Elijah Raven Hands-Out Foundation. But I had to admit, having a bed is nice. I've spent many bone-flattening, sleepless nights on concrete-hard floors.

The furniture donation included a cherry wood four-poster bed, matching night stands and dresser, a brown wing-back chair, two cherry wood bookshelves, and a three-foot high wooden representation of Albert Einstein, in which he's holding a stack of books that opens to a not-so-secret compartment. Inside the compartment is a racquetball within a glass case, a memorial to a lost friend. A small table and matching chairs sit just outside my galley kitchen. A stone fireplace faced my door on the opposite side of the room.

I had a hunch Uncle Joe decided to remodel as an excuse to help me acquire more items than what fit in my backpack.

I don't have any pets, but I actually *like* animals. Yet because of my "gift," I stay away from them, as if I would get leprosy just by eye contact.

Well, I do have one pet: a rock named Rocky. He's house broken, always smiling, didn't eat much, and never tried to project thoughts to me.

For cover, when asked why I have a problem with animals, I tell people I have zoophobia. That is the actual name of the phobia meaning fear of animals. Since dogs communicate with me more than other animals, if a dog is around, I claim to have acute cynophobia—fear of dogs.

I have some ugly scars on my left arm, which I show as evidence for the reason of my phobias, fabricating a vicious dog attack. In truth, the scars were a souvenir from the time Allister beat me with a hacksaw when I was ten. He was so enraged that he just picked up the closest thing to him at the time. I'm lucky he didn't grab a baseball bat.

Or an axe.

That's the day my best friend, Billy, saved my life and died.

I wear long sleeves to hide the scars, which make me look a bit odd in the summer. It's easy at work thanks to the long-sleeved dress shirts.

Sometimes, I feel the scars act as an early warning system. A portent of danger. It's bizarre, but they seem to burn slightly when there's a looming threat or hazard.

Maybe it's some form of compensation from God for the disfigurement and pain. But I have a hard time accepting that theory, as there are so many who have suffered far worse than scarring. They deserve more from God than I do.

Or possibly the burning is somehow an extension of my gift. The day I discovered the gift is the day Allister attacked me. Not just a regularly scheduled beating, but an attack.

Mr. Broxton was right; his dog Tyler is indeed a good dog. A great dog. I've talked to Tyler a few times. He's incredibly intelligent, and also mischievous. He escaped the backyard—oh, sorry, the *rear grounds*—on occasion to roam the surrounding neighborhoods, hunting and exploring. Yet, it's not entirely his fault. Mr. Broxton, who has no immediate family and, other than Tyler, lives alone, is gone frequently on business, which sometimes leads to extended periods away from home. Tyler gets bored. Neighbors check on him, and he has a better crib than some humans. If he gets too hot in the brutal summers, he has access to an environmentally controlled mudroom just inside the mansion. That room is as big as my apartment.

Anyway, he's a black Labrador retriever. It's in his blood to explore.

Tyler has described some of his adventures to me. It's our little secret. Mr. Broxton doesn't know Tyler is an escape artist.

I sat on the bed, trying to decide what to wear. Brooding, actually. When you look like me, vanity isn't an issue. And I'm not indecisive. So I didn't understand my apprehension.

I had no reason for trying to impress Mr. Broxton. Just one of his suits costs more than everything I own. Hell, just one of his *socks* does.

My alarm clock displayed *7:15PM*. I'd been sitting on the edge of my bed for half an hour. My apprehension had progressed into irrational fear. I felt like I'd just returned to the real world from a horrific nightmare.

I placed my hand on my chest to feel my heartbeat. A hummingbird would be proud.

Things normally don't get to me. I've been through a lot, more than most people. Your perspective changes, your perseverance.

I forced myself to calm down. Deep breaths, imagining a big blanket of cottony calmness floating down over my body, and an angel smoothing out my feather-duster hair. Something I learned in therapy as a child. It's stuck with me, and it works. As an adult, it felt childish. Rarely did I ever have to use the technique.

Sometimes the angel was Mom. Before drugs ruined her.

Thunder hammered the roof and Niagara moved from New York to right outside my window.

Able to function again, I decided on black jeans and a dark blue sweatshirt with my black hiking boots.

Umbrellas don't like me and I feel the same about them. We have a mutual understanding. I grabbed my hooded heavy coat and my backpack of tech goodies, then descended the stairs to the *Beast*.

Chapter Five

Mr. Broxton is a good guy. When someone has a commanding presence *and* is amazingly wealthy you automatically feel a little frightened of him or her.

Seemingly aware of his combination of fear inducing characteristics, Mr. Broxton strove to be affable. Yet he didn't have to strive to be kind. It came naturally.

He knew more about my past than most people. Not because I'd talked to him about it, but because Uncle Joe had. Though, Uncle Joe didn't share things too personal to me, just basic history. And even Uncle Joe doesn't know everything.

People who have some level of knowledge about my childhood seem to look down on me. I don't think most of them do so intentionally, but it's as if I'm less of a person, not as *whole* as they are, since I bounced around from place to place growing up and didn't have "real" parents.

They don't know about all of the violence and death, or they might then think of me on the same level as the family of *Cricetidae*, or rats.

On numerous occasions, Mr. Broxton has admonished me to call him Nicholas, or Nick. I just can't bring myself to do so. It seems akin to approaching the President of the United States and saying, "Wasabi!" The Secret Service would interpret that to mean, "I have a bomb!" and the next thing I know I'm sniffing dust on the White House travertine floor (in truth, I don't know if it has travertine floors, but it sounds appropriate) with a half-dozen agents piled on top of me playing real life Kill the Man with the Football.

Somehow the scene would end up on YouTube. Jenny would see it. I just know it.

So, with a pervasive fear of travertine floors and footballs, I call Mr. Broxton, Mr. Broxton.

Nightfall had dropped its natural shroud over the land, which covered the unnatural shroud caused by the armada of clouds. The *Beast's* headlights barely penetrated the night and storm. Xenon they were not. Rain still fell, but it had lightened considerably. I had to do the manual on/off intermittent wiper thing.

Mr. Broxton lives on an estate with a few acres. The roads did not have streetlights.

Just before turning onto his street, I passed a black Suburban parked to the side, partially in the road. Tinted windows, black bumper, black non-glossy paint. If there was a license plate, it was hidden behind a black cover of some sort. The only reason I noticed the truck was because it surprised me a little in the absolute dark with no reflective surfaces.

As I pulled into Mr. Broxton's long driveway, I noticed another black Suburban parked at the top of a hill farther up the street, but the oddity of two monoblack Suburbans didn't register in my brain at that time.

An eight-foot high, stone wall surrounded the estate. A wrought iron security gate blocked the entrance. Expecting my arrival, Mr. Broxton had left the gate open.

Cameras kept watch from a security hut on the right. The few times I'd previously been here, the hut was manned. This time it was empty. And dark inside.

After pausing by the hut to peer quizzically into the darkness, I continued along the flagstone driveway. I checked my rearview mirror to see if anyone stepped out of the hut behind me or if the gate closed, but it was too dark to see. I applied the brakes to create light. A red hue brightened the immediate area behind the car, but still did not provide enough light to see the hut.

As I sat watching, the bright red seemed to darken and darken until it appeared to flow down in a blood red. My imagination entered the room in my brain where regular thoughts mingled, and announced its presence. Loudly.

I locked my doors. Since the *Beast* didn't have electronic door locks, this meant I had to dip below the viewing level of the windshield and side windows to stretch to the passenger door lock, which I was wary of doing. I wanted to know when a rabid group of spider monkeys were going to descend on me, screaming, bearing their teeth, jumping up and down on the car until they broke through the glass, chewing on me like a fresh batch of fried chicken.

I've never talked to a spider monkey and I don't know if they eat fried chicken. My imagination doesn't care about being factual.

The driveway curved around the heavily wooded front grounds. I'm not sure how absolute darkness could get darker, but it did. Then I realized the exterior lights that normally illuminated the trees along the drive were dark. As was the water fountain up ahead.

Not knowing why all the lights were off, or if rabid spider monkeys waited for me in the darkness, I wanted to turn off the headlights, but I was afraid there wouldn't be enough light to see the driveway.

I switched off the lights anyway. I felt like a target with them on. It's not whether you're paranoid, but whether you're paranoid enough.

I let my eyes adjust in the oppressive gloom and crept forward in the car.

No wildlife. No birds, squirrels, opossums… Not even spider monkeys. I was the only thing alive on Earth, and beginning to fear I wouldn't be for much longer.

The scars on my left arm started to burn. Trouble. The fight or flight adrenaline started streaming into my blood.

Monoblack Suburbans. Two of them, flanking Mr. Broxton's mansion. The security guard, gone. Lights out everywhere.

Mr. Broxton is a friend.

Fight.

I drove a little faster and followed the flagstone drive as it circled the water fountain in order to point the *Beast* toward the street for a fast getaway if necessary.

I've seen a few thriller movies. That's what they would do.

I pulled the hood of my black coat to cover my head from the rain and grabbed my black backpack. With my black jeans and black hiking boots, I'd never been more thankful for having an affinity for wearing dark clothes.

I grabbed the keys—they weren't black—and tucked them in my jeans pocket. Now if I could only cover my lighthouse-white face.

The dome light in the *Beast* didn't illuminate when a door opened. I still didn't know for sure whether I was being watched, but my burning scars seemed to be a solid indicator that I was.

Darkness consumed most of the mansion, with just a few faint lights seen through second floor windows.

Chapter Six

The front door stood slightly open. My scars burned hotter. I knew from experience touching them wouldn't help, nor water, ice, lotion... I eased through the open doorway. I had a flashlight in my backpack, but didn't dare use it. I wished I had night vision goggles.

Though sightless in the gloom, I knew I was in the foyer. Marble columns spread out left and right. To the left was one of the formal living rooms. To the right was a gallery which narrowed into a wide hallway leading to another wing. Stairs wrapped majestically around the room, and a passageway straight ahead led to the far side of the first floor.

Mr. Broxton had four computers in various locations, each one set up by me. The computer he used the most was in his study on the second floor. That's where the only light shined.

It didn't take instinct or a burning scar warning system to know things were not right. I thought about returning to the *Beast* and calling the cops. I may have super geek skills, but not super ninja.

No, Mr. Broxton might be hurt, or worse.

Or Tyler. I wondered why I hadn't seen or heard the dog. Mr. Broxton must have left him out back.

I groped in the gloom for the newel post of the stairway, then ascended to the second floor, staying close to the side to lessen the chance of creaking.

I didn't worry about clearing the first floor. If unseen enemies waited to jump me, they were going to whether I knew they existed or not. Besides, that would delay my arrival to the study, where I hoped to find Mr. Broxton unharmed.

Yet my burning scars told me I was probably wrong.

Not wanting to make any noise as I ascended, I held my breath. At the second floor landing, that proved to be a big mistake because now I couldn't breathe after climbing the stairs. I paused long enough to catch my breath without sounding asthmatic.

Two hallways, one to my left, one right, fed additional rooms. Small, recessed lights in the walls dimly illuminated the floor in spots. I stepped off the carpeted stairs onto the wooden floors of the landing toward the left hallway. I walked on my tippy-toes with arms spread like wings for balance so that my wet hiking boots didn't squeak on the wood floor, praying there were no low-light surveillance cameras recording my actions. That video would also end up on YouTube.

After reaching the hallway's long carpet runner, I moved to the third door on the left, the study.

Under normal circumstances, this was my favorite room in Mr. Broxton's mansion. Modeled as a smaller version of the library in the Biltmore Estate, though still huge with a twenty-foot ceiling. The room had floor to ceiling bookshelves and a balcony that wrapped around the upper half. Spiral staircases led to the balcony in two corners. A bookshelf in a prominent location displayed all of Uncle Joe's books.

A six-foot high ornate fireplace was on the wall to the right. To the left was a stately desk. All of the wood in the room was mahogany. A Tiffany desk lamp provided the only light in the room.

I heard, "Oh my God," fall out of my mouth, then realized I said it. Mr. Broxton lay on his side on the floor fifteen feet away. A pool of blood glistened sickly underneath his body.

Tyler was on the floor a few feet away.

I got to Mr. Broxton's side in three long steps and a slide on my knees, searching for his carotid and a pulse. He opened his eyes and weakly grasped my arm.

"Thank God," I said. "I need to get you an ambulance." I put one foot in front of me to stand—

"No time," he said, in little more than a whisper. He glared at me in desperation, commanding obedience.

He got my attention.

"Hidden folder… recipes… remove." He had a hard time sucking in enough air to talk. His face a pallid grey.

"Who did this? Why?"

He closed his eyes. I tried to find a pulse again, then I heard him talk more. "Take Tyler…dart…they"—cough—"they're returning." He had opened his eyes to make sure I heard him. The brilliant green was dull and flat.

Death grabbed Mr. Broxton's soul, trying to separate it from his body. Mr. Broxton desperately tried to hang on to this Side, but Death would not lose.

I didn't know what he meant by dart until I noticed a thin needle sticking in Tyler's neck. They must have just used a tranq gun on him instead of killing him. Afraid to touch the dart in case some fluid leaked, I removed tweezers from a toolkit in my backpack and also got a plastic tube used for extra screws and jumpers. I didn't know why I wanted to keep the dart, but I put it in the tube and closed the lid.

One of them left a tranq gun on the desk, which I pocketed.

I gently but firmly shook Tyler, trying to rouse him. He's a big dog, about 90lbs. We wouldn't get very far if I had to carry him.

Mr. Broxton's eyes were closed again.

I'm used to multitasking, but this was too much. I needed to try to save Mr. Broxton's life, wake the dog, get the secret files off the computer, prep it for my later use, and get Mr. Broxton, Tyler, and my sorry butt the hell out of there before whoever did this returned. All within the same second.

Mr. Broxton seemed to know my thoughts. Without opening his eyes, no longer trying to conjure a voice, he whispered, "Files…now…fake FBI…Meredith next…warn…" He hitched an inhale and then nothing.

I didn't bother taking time for a pulse. I'd been around death multiple times, witnessing it firsthand, on the scene when the Reaper came to collect.

Mr. Broxton was gone.

There was no time to mourn. Or get angry. I could do both later.

I vigorously shook the dog, this time getting a response with a leg twitch and eyeball movement under heavy lids.

Get the files, return to Tyler. I pushed a 2TB thumb drive into a USB slot on the computer, thankful both were USB 3.0 because it's much faster. I knew Mr. Broxton did not cook, so I figured the name of the hidden folder was *Recipes*, with a $ after the name so it wouldn't appear in the folder structure. Bingo. I was surprised Mr. Broxton knew how to hide folders. After checking the size—300GB—I started the transfer, doing a simple cut and paste to remove the directory off the hard drive.

That alone wouldn't keep someone from accessing the data even after it had been removed/deleted if the person knew what he or she was doing. I had previously installed a second network interface card, or NIC, into the computer with its own static IP address so I could access the computer remotely through a back door if Mr. Broxton ever needed my assistance at, say, 2:00AM. I instructed him to leave the cable unplugged when not in use so he wouldn't worry about my access. Not that he would. He trusted me. But that was also for my own conscience. When you've been an orphan much of your life, many people automatically distrust you. I didn't ever like having the keys to the kingdom. No suspicion.

I plugged the loose cable into the second NIC, then unplugged the cable from the first NIC as well as from the wall jack and took it. The first NIC was for Internet access. The second NIC didn't provide direct access without "cheating." I hoped these people didn't know how to cheat. I uninstalled the first NIC from Device Manager and disabled Plug and Play so the computer wouldn't recognize it had the NIC without further intervention.

Tyler lifted his head, trying to get his bearings.

I looked out the study window. The *Beast* could be seen from there on the other side of the water fountain.

I could barely see two dark figures looking into the car. They didn't use flashlights. That meant the friggers had night vision goggles. Not fair.

"That's it," I said aloud. "I'm buying night vision goggles."

Then one of them knelt next to the left rear tire, and I saw that corner of the car dip down. No! They punctured the tire.

No no no no no! They moved to the remaining three and did the same. Those tires cost a lot of money.

I wanted to break the second floor window and yell obscenities at them. Thankfully, wisdom overruled emotion.

It might seem silly to be so angry about them slashing the *Beast's* tires. That was an anger my psyche knew I could deal with at that moment. I had to stay sharp. My anger over Mr. Broxton's death was infinitely stronger, and not something I could rationally control.

Obviously, the air had been let out of my quick getaway plan, pun intended. I needed a new plan, fast. If they didn't know anyone else was in the house before, they did now. They'd be searching for us soon.

Tyler whined behind me. He'd gotten to all fours, steady, and nudged Mr. Broxton's chin, trying to wake him.

I said, "He's dead, Tyler."

I don't know if Tyler intentionally projected his thoughts to me, but I picked up on them. *My Master is dead. I am sorry. I failed you.*

I almost lost it—right there—and started to cry. *Feeling* Tyler's anguish, despair. Even as I knew the murderers were just outside the house.

The last time I really cried was right after I killed Allister when I was ten. Not because of remorse. But because it was finally over. There have been a few tears here and there since then, but I got over them quickly.

Some dogs cannot use first person pronouns, like *I, me,* or, *my.* I'm not sure if it's a self-awareness thing, or maybe even a form of subservient humility. Tyler's understanding is beyond most dogs. But, that also means his hurt—his grief—was more pungent. Stronger. With greater understanding comes greater pain.

I heard a noise downstairs. I looked out the window to see if the men were still there. Gone.

"Tyler, we've got trouble. They're back in the house."

He licked Mr. Broxton on the cheek. I heard *Bye* and then he looked at me. *Come on, follow me.*

I made sure the file transfer had finished, grabbed the flash drive, and followed Tyler into the hallway. I heard feet ascending the stairs and looked right in time to see a pair of disembodied red glowing eyes. Lights to create an infrared field visible with night vision. *Crap!*

I aimed the tranq gun at torso level of the red eyes and fired. The eyes dipped and I thought I scored a miraculous hit, but instead the eyes rose back up, then dipped, rose in rapid succession. He ran toward us.

I could hear Tyler running to my left and followed him down the hallway until we came to a stairwell. A couple of seconds later I heard his nails ticking on the tile floor in the kitchen. These stairs were in a curved four-foot wide hallway with railings on both sides. I grabbed each railing and descended as fast as I could.

On the way down I heard a cabinet door close and the crinkling of a plastic bag. I didn't know if the noise was caused by an intruder. Tyler didn't bark or growl, a good sign.

The kitchen was a shade brighter, yet still not enough for me to see well. There were a lot of windows, but with the clouds blocking the moonlight, little light filtered in. I didn't take the time to get out my flashlight, but instead briefly turned on the flash of the embedded camera in my iPhone. I just needed a quick snap of light to see where to go.

Tyler was already through the open door to the mudroom headed toward the dog door leading to the rear grounds of the estate. He waited for me just outside the door, then said, or in other words, projected to me, *Come on.*

I started for the back door and noticed red glowing eyes reflecting in the windows. I couldn't tell how many. But hoping for a brief distraction, with one hand I turned on the bank of light switches, flooding the kitchen with bright white light, and ran out the door not waiting to see what happened.

Tyler being a black Lab in a lightless night was just a shadow. But in the distance I could see the cream colored wall that surrounded the estate.

Now, despite my geekdom, I'm a good athlete. I got ups. I can dunk a basketball on a nine-foot goal, and can come close on a ten-foot. Plus, learning to quickly scale walls is a required survival skill when you grow up running away from neighborhood kids twice your size.

It would take little effort for me to jump up to the wall and scamper over. But Tyler?

I wasn't lifting a ninety-pound dog over an eight-foot wall. Or throw, for that matter.

"How are you getting over?"

Jump.

"You're going to jump over the wall?"

He chuffed. It sounded kind of weird so I knelt next to him and saw a big bag hanging out of his mouth.

"What is that in your mouth?"

Cheetos.

What! "You have a bag of Cheetos in your mouth?"

Stop asking so many question. With that, he was off.

I was so surprised, I laughed. I couldn't believe I just got chastised by a dog. I fastened my backpack around my waist so it wouldn't jostle as much when I ran, and chased Tyler.

The rain had stopped, but the ground was still soggy. My hiking boots sank a little with each footfall, making a *squish squish squish* as I ran. The air still had that damp coldness and felt thick.

I couldn't really see Tyler, but I could hear the Cheetos shaking inside the bag. I still wondered if he could jump the wall. Somewhere I read that the original Rin Tin Tin German Shepherd could jump over eleven feet. So I guessed it was possible, but it just boggled my mind.

As we approached the wall, Tyler stopped. He studied the top, backed up a few steps, then ran forward and launched himself. Cheetos and all. His front legs landed on top, his back legs acting as shock absorbers against the side of the wall. He hung there for a second then scrambled to the top.

Wow.

My turn. Because I had a small laptop in my backpack, and other breakable items, I didn't want to toss the pack over the wall. But when I'm playing hoops, I don't typically have a twenty pound pack hanging over my shoulders. I also had just remembered that rain makes things wet. By inductive reasoning, because it had rained, I figured out the surface would be wet. I'm smart like that.

Okay then.

All right.

I moved away from the wall a few steps and looked up at Tyler, who wagged his tail and seemed to be grinning even with a large bag of Cheetos hanging from his mouth.

Fine.

I ran and jumped, catching the top of the wall as my body slammed against it. *Ouch.* I didn't have hind leg shock absorbers. I struggled to maintain my grip. I *really* didn't want to fall and have to body slam the rock wall again.

Tyler said, *They're here. Hurry.* Then I heard an impact and bits of rock fragment exploded a few feet to my left.

The filthy-scabby-spider monkey wannabes were shooting at us!

Chapter Seven

  I didn't hear the gunfire, which meant they were using silencers. That would reduce accuracy, but I wasn't going to hang around, literally, to see how much.

  I tried to pull myself over and use my legs to drive up. Hiking boots have great traction on uneven, coarse ground. Even when wet. But on a smooth, slick wet surface? Not so much.

  I looked back at the assailants. I couldn't tell if they were in shape or not, and didn't know if they'd be able to scale the wall easily.

  But I was getting ahead of myself. First, *I* had to get over the freaking wall.

  The life-giving (in this case) fight-or-flight adrenaline kicked in, I grunted and clambered over.

  Tyler still waited on top.

  I looked up and he dropped the Cheetos bag in my hands.

  He quickly located a good landing spot then jumped to the ground. He said, *This way.*

  We ran through the woods. I used my ears as much as my eyes to stick with Tyler, who ran slower than normal to maintain a pace I could handle. And hoped he wouldn't run under branches over his head, but lower than mine.

  I couldn't see or hear gunfire. Either they were unable to get over the wall or we were out of range.

  After running hard for about a mile, I stopped, panting, and between big inhales, I said, "We need to, find a place, to chill for, a minute, to figure out, what to do next."

  Got it, he said.

  Stooped over with my hands resting on my knees, I turned to look behind us. I thought I was in better shape than this.

  No one chased us, but of course it was still hard to see in the pervasive shadow. Especially with the dark clothes the scurvy-stricken monkey-men were wearing. I suddenly had a strong dislike for people who had an affinity for wearing dark clothes.

  I didn't see any flashlights either, but that would make sense if they were still wearing night vision goggles.

  I hate people with night vision goggles too.

  The black clouds *did* seem to be chasing us. No stars were visible. Most of the trees had lost their leaves. Scarecrow limbs reached high toward the shrouded moon.

  I looked at Tyler. "I don't see them, but let's get out of sight anyway."

  Tyler was so intelligent, I had to keep reminding myself he's a dog. He led us to a shallow ditch that fed into a large concrete culvert. Even at six feet, I only had to slouch a little. I pulled out my LED flashlight, and surveyed the area, making sure light did not escape back out the entrance. We went in a few paces and then a connecting pipe appeared to the right. A fresh waterline indicated the heavy rains created a fairly deep runoff, but now the water was gone.

  Tyler walked deeper into the pipe until we came to a cutout for a ladder leading to a manhole. The four-foot by four-foot cutout had a concrete pad, high enough to have remained dry despite the rain runoff. We both sat down, exhausted. The drained feeling of adrenaline ebbing was way worse than a sugar crash. My groin muscles tightened in the cold. I tried to sit Indian style to stretch them before they decided to tighten up completely. There were few things worse than a groin cramp.

I switched the flashlight to a low setting, which emitted a minimal amount of light, and placed it in a corner of our little hideout.

Tyler sat straight up and put a paw on my knee to get my attention, wagging his tail. *Cheetos.*

I smiled. "You want Cheetos?"

Yeah, Cheetos. Love Cheetos. Yeah. Yeah.

He stood on all fours, his tail wagging so enthusiastically that his rump swayed from side to side.

I'd placed the Cheetos in my backpack as we started to run so I wouldn't have to worry about holding them, wanting both hands unencumbered in case I fell, and to help prevent getting decapitated by a branch. Tyler bent forward and sniffed even though the bag wasn't open yet. I opened it; Tyler's tongue lolled out of his mouth. I said, "Sit."

He cocked his head, *Are you really going to make me do tricks?*

"Yep."

He jerked his head and peered down the pipe as if hearing something. *What's that?*

I tensed and looked in the same direction, staying quiet. Out of the corner of my eye, I saw his muzzle spring for the Cheetos bag—I yanked it out of his reach.

Ah man.

I laughed, shaking my head. "You... are a bad dog."

He grinned.

I said, "Sit."

If a dog could roll his eyes, he would have. He sat, then chuffed.

"Good boy." I grabbed his neck and gave him a soft noogie. He wagged his tail, enjoying the attention.

Opening the bag, I poured a small pile of Cheetos on the ground.

He attacked the pile. *Crunch crunch, slurp, crunch.*

"Chew with your mouth closed."

Tyler said, *Yummy.*

I discovered I was pretty hungry too, but I wasn't going to eat Cheetos off the ground. I grabbed a couple and tossed them in my mouth. Contrary to Tyler, my crunching was silenced with closed-mouth chewing.

I said, "You're right. Yummy," as I chomped on some more.

The only bad thing about Cheetos is the orange, sticky residue that's left on your fingers. I wondered briefly if I *should* eat them off the ground, but my inner germophobe screamed in panic. Yet I hate having stuff on my hands. Lotion, chocolate, Cheeto dust... Not even hand sanitizer. I'd much rather wash my hands with soap. I also don't like wiping my hands on my clothes. I never lick my fingers. And I wasn't about to let Tyler lick them. This presented a quandary. The concrete surface wasn't suitable for wiping off the Cheeto dust.

I stared at my orange fingers, then sighed. I swallowed my dignity, and also Cheeto dust after sucking my fingers.

I guess when you're on the lam, you do what you've gotta do.

Between the two of us, we finished the large bag. I soon discovered a second negative of Cheetos: they also make you thirsty.

Tyler had a simple solution to the problem. He jumped down from the raised concrete pad and lapped some leftover rainwater which pooled in the culvert.

The water was probably just fine for me too. But my inner germaphobe spoke up again—at least this time not screaming—and reminded me of what potential bacteria could do to my intestines after the water mixed with loveliness left in the pipe by insects and animals. Being on the run would be the worst time to get the runs.

After the things I've gone through, the various levels of squalor I'd been forced to live in, you'd think I'd get over being a germaphobe.

Nope.

If I could have collected the rainwater before it hit the ground...

After a few more moments, I'm not sure if it was psychosomatic, but I could just *feel* the Cheeto dust cloying in my throat. I was going to die of asphyxiation. Water... *water...*

Whatever.

I walked up the dark pipe a little bit, got on my hands and knees and slurped rainwater.

Tyler gave me a look that seemed to portray both amusement and pride.

Returning to the platform where my still-on flashlight provided illumination, I said, "We need to figure out what to do next."

Get more Cheetos.

"Well, that *is* a solid plan, but I don't think it'll be too easy to forage for Cheetos out here."

Reality—bad reality—came back to light as I sat in the mild glow of LED's. There were so many questions. Why did they kill Mr. Broxton? Hell, who were *they* to begin with? Why didn't they kill Tyler? Why leave and come back?

What... is on that flash drive worth killing for?

Who was Meredith? I don't know anyone named Meredith. How could I warn her?

During this question and non-answer session with myself, I had shifted on the concrete ground to sit with my back against the wall. I wanted to sleep. I was so tired. Drained. But I knew even if I was in my bed, I wouldn't be able to sleep.

Tyler lay on his stomach, his head flat on top of crossed forelegs, eyes open, just staring at concrete.

I know what dogs are thinking only when they project their thoughts to me. I'm not a mind reader. It might sound similar, but there's a distinct difference.

But I didn't need to be able to read minds to know his thoughts.

How do you console a dog who just lost his closest "relative"? Even a dog who's smart enough to understand what you say. How do you console a human who just lost a spouse? A parent, a sibling, a child, a best friend... You say, "I'm sorry." But it doesn't really mean anything. There is nothing you can say that can do more than provide surface comfort. The void—chunk of your soul—that had just been ripped out of you will never be replaced. Time will cover it, but the hole will always be there.

God may bless you with as much of an understanding as we can have about the ways of life. Or He may not.

Some people tried to console me after the death of my mother, the death of my siblings. Meaningless.

They meant well, sure. We're conditioned to offer comfort to the survivors, and conditioned to accept that comfort when we're the one left behind. This conditioned offer and acceptance is simply the way of things. But it has no true essence. *Life and* then *death* is the true way of things. And we will never understand as long as we ourselves are living.

24

I didn't bother trying to console Tyler with words about his loss. I stroked his back and gently massaged his neck and ears. He let out a long, forlorn sigh.

But I didn't want him to think this was his fault. I have carried that weight for years. Often punishing myself. Sometimes without even knowing it.

I wasn't going to let Tyler do the same. Even if he got over guilt much faster than a human would, he had no reason for the blame.

I scratched behind his ears. "Hey, you are not at fault for Mr. Broxton's death." I felt silly calling him Mr. Broxton. But I also felt silly referring to him as Tyler's master. He was more than just a master, he was family. The dog's only family.

He wanted you to call him Nick.

I said, "I know," then paused, trying to think of something else to say. I couldn't, so I just dropped it. "The important thing is his death was not your fault. You've got to understand that."

I am supposed to protect. I need to protect.

Tyler may have been smart for a dog, but he was not a human. He couldn't process his thoughts. Some humans can't either. He felt he needed to protect because that's how he showed love. Dogs can't talk. They can run up to you and make you smell like dog breath, expressing love with copious amounts of saliva painted on your face. But they can't verbalize, "I love you."

They are pack animals, social animals. They need to belong. And the pack, or family, they belong to, they protect.

"Yes, but you cannot protect if you're drugged." I didn't know if he knew what it meant to be drugged. "They shot you with a gun that makes you go to sleep. It's called a tranquilizer gun. It's used a lot on animals in the wild to capture them and transport to zoos."

I got the tube containing the dart out of my backpack and showed it to him. "See?" I rattled the tube to get his attention. "They shot you with this. It made you sleep."

He raised his head and turned so he could look at the dart and then looked me in the eye. He held my gaze for a beat and then dropped his head back on his legs. He didn't project any thoughts to me. I guessed he was trying to see if I spoke the truth. Satisfied, he resumed staring at the concrete.

There was no point in repeating what I'd said. He understood. Time would have to cover the void.

"Did Mr.—did Nick ever say anything about a person named Meredith?"

I heard him say Meredith talking on the phone.

"Do you know who she is?"

No.

Then I said as much to myself as to Tyler, "We've got to figure out who she is. Warn her about the fake FBI, or whoever they are. Maybe we can get some answers too. She's obviously involved."

Time to do some digging. I retrieved my laptop from the backpack, opened the lid and slid my right index finger over the biometrics fingerprint reader, a small scanner built-in to the wrist rest by the keyboard. If a successful read was made, and the scan matched the credentials I'd set, it then powered on the laptop and logged me on.

I just had to make sure no one stole my laptop and my finger.

I planned to reconnect to the computer in Mr. Broxton's study to see if there were any attempts to retrieve information, other than mine. Then investigate the flash drive.

As I watched the screen come alive, casting a bluish light on the walls in our cubby hole, a light suddenly shined in a previously dark room within my brain. And what I saw startled-horrified me.

"Oh no! Not Meredith—" before I could blurt anything else, I spasmodically clamped my hand over my mouth.

Chapter Eight

I'm an idiot. I freely admit it, though there's plenty of evidence to figure it out without my declaration. The identity of Meredith should have been obvious to me. I was surprised when Jenny recognized Mr. Broxton, to which she explained the connection between him and her dad. With Mr. Broxton's dying words, I was so focused on Meredith being a first name, I didn't get it.

Jenny is Jenny Meredith.

I repeat: I'm an idiot.

By now, the fake feds had already run the tags on my car and have chased down the title owner: me. I didn't submit a change of address with the Postal Service when I moved to Uncle Joe's. No one knew me and I paid all of my bills online. I couldn't easily be traced to Uncle Joe's address. He would be safe, at least for now.

I retrieved my cell, started to call Jenny and then realized… bad idea. With car ownership they got a name. With a name they would query databases for cellular users, even unregistered. There weren't too many Elijah Ravens in the world. I couldn't use the phone without leading the killers to whomever I called. Mr. Broxton's warning suggested they potentially already knew about the Merediths. But no point in sending an invite.

The cell's display showed 11:04. Three hours had passed since I arrived at Mr. Broxton's house. Just a few minutes before that, Mr. Broxton was still alive, Tyler had a master, and I was simply on my way to helping a friend with his computer. It's amazing how our lives could change—or end—over the course of just a few minutes.

With enough determination, the unknown enemy could identify my cell and find me by using the phone's GPS to isolate my location, like a Greek god peering down from the clouds, pointing, and with a victorious roar, shouting, "There he is! Off with his head!" Okay, maybe a Greek god in Wonderland.

Mr. Broxton's murder meant they were determined.

My phone could also be used for other nefarious activities. It was too dangerous to keep. Since it could be traced even while powered off, as long as the battery had juice, I turned it off and left it in the pipe as a decoy. I never kept data on the phone I feared losing.

I powered off the laptop and shoved it in the pack. I said, "Let's get out of here," and nudged Tyler in the opposite direction of the pipe entrance.

Tyler looked back from where we came, looked forward, and then back again, seemingly to orient himself. I could hear him sniffing. *This way.*

I grabbed the flash and we ventured deeper into the pipe. Thankfully I'm not claustrophobic. In fact, under different circumstances, I'd actually enjoy being in a dark, isolated, closed-in place. Somehow it made me feel protected. A Freudian psychosomatic longing for my mother's womb? Nah. Freud was nuts.

On this occasion, though, I just wanted to get out of there and hoped Tyler wasn't taking us on a route that would take a long time, or worse, get us lost.

After what seemed like half an hour, but more likely just a few minutes, we exited the darkness of the pipe into the gloom of the chilled night. I looked around wearily, doubtful the killers were waiting to waylay us, but too paranoid to completely dismiss the possibility.

Satisfied there were no killers in the area, including spider monkeys, I straightened my back and stretched my arms upward.

Once I put things together, I didn't want to talk aloud in the vicinity of the phone. Now that Tyler and I had cleared the pipe on the opposite end, I said, "We need to get to Jenny Meredith's house. That's where the bad guys are headed—if they're not already there. It's on Monticello Street, but I imagine that doesn't help you much."

What does it look like?

"Big southern colonial, three stories, with wide, white columns in front. Big trees and bushes on the sides."

Got it. Fat squirrels in those trees.

Tyler raced and I chased.

The clouds had started to clear, and what heat they blanketed escaped to the stars. I had lost my electronic tether to the world when I left my cell in the culvert. Without it I couldn't check the temperature. But I imagined it dropped two or three degrees, yet still above freezing, a big break for us. The challenge of running on ice through the woods and streets might have been impossible to overcome, certainly with any speed.

I continued to run like a hunchback while using my arms to block unseen branches from decapitating me, but Tyler seemed to sense which path to take that would leave my head where it is.

Brilliant dog. I was breathing too hard in the cold to talk, but I would make sure to tell him. And get him his own bag of Cheetos.

We cleared the woods into a neighborhood. I didn't know where we were while running between trees, but now with streets and houses as landmarks, I knew we were close to Jenny's house. I'd driven these streets a few times for no other reason than to see her house.

No, I wasn't stalking her. Just driving by to see where she lived. A few times.

We ran up the hill on Montgomery Street to turn onto Monticello when we saw death on four wheels. A black Suburban a hundred yards ahead and a few houses down from Jenny's.

No!

Without thinking I started to bolt up the street. Just pure reaction. But then I saw light approaching from behind. If it had been the second Suburban, I wouldn't have gotten very far. Thankfully I was clearheaded enough to run for cover and Tyler followed me without being told.

We were powerless to do anything. If we charged the house and got shot, we weren't going to save anyone. If we sat there and hid, we weren't going to save anyone.

I hate feeling helpless. Absolutely *hate* it.

But then, a miracle. The car driving up wasn't a black Suburban. It was a green BMW. Jenny's car!

The right hand turn onto her street from the hill on Montgomery was a blind turn, which made the driver slow more than usual. I could run faster than she was driving at that moment.

Not wanting to startle her, or get run over, I approached the street at an angle to the side of her car and knocked on the passenger window.

Of course, this startled her and she slammed on the brakes, but not with enough momentum to make the tires bark.

I quickly pulled my hood back so she could see my face. In the glow of the instrument panel, I saw her facial expression transition from the shock of fear to shock of surprise. On her expressive face, that was a dramatic difference.

She unlocked the doors.

I first opened the back door for Tyler, who again knew what to do without instruction. Then I jumped in the front seat.

She said, "What in the world—"

I put up my hand to stop her. "Sorry, I love you—" I put up my hand to stop me, then smacked my palm on my forehead.

Tyler said, *Doh!*

I didn't know "doh" was in a dog's vocabulary.

"That is *not* what I meant to say."

She laughed and with her left eyebrow arched, asked, "What is going on here?"

Trying to recover from an acute case of idiocy, I looked at her and said, "Please, trust me, we have to back up now. Don't ask questions. I'm being serious. I'm sorry for my stupid mouth, ignore that. I'll explain everything in a few minutes."

"What part am I supposed to ignore? Your declaration of love, or the stupid mouth part?"

"Jenny, *please*."

I guess she saw something in my face, because her expression abruptly changed from embarrassed amusement to alarm. To her credit, she didn't ask more questions, but put the car in reverse and turned to roll back down the hill on Montgomery.

I motioned for her to stop. Her cell sat in a cup holder. I put a finger to my lips, then grabbed the phone and took out the battery.

Her eyes flared.

I put my finger to my lips again to silence her. After verifying a secondary battery didn't exist on the phone, I said, "Pull over here and turn off the lights."

She followed directions. This was a great test of our friendship. I was glad, and surprised, she didn't start to beat me over the head with an umbrella or something.

Then she looked at me and said irritably, "Okay, what the hell is going on here?"

I quickly searched for umbrellas.

"I'll explain the phone bit later. They can hear whatever we say—"

She turned to face me. "Who are *they*? Hear what? What's happening?"

I decided that being blunt was the best plan. "Mr. Broxton was murdered."

She sank back in the seat. "Oh my God."

"*They* killed him. I don't know who *they* are yet. They shot at me and Tyler, he's the dog in your backseat, and chased us but we got away. Before Mr. Broxton died, he told me to get some files off his computer and to warn Meredith."

She gasped. "Daddy." She looked in the direction of her house, but it wasn't visible over the rise of the hill. "So what are we going to do? We can't just sit here."

"I know, Jenny, I'm sorry, I'm trying to think of what to do. There were two black Suburban's at Mr. Broxton's house. One of them is close to your house—"

"No. I'm—" She reached for the door handle but I grabbed her right arm.

"We can't just go charging in. They'll kill us. We can't help your dad if we're dead. He may already *be* dead."

She yelled, "No!" with such defiance I thought she might actually know whether he was alive or not. She opened her purse and pulled out a pistol.

"Whoa! What's that?" I don't like guns. I used one once. The experience cut a slice out of my soul.

"It's my turn to explain later. We have to get to my house."

29

This crisis had suddenly taken a turn I didn't expect.

She popped open the door and exited before I could say or do anything else, then quietly yet urgently shut the door.

I jumped out and opened the door for Tyler. I scurried after Jenny, yelling in a whisper, "Jenny! Jenny, stop!" I thought the effort would be futile, but she surprised me by turning around.

She said, "There's a secret entrance to the house on the back side."

My jaw dropped.

"You couldn't see it as you drove by my house," she continued and then patted me on the shoulder.

A train could have used my mouth for a tunnel. "Wait, how did you know—"

"No time. Follow me. Don't get killed."

Tyler and I fell in line after her as we ran, Quasimodo-like, up the hill onto her street. She wore dark clothes as well, so none of us stood out in the gloom. We crossed to her side of the street and then stayed close to the houses from yard to yard. Most of these houses had landscape lighting, but the lights were all pointed straight up, illuminating the house or trees. We were only visible in shadow form if someone briefly saw us block a light.

The house next door to hers was dark. She walked to the front door, pulled out a key and unlocked it, letting us in.

"The Foremans live here. I watch the house when they go on vacation. Right now they're in Berlin."

The only lighting came from low-wattage lights set into the floorboards along the walls, and the interior seemed to be made with dark materials, so it was hard to see what the place looked like. But it was cavernous.

Jenny led us through the house to the back door and we exited. A brick wall surrounded the yard, though the lot wasn't as big as Mr. Broxton's.

I looked at Tyler. He looked at me. He said, *Oh boy.*

I said to Jenny, "We don't have to climb the wall, do we?"

"No, there's a gate leading to our yard."

Whew.

No landscape lighting illuminated the backyards. As we approached the gate, I said softly, "Let me get this straight, you have a secret entrance to your house?"

She smiled. "Doesn't everybody?"

"Um, no. Why?"

"My father loves spy stories. When you have play money, imagination, and are drawn to espionage, you build secret entrances."

"Oh, sure, when you put it like that, makes perfect sense." I looked at Tyler. If a dog could shrug his shoulders, he would have.

A thin fog covered the neighborhood. Either it had just started settling, or I hadn't noticed it as we ran to Jenny's house. Thankfully there was no fog while Tyler and I were in the woods. It was already hard enough to see his pure black coat in the moonless night.

We snuck through the gate and inched up to some shrubs that hugged the back of the house. I didn't see any movement anywhere and the fog hushed noises. The quiet seemed ominous, though I'm sure my imagination contributed.

My scars burned slightly.

30

I whispered to Tyler, "Smell anything?"

Squirrels.

No help.

Uncle Joe is the only person who knows about my ability to communicate with animals. But Jenny did not give any indication she thought it was unusual for me to be asking Tyler a question. She probably talks to a cat.

The roots of the shrubs were about three feet from the house, growing in a tight bundle at the ground, then flared out as the branches grew leaves. This created a near perfect tunnel-like space. I'd state the name of that type of shrub, but the extent of my horticulture expertise ends at tree, bush, grass. The only plant I can readily identify is poison ivy. It loves me. It should make me feel good to be loved, but it doesn't. This time of year, nothing to worry about.

Jenny dropped to her knees and crawled into the tunnel. I followed, then Tyler.

Despite the heavy rain, the ground felt just slightly damp.

For me, curiosity is a basic emotion, right up there with happy and sad. Intrigued by the *tunnelainvillea hibiscumus,* I touched the plant, tilted my head, looked at my fingers, and touched the plant again. Plastic. The bush was plastic. Of course, in such low light, it was hard to judge the quality, but it sure looked real.

"Why are the bushes plastic?"

Jenny glanced back at me and said, "Why wouldn't they be?"

I thought about that for a moment, then said, "Uh."

She said, "Not everything is always as it seems."

"You're not a man, are you?"

She stopped, half-turned, and looked at me as if I were an idiot and said, "No." Then continued crawling.

Whew.

We went a few more feet and then stopped. I couldn't see what Jenny was doing, but a second later, a three-foot by three-foot panel slid to the side. She crawled-rolled feet first into the opening and said, "Come on."

Jenny stood in a sunken corridor inside the house. The outside ground was level with her midsection. I hopped down and Tyler followed, then Jenny closed the panel.

"You are the first person besides my parents and me to go through this entrance."

I realized I'd never heard anything about Jenny's mom before. But now was not the right time to ask.

"When I was little," she continued, "I used to daydream about sneaking my husband through here, as if having a husband was something to hide." She smiled.

We were in a forty foot corridor with concrete floor and walls spanning east-west. There were no sounds. It smelled like what you'd expect: damp and musty. On each end of the passage were 90° turns toward the center of the house.

A cat rounded the east end, which commanded Tyler's attention. To his credit, he didn't attack, but it seemed like an internal struggle. To be safe, I said, "No Tyler. This one's not for you."

Jenny said, "Watson, go away."

I looked at her. "Watson?"

"*Dr.* Watson, actually."

Tyler sighed deeply, almost whining. *Please?*

31

"No."

I don't want to eat it. Just chew on it. Promise.

"No."

Dognip. Get it? He looked me in the eye, and I could swear he actually smiled at me.

I stifled a laugh. "No."

Bugger.

Watson moved closer, paying Tyler no regard. He obviously knew the big dog wouldn't be able to catch him inside the house. But when Watson looked at me, he stopped. And stared. He studied me for a long, weird moment, long enough for me fake an air of disinterest, then said, "I guess I'm spooking Dr. Watson for some reason."

Then the cat projected, *You hear.*

I don't understand how animals know I can *hear* them. There are a lot of things in the animal world that we, as humans, don't understand. They are inferior to us in most ways, but superior in others, including the senses.

My best guess is by detecting a chemical I emit that's imperceptible to humans. Even that doesn't make sense, but it makes more sense than anything else I've been able to come up with. And believe me, I've spent years trying to figure it out so I could find a way to stop it.

It's been my experience that cats are inherently infatuated with facts. This explains why many of them have this sense of haughtiness, believing they are smarter than other creatures. Year after year they gather facts by their observations. When an older cat observes from his perch a kitten going absolutely bonkers over a piece of string, you just *know* the wise, aged feline is thinking, *Stupid cat.*

This is also why a cat loves to stare outside through a window. If it could talk, it would be like a news reporter, studying the world from his newsroom, reporting on the events outside: "It is raining. Car drove by. Yellow bird in tree. Looks tasty."

The cat continued to stare at me. *Three men. He is hurt. Gunshot. In study.*

Chapter Nine

"Mr. Broxton was murdered in his study. Do you have one?" I said, trying to sound vague.

"Yes," Jenny replied. "First floor."

The cat turned and ran down the corridor.

Jenny, Tyler, and I followed. After turning the corner, there were four steps leading to a small landing in an alcove with dark wood paneling. Jenny approached the left side and pulled on a ring set inside a recessed hole, which opened a door. Light spilled into the alcove.

Watson was gone. Evidently he had a different path into the house.

We went through the door into a large pantry. Floor to ceiling shelves were loaded with dried foods and cans of soups, vegetables, fruit… There was a section of Wolf brand chili. I love Wolf brand chili.

Tyler said, *Is that Wolf brand chili?*

I whispered, "Yes."

Chomp.

No doubt I was going to love this dog.

We entered the pantry, stepping over a large basket full of potatoes.

Jenny led us into the bright kitchen. Light pinewood cabinets covered the walls and Baltic brown granite countertops provided contrast. Brass pots and pans loomed over the center island, but judging by the quantity of canned foods in the pantry, they were probably meant more for decoration than cooking.

The kitchen led to a butler's pantry and then the formal dining room. These rooms were dark, but crystals on a large chandelier hanging in the dining room twinkled, reflecting light from the kitchen.

As we stepped into a long hallway, voices could be heard at the other end, but not loud enough to pick out words.

Jenny whispered, "That's where the study is." She reached into her jacket and pulled out her gun.

I didn't think that was a good idea, especially if the three bad guys in the study had guns. I doubted Jenny would be able to shoot all three before they shot her, and us. And they would be trigger happy upon seeing her armed.

Or, they may just shoot anyway. And we'd be walking into the room defenseless.

I didn't tell her to put the gun down.

We snuck down the hallway. French doors opened into the room, but were nearly closed, so that only a thin slice of the room could be seen.

The voices grew louder as we approached, but still too soft to understand.

Tyler sneezed. *Sorry.*

"Aha! *Zey* are here!" said a man in a thick German accent.

"Jenny! Run!" There was a loud smack followed by an "*Oomph.*"

"Daddy!" cried Jenny.

"Wait!" yelled the German. "Don't make me kill your father! I want to talk to you. A nice little chitchat. Your father said you would have a gun. I suggest you drop *ze* gun."

Jenny looked at the pistol in her hand, but didn't drop it.

33

"He saved your life, *zis* loving father of yours, by telling us you had a gun. I can *zen* warn you. If not, and you walk into *ze* room, my two comrades would shoot you on sight. *Zey* are not too smart like that. *Zey* see someone with *ze* gun, and *zey* shoot! Before *zey* are shot. Hmm, maybe that *is* a good plan."

The direction of the German's voice changed. "Tell her to drop *ze* gun."

"Jenny, leave the gun on the floor, honey. There are three men in here armed."

Jenny looked at me.

I said quietly, "If there are three guys in there with guns, our best chance is to negotiate, see what they want."

She thought about that for a moment, then ejected a chambered round, catching it in the air, and ejected the magazine. She pressed the round into the magazine, shoved the mag in her jeans pocket and put the gun on the floor. "Okay, the gun is on the floor."

Jenny obviously knew how to use a gun. Maybe she could actually take them. But they were professional killers. And just because she could snatch ejected rounds out of the air, didn't mean she could aim. Still, I was impressed. If she knew how to cook those cans of Wolf brand chili, there wouldn't be a more perfect wife in the world.

The German said, "Please come join us. We are having a nice visit." Someone snapped fingers and then heavy feet walked across the floor.

Jenny looked at me. I didn't know what to do either. I'm an IT geek, not a superhero.

I got down on one knee, eye level with Tyler and cupped his muzzle with my hands. I knew he would understand everything I was about to say to him, and I also knew that Jenny would think I'm some sort of freak.

She'd be right.

"I need you to stay here. If you go in there, they will shoot you. I don't want to take a chance of that happening. We need to talk to these people so we can find out what the hell's going on. But if you hear us scream, then run in there and bite someone's ass. Preferably not mine."

"Or mine," Jenny agreed.

Tyler locked eyes with me. *I understand. I want to kill them. But I have no chance against a gun. Humans hide behind weapons. Cowards. I mean no offense.*

I nodded. He was right. Humans hide behind weapons. Yet you could also say that without the higher intelligence of humans we wouldn't have the weapons to begin with. But that certainly doesn't make us nobler. In fact, the opposite.

I didn't admit to him that if I saw a 90 lbs. growling beast jumping for my jugular and I had a gun, I'd shoot. That may make me a coward, but I'd be a breathing coward.

I stood and walked with Jenny into the study.

As soon as we entered the room, a humongous man aimed a silenced pistol at my head and a gigantic man aimed a silenced pistol at Jenny's. I could not tell if either of these men were the two that chased Tyler and I. They seemed bigger in person, yet I had only seen the killers in the dark and from a distance.

Another man pointed a gun at a figure on the floor, I assumed to be Jenny's father, Mr. Meredith. The man was much smaller than the goons, splinter-thin with bright white skin, a long thin nose, thin lips, and slits for eyes. He smiled.

Mr. Meredith lay in a fetal position so both of his hands could plug the hole in his right thigh and keep the blood in. It didn't work as blood seeped between his fingers and pooled on the floor. A lot of blood. I wondered if the femoral artery had been pierced. I didn't know how long it would take a person to bleed out. Five minutes? Fifteen minutes? He looked bad. His greyish hair matted with sweat, and his skin was pale except the red swelling of his left eye.

Tears shimmered in Jenny's eyes. She stepped toward her father.

The presumed leader of this group raised his hand and shouted, "*Nein!*

Jenny stopped.

I stepped forward and yelled, "We need to help him!"

"*Nein.* He is already dead. He just doesn't know it yet."

"Who are you people?"

"I am Francisco." He pointed to the goons and said, smiling, "This is Jose and this is Pedro." To Jenny, he said, "You are very pretty. These pictures are inadequate." He gestured at the various family pictures in the study. "You are much more appealing in *ze* flesh." The corner of his mouth curled upward. He snapped his fingers.

One of the goons approached Jenny.

"Don't worry," said Splinterman. "He is only going to pat you down for concealed weapons and will not touch you inappropriately. I on *ze* other hand…"

I thought about impressing them with my bravado and saying something like, 'If you lay a hand on her…' but this wasn't the movies and they weren't going to hogtie me to keep me still, after which I would have deftly produced a razor blade from my mouth and sawed through my restraints and rescued us all in a barrage of bullets with the gun I wrestled away from Francisco that I didn't know how to shoot well.

The goon took the clip from Jenny and patted me down, finding nothing of interest.

"Very good," said Splinterman. "Now we can have our chitchat. I like that word, chitchat. Your father has some very important information, *my* information in fact, and I want it. He is stubborn."

Splinterman shot Mr. Meredith in the other leg.

"*Aaugh!*"

"Daddy!" Jenny fisted her hands and looked as if she was going to charge the lunatic.

Splinterman aimed the silenced pistol at Jenny and fired, missing over her left shoulder.

Jenny clapped a hand to her left ear, evidently hearing the bullet wiz by.

"Maybe you can persuade him otherwise," said Splinterman, still smiling. "Maybe he will be sensible instead of making me hurt you. I am in a… how do you Americans say it? A win-win situation. I get *ze* information. If he does not tell me, I have fun with you, and I get *ze* information. In fact, I hope he does not say anything." The disgusting man let out a high-pitched cackle.

I wished I had some trained spider monkeys.

Jenny's father looked at her beseechingly. Staring. "Jenny, I love you, there is no time for me. Just do what he says. He's right, I'm already dead. The data he wants is on a flash drive on the fourth bookshelf by the wall. Give it to him."

She looked in the direction her dad indicated. "No. I can't." She made a fast swipe at her face to remove a tear.

"Yes. I will see you again. It is not forever. I will see you in Paradise. Now I can be with your Mom, and I will someday be with you again. Trust me. But I want you to have a full life here first. Get—*aangh*—get the data. *Please.*"

I looked at the large bookcases, just now seeing them. Funny how walking into a room at gunpoint and seeing a dying man on the floor keeps you from noticing your surroundings.

The study was large, with a ten-foot ceiling. One wall was all windows, with heavy green drapes. A massive U-shaped cherry wood desk sat next to the windows with a bank of four flat screen computer monitors. Another wall was covered with family pictures, a beautiful woman in some of them—obviously Jenny's mother. She looked just like her.

Mr. Meredith and Splinterman were by the desk. The goons stood next to us by the door.

Jenny grabbed my hand for support. She led me to the bookcases on the opposite end of the room and said without moving her lips in a whisper loud enough that only I could hear, "Get Tyler."

I couldn't think how that would possibly help. I did not want to call Tyler's name and thus alarm Splinterman, making him think our savior was going to walk into the room. I had no doubt he would shoot whatever entered the room if alerted first. I gambled that seeing a dog walk straight to us would be less threatening and make him not as inclined to be trigger happy.

I had seen Mr. Broxton snap his fingers and then Tyler appear at his side from wherever he had been. I hoped the dog would do the same for me.

I waited until Jenny picked up the flash drive and then I snapped my fingers. Tyler trotted into the room straight to my side standing on a carpet runner. I didn't know Jenny's plan, assuming she even had one, but I prayed it would work. I couldn't see how we were going to get out of this either alive or with Jenny unmolested. I felt like the bottom had disappeared from under our feet, dropping us into an abyss from which we had no hope of ever returning.

Jenny squeezed my hand uncomfortably tight. She looked at her father. "I love you, Daddy."

Her father managed a weak smile.

She stepped toward Splinterman, then thrust out the flash drive with her free hand and yelled, "Here, you worthless son of a—"

"Thank you my sweet—"

He disappeared—the whole *room* disappeared!

Chapter Ten

We slid down a polished metal tube. Not fast, but with enough speed to keep us from braking with hands and feet.

Tyler tried to dig his claws into the tube but slipped and went the rest of the way on his haunches.

I turned sideways to make an awkward attempt to see if Splinterman or his goons followed, but the opening had closed. After what seemed to be two seconds but was surely more like three (my timekeeping skills are not as accurate as Jenny's), we ungracefully slid to a halt as the tube opened into a small room with a tile floor.

I jumped up. "Woo! What was that! Did you see the looks on their faces? Did you see the look on mine?"

Tyler panted with excitement, face grinning. I don't know if he actually enjoyed the slide or if he just fed off my enthusiasm. I patted him brusquely on the side as his tail wagged.

Jenny didn't smile. Oh yeah, her father was bleeding to death right in front of us, and we left him there with a maniac who'd already shot him twice.

And there I cheered.

My score on the Idiot Index climbed in dramatic fashion.

"I'm sorry, Jenny. I'm sorry about your dad."

She walked to a console on the wall and pressed a button. A panel slid down closing off the tube, like a small garage door.

The barrier also closed us off from helping her dad. Forever.

"And I'm sorry about my selfish reaction just now."

She made brief eye contact and flinched a smile.

The first thought that popped into my head was that I'd blown it. Followed quickly by how silly I am to think there was anything between us to mess up. Followed again by another revelation about how selfish I am.

And it was the second time within a few seconds I'd thought of myself instead of her loss. I know about loss. I've lost *a lot* in my life already, which has given me a greater empathy for others. I don't know why my thoughts at that time indicated otherwise.

And now Jenny had lost a lot. Her dad… and it seemed like her mom was no longer living either.

Sometimes life sucked.

Jenny grabbed some keys from a workbench next to a small tunnel. "We need to put some distance between us and them. That is, assuming you want to leave. You can stay here with them if you want." She walked off.

Well, at least she talked to me.

Tyler and I followed. I wanted to ask where we were going, where does the tunnel lead, *why* was there a tunnel, what were we going to do next, did she know who those people were— oh no! I'd left my backpack in her car. The data from Mr. Broxton's computer was in my backpack.

A large bang boomed behind us as something heavy crashed into the panel door.

All three of us twirled around. One of the goons must have jumped into the tube to chase us, slamming against the door.

"Crap," said Jenny. "They've already figured out how to open the trapdoor." She turned back to the tunnel and ran, holding a flashlight in front. "Come on!"

Since both Tyler and I had intellects more advanced than your basic paramecium, especially Tyler, we ran after her. The sound of our shoes slapping the floor echoed like reports from a semiautomatic pistol.

Jenny yelled between breaths to be heard over our footfalls, "We need to call 911."

I responded in like volume, "We should get clear of your house first. And my backpack is still in your car. I have to get it."

"Crap."

Another thing we had in common in addition to both being human was a similar vocabulary.

The tunnel ended at a metal gate. Jenny unlocked it with a key, then locked it after we exited. We were now in a sewer.

We went left and followed this section of tunnel as it curved. I wondered if you could develop a phobia about having a phobia many people have. I wasn't claustrophobic yet, but I was sick of being in so many tunnels in one night. Craziness.

This one ended at iron bars set horizontally in the concrete wall, making a crude stepladder. A manhole cover capped the top. The thing weighed over a hundred pounds. Here was my chance to impress Jenny with my brute strength, acquired from years of sitting at a keyboard. Yeah.

But I was being too hard on myself. I really was in good shape.

Jenny looked at me with one eyebrow raised.

Tyler looked at me with both eyebrows raised. *Want me to get that for you?*

I looked at both of them and said, "I guess I should get that, huh?" Then I said in a lowered voice, but enough to be heard, "Impress the lady. Drive with the legs." I pretended to spit on my palms, then slapped them together and swiftly rubbed.

I looked at Jenny and winked, then almost laughed at my stupid macho act. Grabbing the first of the iron rungs, I climbed as high as I could go without bending over, and took an extra step to force up with my legs.

Then I had a sudden insight: "Where does this lead, a street? Am I about to get tread-head?"

In spite of everything else, she laughed. "It might look good on you."

Taking that as a no, I lifted the lid, trying my hardest not to grunt. I pushed the lid to the side and climbed up. It was a storm drain.

I looked down at Jenny and said, "All clear." Then realized I'd have to carry Tyler up the steps. Joy. He was way too big to tuck under an arm and climb. I'd have to be able to grab the next rung with at least one free hand or we'd both be going nowhere. The manhole wasn't wide enough for me to put him on my shoulders, even if I could climb while making sure he didn't slide off.

"You don't happen to have some rope and a harness, do you?"

Jenny patted her jeans pockets. "Nope."

"Bummer." I looked around me, hoping to find a miracle or an angel. I didn't see any. "What time is it?"

Jenny looked at her watch. "Three o'clock."

Three AM. Ouch. Angels must be sleeping.

"Okay, Tyler. Climb up."

He sat.

Sigh.

I climbed down into the tunnel. "We're going to have to both climb with him. If you can kind of grab under his front legs and keep him from falling backwards, I'll try to push up on his back legs."

"Ooookay." Jenny held the small flashlight in her teeth.

I stood Tyler on his hind legs. Jenny took two steps up, then wrapped one arm around his front shoulder. I lifted Tyler to the first rung.

I said, "Tyler, I need you to keep your back legs stiff," as if he could understand me. Which he could, but Jenny didn't know that.

Tyler said, *If you drop me, your butt is going to have new holes.*

I said to Jenny, "Go up another step and I'll push."

She did so. I squatted underneath Tyler and pushed up on his hips.

"Let's take another step on three. One, two, three. One, two, three…"

No matter how hard I tried to reposition, my face was in the rather unpleasant location of being right next Tyler's rear end. I petitioned God for a gas-free climb to freedom and fresh air.

We ascended in this manner until Jenny could roll out of the way and Tyler could get his front legs on the ground and climb out.

I looked around, trying to get my bearings. "Where are we?"

"Two streets over."

"Let's see if we can get back to your car, if those goons aren't close. Then we can get out of here and call 911."

"This way."

The three of us ran up the street toward Jenny's car, trying to stay in shadows and close to landscaping that could provide cover. Lucky for us the streets were deserted so we didn't have to dodge headlights.

This was a very well-to-do neighborhood. I'm sure the residents weren't accustomed to seeing two people dressed in black and a dog running from one hiding spot to the next along the street. Thankfully no one saw us.

With Jenny's car in sight, we paused *out* of sight and scoped the area for trouble. We tried to quiet our heavy breathing so we could listen and not be heard. Despite the effort, plumes of fog puffed out of our mouths as if we were tiny smokestacks.

I gave the all clear sign with an upturned thumb, then we sprinted to the car. I ran so fast to the BMW I couldn't slow down in time and slammed against the side with an *oomph!*

After opening the door for Tyler, I jumped in and noticed Jenny was already in the car, started, belted, and shifted in gear.

How did she do that?

She turned on the lights and hit the accelerator.

A goon stepped into the middle of the street about fifty yards in front of us, taking aim with his gun.

Jenny started to swerve but I yelled, "Hit him!"

The gun flashed followed by a metallic *thwack!*

"Hit him!"

"I'm trying!" Jenny steered toward him and pressed harder on the gas pedal.

"Turn on the brights!"

The goon lit up like he was on stage. He used one arm to shield his eyes, aiming with the other. Another muzzle flash, but nothing happened.

Evidently it's harder than I thought to hit something the size of a car bearing down on you while blinded.

The goon made no effort to get out of the way, probably thinking these two nice kids wouldn't actually run him over.

He was wrong.

Sort of.

At the last second, Jenny slammed on the brakes, but too late to keep from hitting him.

The front bumper hit his legs with a sickening thud, then his face slammed against the hood, his body rolling onto the car. He bounced off the windshield just as the car stopped and then slid to the side on the street, unmoving.

Jenny shrieked, "Oh my God oh my God oh my God!"

"It's okay, we're okay, we need to go."

"Oh my God is he dead?"

"I don't know, but we can't stop to find out. His buddies will be here any second. They won't stop to find out if we're dead, they'll just kill us!"

For most well-adjusted individuals, it's difficult to purposefully kill someone. The Kill People switch in our brain stays off. Taking someone's life is shocking even in self-defense, or when trying to save someone you love.

Obviously, we can be trained to overcome the obstacle, and some non-well-adjusted people flip the switch on with intent.

I didn't know for sure, but I doubted Jenny had ever killed anyone before. I feared she was going to shutdown.

I *had* killed. A part of me died simultaneously.

But for better or for worse, I wasn't shutting down. I had to get Jenny going. She just sat there, bone-white hands squeezing the steering wheel so tight that blood couldn't flow into fingers.

The rear windshield exploded.

Chapter Eleven

I smacked Jenny on the shoulder, hard, and yelled, "*Go go go go go!*"

Another bullet hit the trunk.

"Tyler, get down!"

I made a feeble attempt to look behind us to see who shot, but it was too dark to see at a glance. Then decided it didn't make a difference.

Jenny stomped the gas pedal. The tires screeched briefly before biting pavement and the car shot forward. She fishtailed a right onto the street exiting her neighborhood.

I looked behind us. "I don't see any headlights. They're not following us."

We took a left onto the highway away from town. I looked behind us again and took a deep breath, relaxing a little with no sight of pursuit. "I think we're good."

Wrong.

I caught a glimpse of a hard-to-see black Suburban waiting for us, lights dark, on the shoulder. Then headlights on and gravel spewing.

"Crap!"

Jenny pressed harder on the accelerator. Thankfully the car seemed to be unharmed by the bullets it took. German engineering.

But Jenny's BMW wasn't a racecar, and the Suburban, though still a few hundred yards behind us, would overtake us on this two-lane highway.

I wished we were in the *Beast*.

We rounded a long bend and over a hill, then Jenny abruptly cut the lights, slammed on the brakes, yanking the steering wheel left, and drove into brush in between trees.

The car whined in protest as bushes and tree limbs scratched the roof and sides. With no headlights, it was too dark to see small things, but Jenny weaved around slightly visible car-stopping trees. We bounced over the rough terrain; our seatbelts kept us pinned to the seats. *Crunch-pop-squeal* the car dutifully plowed through the woods and underbrush.

A large branch lodged against the right rear passenger window sill, pressing until the window gave in. Glass shards showered the backseat. Tyler moved to the other side, his coat too smooth for any of the glass to stick.

We eventually rolled to a stop. Jenny didn't use the brakes so we wouldn't light up like a Christmas tree.

She put the car in park and turned it off.

Then we all turned around in the seats and held our breath. We couldn't see the highway, and I couldn't tell if we'd see any car headlights drive by.

This was our only hope. We were all in. If they found us here… dead.

But still a better plan than trying to outrun them, especially when they cheat with guns.

The gaping hole where the back windshield used to be made it easy to hear. A car drove by in the opposite direction. The thick brush blocked the light low to the ground, but light could be seen reflecting off the trees. And sound carried well.

Almost immediately, a large-engine vehicle screamed by with deep sounding tire noise, probably a truck. We couldn't see it, but it had to be the killers.

We continued to sit in silence.

Two minutes.

Five minutes.

Eight minutes.

At some point, they'll realize they'd been duped, but when, and what would they do? Would they double back? The road curved a lot in this area. Not sharp turns, but long bends and small hills. Line of sight travelled a short distance.

A strong musty smell from damp trees and ground settled into the car.

Everything was silent. The wildlife had either gone to bed or had left, scattering when we drove into their living room.

I turned to face forward in the seat. Jenny did the same.

I looked at her and said, "When did you learn to drive like that?"

"Just now."

"Oh."

Tyler said, *I need to pee.*

I thought of checking the time on my phone and realized I no longer had a phone. So I thought of checking Jenny's, then realized she no longer had a phone. Oy. Stupid GPS-enabled cellphones. I made a mental note to get a sundial.

But then I remembered Jenny had a watch. I was getting tired and not thinking straight. I asked her the time.

The watch face didn't illuminate. She reached into her glove box, retrieved a flashlight and deftly looked at her watch. Yes, deftly. I would consider *any* action someone successfully completed this early in the morning with no sleep to have done so with deft.

"Four-thirty."

"It's probably all right, but where's your switch to turn off the dome light?"

She reached up to the light above my head and slid it to *Off* so the light wouldn't illuminate when a door opened.

I got out and opened the door for Tyler, who found the closest tree suitable for relieving himself.

Jenny walked up next to me. I stared at Tyler.

I turned to give him some privacy, and looked at Jenny. "I'm sorry about your father."

No reaction. I guessed she was tabling the emotions, even the acknowledgement for now. So I moved onto something else. "You hungry?"

I'm always hungry. It only seemed natural that Jenny would be hungry too.

I heard Tyler, *Yes.* I heard Jenny, "Yes."

I retrieved three granola bars from my backpack that I kept for emergencies and passed them out. I left the wrapper on Tyler's granola bar, and he said in response, *I'll bite you.*

"You need to learn patience."

Jenny looked at me.

I said, "Talking to the dog."

Jenny looked at her battered car and rubbed the large indention on the hood. She simply said, "Sadness."

Having a strong affinity for my own car, I empathized with how she felt.

I walked around the passenger side to assess the damage to her Beamer. Deep scratches lined the fenders and doors. At some point during our Texas jungle adventure, the front bumper hit something large enough to remove it.

At least one bullet was lodged in the front of the car. I stooped in front to see if I could locate the bullet entry. It was too dark, and I didn't want to use a flashlight. But the hissing sound seemed to indicate the radiator wasn't happy about something. Plus there was the strong smell of antifreeze. The car would probably overheat if we started it back up.

Just as I'm not a mechanic, I'm also not a ballistics expert. But I couldn't imagine the back windshield could stop the travel of the bullet that shattered it. We might find as many as a half-dozen bullets in the car.

As I continued to inspect Jenny's ride, I marveled that none of the tires were flat—scratch that. The driver side rear tire was flat, the bottom partially hidden by soft ground.

I finished the circuit and walked up to her. She sensed what I was doing and looked at me expectantly, not having the heart to look herself.

"We're not going anywhere in your car. She's done."

"Sadness," Jenny repeated, and closed her eyes.

A deep voice boomed, "What in the blue *hell* are you kids doing!"

43

Chapter Twelve

I jumped at the voice which resounded like a cannon. It startled me so bad I reflexively covered my ears and flinched to drop to my knees and duck for cover, but I recovered before actually hitting the dirt.

I whirled around to see a large man in all black leveling a shotgun at my torso, then Jenny's, then mine, back and forth. He used the front end of the car as a barrier between us.

Tyler had been off exploring and was also taken off guard by the man who manifested out of nowhere, without a noise, like a ghost. The dog ran up to us, walked around the corner of the car, and growled.

"Call off the dog or it's dead." He pumped the shotgun for effect. "It's been awhile since I had dog stew."

I wondered why it always seems more ominous when someone pumps a shotgun after a threat, or cocks a revolver. The gun will kill you just as dead either way.

There was such little light, the man's outline could barely be seen. He seemed to be wearing black fatigues. Just a large mass, features blending into the darkness. He said, "You two keep your hands up," as he aimed down toward Tyler.

Jenny and I raised our hands over our heads.

I said, "Tyler, come here. Come on."

I got him. Tyler continued to growl.

"Tyler, no. Come *here.*"

I didn't really know if Tyler would obey. I hadn't been around him enough. And just earlier that night—it didn't seem possible that everything had happened in just one night—he failed to protect Mr. Broxton, and thought it was his fault.

"Tyler, you're not faster than a gun—"

"—darn straight—"

"—come here before he shoots you."

"Boy's talkin' sense, dog. Listen to'im."

Tyler stopped growling, but didn't move and didn't avert his eyes. I heard him sniffing.

I am amazed at how well dogs can judge a human's character. I don't have scientific proof, but it's been my experience, that dogs have an uncanny ability to sense whether a person is good or bad. I trust a dog's initial *impression* on whether to trust that person or not.

If the dog does, I'll be more likely to follow suit. If the dog doesn't, I won't be friending the person on Facebook.

I said, "What do you think?"

Jenny looked sideways at me, not knowing if I was talking to her.

The stranger glanced at me as well.

I smiled and nodded toward the dog as if to say I'm talking to him. It sure would've be nice if I could communicate silently with Tyler like he could with me.

Tyler said, *Difficult to know. I think he's okay. Could be wrong. I need to smell his butt.*

"Not going to happen. Get over here."

Jenny looked at me again.

Tyler backed a few steps, still eyeing the armed stranger, then moved quickly to my side.

I said, "Good dog." I would have reached down to pat him, but we still had our hands up. Even if the stranger wasn't planning on harming us, it didn't mean I should test him.

He pointed the shotgun at the ground and said, "Now what're you kids doing out here?" He had a heavy southern accent, even for the Deep South.

Jenny and I exchanged glances, neither one of us knowing what to say or not say.

He turned his head to take in the car. "Looks to me like you're running from something. I ain't never seen someone crazy 'nuff to drive through my woods. Yep. This here's a first. And you sure as hell picked a bad car to go offroadin'."

I noticed he didn't seem to have trouble seeing in the dark. Then I noticed the contraption over his eyes. Night vision goggles.

I said, "Does everybody but me have night vision goggles?"

Tyler said, *I don't.*

I extended my leg sideways to kick him on the hip.

"Oh, you like these?" he said as his finger tapped the side of the goggles.

"Yes, sir."

"Military grade 3rd Gen AN/PVS-7D dual eye tube goggles. I can see better at night than you can during the day and I ain't gotta squint to do it!" He relaxed the arm holding the shotgun allowing the barrel to point straight down.

Detecting an opportunity to win his favor by appealing to the obvious pride in his goggles, I said, "Very impressive, sir. I've wanted to get night vision goggles myself. Where can I find goggles like yours?"

Again tapping them he said, "These here I bought from a Nam buddy of mine online. I gotta deal. They'd cost you close to four thousand dollars with the features I have. Shoot."

I tried to be impressed—which was easy since I was—without going overboard. "Wow, four thousand dollars? The quality of those goggles must really be outstanding."

"Yep."

I thought I heard the pitch of his voice change as if smiling. I was winning his favor.

Then he raised the shotgun and said, "Now quit trying to change the subject!"

Or maybe not.

We had gotten back to that again. I still didn't know what to say. Jenny stood next to me, arms raised, as soundless as a fallen tree.

The stranger prodded, "Why are you two crazies driving through my woods in one of them German cars made for valet parking?"

I wanted to say, 'It's Jenny's car, sir. I wouldn't own a German car. American made, all the way.' But I'd be lying because I would like a Mercedes and if the stranger didn't kill me, Jenny would.

So instead, tapping into the shallow well of discretion I possess, I said, gravely, "I understand you think we are crazy. And to a point I agree with you, sir. But please don't let your initial perception influence your thoughts regarding what I'm about to tell you, which, sir, is the truth."

I paused to give my request added weight.

Tyler said, *This ought to be good.*

The dog just lost his chance for more Cheetos.

"It's a long story; may we put our hands down, sir?"

He stood silent a time, then sighed. Finally, he said, "Fine. But I'm warning you, if either of you so much as fart—sorry little lady—I'm gonna blow yer intestines out. It'll be the last time you ever pass gas."

Trying my best to make sure lowering my arms didn't press gas into my colon, I rubbed each arm to get the blood flowing again. "I went to Tyler's house, that's the dog, to help his owner, Mr. Broxton, with a computer problem. When I arrived, Mr. Broxton was on the floor in his study, wounded by what would be a fatal gunshot. There were two black Suburbans at his house, and at least two people dressed in black on the premises. Before Mr. Broxton died, he told me to get specific data off his computer and warn Mr. Meredith."

I paused there to make sure the vet was with me so far. I used names, since even using fake names added legitimacy to a story. But I used real names because I was too tired to put on a good act.

He said, "Go on."

"I got the data as instructed and Tyler and I fled the house. The two dressed-in-black bad guys saw us and tried to shoot us." I wondered if I should omit Tyler's wall-jumping bag-carrying Cheetos-scarfing abilities. "Do you like Cheetos, sir?"

"Huh? What do Cheetos have to do with anything?"

"It's a weird question, sir. Never mind. I'm nervous."

Despite the Cheetos question, the vet seemed to be interested. "I guess you got away since you're standing here."

"Yes, sir."

"I wouldn't have missed."

"I'm sure you wouldn't have, sir. We ran through the woods and drain pipes until we got to Jenny's house, this is Jenny—"

Jenny said, "Nice to meet you."

The vet said, "Likewise, ma'am."

This whole scene was just too bizarre. I continued, "We ran into Jenny outside her house. A solid black Suburban was outside. Jenny, and I know this sounds crazy sir, but it's the truth, led us through a secret entrance into her house."

"What's crazy about that?" said the vet. "I might have one or two myself."

Jenny backhanded me on the shoulder.

Pressing on, "We found Mr. Meredith, her dad, lying on the floor in his study. He was bleeding to death from a gunshot in the leg. A German man—" I didn't know if the southern stranger had something against Germans, but I made sure the supposed European heritage of the bad guy was described— "and two of his goons, probably German, were there waiting for us. The main German bad guy tried to get the same data—I don't know what's so important about it—and shot Mr. Meredith in the other leg because we didn't give it to him."

I paused again, hoping we were winning him over. The more I thought about it as I told the stranger our story, the more the realization grew that we needed an ally. We had nowhere to run and no one to ask for help. It was obvious we weren't going to beat the killers on our own. I didn't know in what way the Viet Nam vet could help, and I'm assuming he was a vet, but it didn't make a difference. We were desperate. If he became an ally, we'd certainly get more assistance from him than we would from any one of the many trees in the area.

The vet said, "Then what happened?"

"Jenny tricked the evil German leader, doubtless a Nazi sympathizer and worshiper of Adolf Hitler's spirit, by feigning to hand him a flash drive that was instead a remote for a trap door."

I couldn't see, of course, but I imagined his eyebrows rose. "We fell into a tube and the trap door closed cutting off the chase."

For the first time since we started talking, the man shifted his weight. He turned to place the shotgun leaning against a tree within easy reach, then turned back and folded his arms to listen.

"The tube dumped us into a small chamber. Jenny closed a door behind us a minute before one of the goons slammed against it. We escaped through sewer tunnels until we got to Jenny's car." I pointed to the poor Beemer's remains next to us. "But by the time we were able to get to the car, the goons were waiting for us."

"An ambush," replied the vet just before the sound of spit hitting the ground.

"Yes, sir. One of them stood in front of the car and tried to shoot us, but Jenny ran him over."

"You don't say... well that's mighty 'pressive."

"Thank you," said Jenny.

Yes! He seemed to be genuinely impressed.

"But the other goon started shooting at us from behind. We got the hell out of there and onto the road feeding the neighborhood. I guess the German leader was in the second Suburban, which waited for us on the side of the road. But we had a head start, and Jenny managed to get us into these woods to hide, evading the evil Gestapo-loving German in the Suburban."

"Well, sounds like you did a fine job, ma'am. Took care of everything. What did this beau of yours do to help out?"

Jenny remained silent. Fallen trees everywhere would be proud.

"I, uh..."

Jenny turned her head to look at me. Even in the dark, I could see a perceptive smile. Or maybe I imagined it.

No, it was there.

She said, "Ellie—I mean, Elijah—saved my life. If he hadn't stopped me from going to my house, I'd be dead."

I smiled. Mine wasn't perceptive, it was as bright as any neon sign. Then I remembered the vet could see in the dark. I pulled the plug on the sign.

Jenny patted me on the back which felt like a I'll-take-over-from-here gesture.

She said, "Mr... what would you like for us to call you?"

"Thompson. Charles Thompson. Please call me Charles."

"Thank you, Mr. Charles. If you would be in a position to help us, we would be greatly indebted to you. You see, we're out of our league here. Those bad guys, or evil Germans, may be coming back for us. They'll want to kill us, just like they killed my..." She stopped and placed her face in her hands, sobbing quietly.

She was good. I didn't know if this was an act or not. She wouldn't have to fake it. Regardless, she was good. There was no way Mr. Charles could deny helping us at this point.

Charles Thompson, Viet Nam vet, pulled a handkerchief, stepped to Jenny and lightly tapped her shoulder with the offering so she would open her eyes and look up.

"Thank you. I'm sorry."

47

The vet looked at the ground, looked at Jenny, looked at me, then Tyler, looked back at Jenny, looked at her car, looked at his watch, and then took a deep breath. "Come on, follow me."

Chapter Thirteen

Charles said, "I know it's plumb-near impossible to see, and I have a flashlight with me, but if'n there might be some miscreants around here, best not to use it. Just try to step where I step."

Charles was right, very hard to see. The woods thickened as we followed him.

As bipeds, Jenny and I did our best to keep from landing on all fours. Our feet kept getting caught in vines, we stumbled over fallen branches, tripped over tree roots. Tyler, with the unfair advantages of having four legs, and better eyesight, had little problem. Maybe Jenny and I *should* have gotten on all fours.

I didn't think the temperature had dipped lower, but the cold and damp were really starting to sink deep into me, down to my bones. New meaning to shiver me timbers.

After a lot of crunching, grunting, stomping, and arm flailing, we arrived at a gate. Charles led us through and twenty more yards of smooth terrain brought us to a porch.

Faint lights were visible through the windows, but still not enough light outside to see the house.

Upon closer scrutiny, at least some of the faint light was caused by a fire in a huge fireplace.

Hallelujah!

Charles retrieved something from his pocket, and though standing a few feet from the door, it opened on its own. "Come on in. The dog will need to stay in the back room."

Tyler said, *Bugger.*

I laughed. Charles and Jenny looked at me curiously. "Sorry."

Charles closed and latched the door, closed some blinds, then walked over to what looked to be a coffee table and grabbed a big remote. He pressed a button and solid metal shields dropped into place covering each of the visible windows and the back door.

Jenny gasped.

We were trapped.

Hansel and Gretel.

Maybe allying with Charles wasn't such a good idea.

He had removed the nightvision goggles and busied about lighting candlesticks dispersed throughout the room. He moved quickly and silently.

Jenny and I exchanged glances. Tyler sat on the floor between us.

Charles said, "Go ahead and sit in those chairs by the fire. I'll make some hot cocoa." Finished with the candles, he walked over to the chairs, gesturing with his hands.

I knew I was cold, and figured Jenny to be more so. She's always cold at Buy City.

Man, Buy City felt a million miles away.

I took Jenny's hand and led her to the chairs. Tyler padded slowly behind us.

Charles smiled as we approached, if you could call it a smile. It might have been a sneer. This was the first time I'd seen his face. The flickering light from the fireplace and candles made his features waver, phasing in and out. The effect did not put me at ease. He had a shaggy brown beard that made him look like a grizzly bear, with slits for eyes that seemed to be in a constant squint. There wasn't enough light to see the color. Deep creases outlined his nose. And bushy eyebrows that seemed to leap off his face in moments when firelight intensified.

Yet it was his size that took me by surprise. He'd taken off his black jacket, and was *still* huge. I'd assumed the jacket made him look bigger than he was as his outline faded into black outside.

The sneer-smile didn't soften even as he asked, "Y'all want some hot cocoa?"

I looked nervously at Jenny. She looked nervously at me.

Not wanting to offend Charles, I nodded and said, "Yes, sir. We would love some."

I couldn't get Hansel and Gretel out of my mind. But I figured if he wanted to off us, he wouldn't need poisonous hot chocolate to make it happen. The shotgun would do just fine. Though the cleanup would be more of an undertaking. At least he wasn't offering cookies.

He set off for the kitchen. "Do you want some chocolate chip cookies?"

Eek gad!

I pondered our situation. I could say yes and then run to the kitchen, shoving him into the oven just as he opened the door. No, he wouldn't fit. Even if it was a double oven and I cut him in half. And that would be messy. With my luck, I'd only find a butter knife to saw him in half. How long would that take? How long could I saw on him before the sneer-smile turned into an all-out dirty look?

I must have been pondering for a while because Jenny whispered, "Aren't you going to answer?"

I snapped out of it, then said quietly, "You can answer too, you know."

She folded her arms and turned away from me.

Women.

Charles was probably some sort of warlock from the Sixth Circle of Satanic Acolytes, who met biweekly at the local VA to accommodate Charles the Nam Vet, and intent on killing us then skewering our chopped up body parts—alternating white and dark meat—with some shrimp, and Jenny won't say whether she wants cookies with her cocoa.

Speaking of food, I've got to stop feeding my subconscious with an enriched diet of horror novels.

Tyler said, *I want cookies.*

Charles raised his voice to be heard from the kitchen. "Hello?"

Tyler said again, *I want cookies. Does he have Chips Ahoy? I* love *Chips Ahoy.*

Speaking of food, again, I was famished. And just a wild guess, but I had a feeling Tyler wanted cookies.

"Yes, sir, Jenny says she wants cookies."

She backhanded me hard on the shoulder and gave me a dirty look.

Ouch. "Please?"

"That's not what I meant, Ellie," she said in a low voice.

"Oh." I smiled.

A couple of minutes later, Charles came out of the kitchen carrying a tray and a bag of Chips Ahoy cookies.

Tyler's tail started thumping the side of the chair. *Oh boy oh boy oh boy.*

The hot chocolate was excellent. I cradled the mug, warming my hands, holding it just under my nose, letting the heat rise into my nostrils.

Jenny seemed to be enjoying hers as well.

I said to Charles, "Is it all right if Tyler has some cookies?"

Charles sat on a couch next to the chairs. He scowled. If you could call what his face was doing a scowl. It looked similar to what I thought was a smile. Actually, every expression was part sneer, part scowl. He looked like he could slit the throats of Sunday school teachers just as easily as Viet Cong.

"Hmph. Cookies are people food. That dog ain't people. In fact, why's he even over here? He's supposed to be by the back door."

Busted.

Tyler whined.

Jenny looked sad.

Charles's scowl softened to a sneer.

Or, maybe his face… I don't know. I give up trying to describe it.

He said, "Fine."

Tyler's tail resumed chair thumping.

I didn't know what Charles had against dogs, but I wanted him to see how well behaved Tyler was. I palmed a cookie, exposing just a sliver beyond my pinched thumb and forefinger, and offered the cookie to Tyler.

He coaxed the cookie ever-so-gently out of my hand with the left side of his front teeth. Once he'd secured the cookie, he tossed it back into his mouth and happily chewed.

Yum. More?

I got another cookie and repeated the process. If Tyler wasn't more self-disciplined, he'd lunge for the cookie and get some of my skin cells with the chocolate chips.

I glanced at Charles. If he was impressed, it was too difficult to tell.

He hadn't said anything about the Fort Knox windows and door shields. I was afraid to ask.

He said, "I'm sure you're wondrin' why I closed up all the windows and doors. If we're gonna have trouble, we're gonna play by my rules. If they didn't see y'all walking in here, they sure as hell ain't gonna see you inside. Or me. The candles make the lighting more cheerful so it don't feel like NORAD."

Cheerful? Did he really just say "cheerful"?

The bear-giant makes hot chocolate, feeds guests cookies, and wants to make things cheerful. With a sneer.

I looked around for doilies.

Then I settled deeper in the chair by the fire, watching the flames crawl up the chimney and jump back down, half-breathing half-drinking hot cocoa. The fire had a mesmerizing effect. I felt really sleepy. All of the night's fear, excitement, and stress had wiped me out. Plus, I'd been up for nearly twenty-four hours. So sleepy.

I looked at Jenny. She reclined on her left side, her hot chocolate resting in her hand on her right hip. She already seemed to be dozing, her chest rising and falling in a slow rhythm. Charles gently removed the mug from her hand before it spilled.

I couldn't see Tyler.

I leaned up to put my mug on an end table, barely having the strength. So tired. I slumped back into the chair. My eyes watched shadows color the ceiling black and then erase the coloring. I let my eyelids slide down.

The last thing I remember is wondering if the cocoa had indeed been drugged.

51

Chapter Fourteen

I woke up some hours later. I didn't know how many. The large fire had burned down to embers. The windows were still covered by the metal shields, so there was no way to know if it was night or day. I tried to lift my head, then let it fall back. The chair was so comfortable. It didn't help that my head felt like an eighteen pound bowling ball. I rested a minute, or twenty, then tried to lift up my head again to look around.

Candles still burned, but I couldn't tell if they were the same candles or replacements.

I shook my head, trying to wake up brain cells. With great effort, I managed to push myself up into an upright position using the chair arms. The effort drained me, and I wanted to go back to sleep again, but I fought the drowsiness, not letting myself succumb this time.

I rubbed my eyes and looked toward Jenny to my right. She was in the same position I saw her last night, or this morning, or whenever it was.

Then I looked left. Charles sat on the couch across from me, staring expectantly.

"You're awake!"

He actually sounded cheerful. Just like when he literally used the word 'cheerful,' it took me by surprise. Anything cheery about the man was a complete contradiction. Like a clock going counterclockwise.

I found myself gaping at him. My head was still too groggy to conjure a reply. But I was clear-headed enough to stop gaping.

I noticed a backpack close to my feet, but it wasn't mine. Then I noticed *my* backpack next to him on the couch. I wanted to object, but didn't really have any grounds, just because it was sitting there. Besides, I was glad to see it. Because, I just realized, maybe a few beats later than I should have, that… I had left the stupid thing in the car again! Unt!… I mean, ugh!

Charles saw me notice my backpack. "After you dozed off, I walked across't to the car to see if y'all'd left anything important. I got your backpack and Jenny's purse. I assume hers. Unless it's yours. It's right here." He held it for me to see. "I also got a mobile phone"—*mobile* rhymed with *go pile*—"with the battry taken out, but I didn't put it back in."

I sat, I'm sure looking dumbfounded, which is easy for me to do, for some time as I tried to decipher what he said. Living in the South, I'm used to the accent, that wasn't the problem. In fact, I could mimic the accent flawlessly. But I just couldn't think clearly.

"If you're wondrin' why you can't think clearly, it's because I sedated you."

How does he do that? Wait—sedated me? "You what?"

"Sedated. That means 'make you sleepy.' Though I thought you'd already know what it meant. It's not that big a word. I put a sleeping pill in your hot cocoa. Well, maybe two. Or three. I didn't know how it would work if you didn't swaller it whole. I have to take them sometimes when I start troublin' too much 'bout the war."

He sure seemed to be talking a lot. But I had no idea at this point if he was friend or foe. He looked like a foe. He acted like both.

I suddenly remembered Tyler, then sat up more to try and see him. "Tyler?"

"Oh, he's over there by the back door chompin' on a heifer leg."

"A what?"

"Boy, don't you know nuthin'? Oh wait, the sleeping pills. I got it. I'll speak slowly so's you can understand: The, dog, is, gnawin', on, a, bone."

Charles also talked louder, as if I was not only dumb, but also deaf.

His volume caused Jenny to stir. He looked at her and sneered. Or smiled. "Anyway, I got your stuff. Yes, I did go through your pack while you were dozin' to make sure you didn't have anything unfriendly."

I started to sneer at him, but then thought better of it. He might just think I was smiling anyway.

"I found something quite near intrestin' in the purse."

I looked at him quizzically. "What?—"

"Ellie?" Jenny tried to sit up.

"I'm right here." I stumbled to my feet and shuffled to her chair.

"Why do I feel so tired?" She put her hands on her head, I presume to make sure it was still there. "I feel like my head is in a vacuum."

I wasn't quite sure what that meant. I looked at Charles. He shrugged.

She rubbed her eyes. "Where's Tyler?"

"Eating a snow cone."

"Huh?"

Charles corrected me, "Chewing on a bone. Man, I gotta see what's in them sleeping pills. I'll get thrown in jail if a cop finds them."

Jenny turned her head to look at me, but kept rubbing her eyes. "What's he talking about?"

"Never mind." I felt like the gaslights were finally getting lit in my brain, illuminating lucid thought. "Do you want some water? Or coffee?"

"Coffee."

I looked at Charles, who was already walking back from the kitchen with a tray and two mugs. I smelled strong coffee. What a crazy-good host. I didn't even hear him get up.

He said, "Don't worry, no sleeping pills in here. Promise. And it's strong, but not too bitter."

I took a mug, sniffed, and my eyes popped wide. I started to sip, but said, "Please forgive me for asking, sir, but how do I know we can trust you?"

"I reckon you don't. But I suggest you do. You ain't got no car, no way to protect yourself. I looked over the trashed heap out there in my woods and found the bullet holes you talked about. I even found one bullet." He held that up so I could see. He was good at show and tell. He also seemed real proud of the find.

"And like I said, I went through your stuff, saw all the techno thingies... Then I found something quite near intrestin' in the purse."

Oh yeah, that. "What did you find?"

"A business card for Bob Meredith. We fought in Nam together. He's also my financial advisor."

Intrestin'. Quite near indeed. I looked at Jenny to see her reaction. She just stared at him. I didn't have a clue what was going on in her mind. She'd been sipping coffee, but stopped to stare at Charles.

For his part, Charles didn't look at her. I'm sure he figured out who Jenny's dad was. He just looked at the floor.

Uncomfortable silence.

Jenny didn't seem to be mad, so I prodded her a little, just to get things moving in a direction, any direction. "Your dad's first name was Bob?" I hated using past tense, but there was no point in denying her dad was dead.

"Robert Meredith. Everyone called him Bob. He was in Viet Nam, though he never talked about it. He did his best to act like it never happened. I wasn't allowed to ask questions about the war. He didn't get mad, but I think he just didn't want to relive the things that happened there. He'd rather ignore it all. He worked in finance, was on the board of a few companies. I know he provided advice for some friends, but that was more of something on the side."

Charles looked up from the floor, but didn't look at either one of us. "Bobby, that's what we called him then, was a rock. We saw some real hellacious stuff happen to guys in our platoon. It never fazed him. The VC set traps all over the jungle. We lost so many men. Hidden pits with metal spikes. You'd fall into one of those pits, and the spikes would pierce through your legs, your tummy, your head. Horrible deaths. Scary as hell to see. Those screams… Bobby would try to save them, even though it was obvious they were dead. You knew that could have been you. Booby traps hit from below, above, the sides… One second, you're creeping through the jungle, the next, your squad mate right next to you is dead with a bamboo spear through his neck. The safest thing was to keep moving, look for traps, hope to God you wouldn't trigger any, hope to God no one else did. That's why he didn't talk about it.

"We'd try to get him to join us when we got together. He never did. He helped with financial planning, even gave some of the guys money when they were down and out. But he didn't want anything to do with the war. We talked on the phone some, but I hadn't even seen him in years, though we live in the same town."

More silence.

Tyler was still content with the heifer leg.

Charles said to me, "You're not drinking the coffee."

I was still trying to figure him out. Tyler wasn't concerned with Charles. I imagine the bone helped. So I figured he was probably all right. Either way, I didn't want to offend him. "I'm sorry, sir, it's not because I think you drugged it, it's because I hate coffee."

"Well why didn't you say so? What do you like?"

"Do you have Coke?"

"I have Coke and DP. But I ain't got none of that prissy diet stuff. You don't drink prissy diet do you?"

"No, sir. Coke would be great, thank you."

Jenny drank prissy diet stuff, but either she wasn't man enough (symbolically speaking) to admit it, or didn't care what Charles thought of her supposed weakness as compared to diet drinks.

Charles returned with a cold bottled Coke and a glass of ice.

I'm sure the level of caffeine in my Coke wasn't as much as the brain cell agitating amount in Jenny's coffee, but it did feel like more of the fogginess melted away.

Charles said, "I suggest you look at the data that is so important that two of my platoon buddies were killed."

Oh yeah, data. Important data. Questions answered. Plans devised. Worlds saved. I definitely needed more caffeine. "That is a good idea, sir." I drained the Coke. "May I have another bottle?" Wait, did he say *two* buddies?

54

Charles sneer-smiled and got up. To Jenny, "Would you like anything else, ma'am?"

It was weird hearing him call Jenny 'ma'am.' I looked at her every time he did to make sure she wasn't suddenly 80.

Jenny said, "The coffee is warm, thank you."

Charles looked at me. I shrugged.

Charles said, "I'll make some breakfast while you check out that data." He walked to the kitchen. "If you need the bathroom, it's the first door to your left down the hallway. Don't go beyond that."

Yikes. Bladder to brain communication was one of the last subnets of my internal network to get powered on after the makes-me-sleepy hot coca. Charles just flipped the switch with the mentioning of bathroom.

I looked at Jenny to defer. She seemed content.

Thank you. My bladder had reached a critical state, and I *did not* want to perform a disaster recovery. I scampered for the bathroom.

Much to my relief, disaster averted. I returned to find Tyler in the kitchen, trying to look inconspicuous, peering around a trashcan so as to not be noticed.

Sausage sizzled. The aroma quite pleasing. Charles was also cooking eggs and pancakes.

Tyler licked his lips. *Sausage! I love sausage! I'll get your slippers for a week if you get me some sausage!*

"I don't wear slippers."

Charles turned to look at me. "Huh? Is that some sort of crack about my cooking?"

I've *got* to remember to stop talking to Tyler in front of people.

Tyler said, *You're in trouble,* in almost a singsong voice. Then, *Hey, can I have your sausage?*

After nearly talking aloud to Tyler again, I said to Charles, "No, I'm sorry, sir. I'm sure your cooking is wonderful. I was just thinking out loud about slippers." Awkward.

He made some indecipherable facial expression and returned to cooking.

I returned to the living room. Jenny was gone, presumably averting her own crisis involving a bladder. The shields were still down over the windows. But for the first time since entering Charles's house, I took in the surroundings.

I half expected to see wood paneling on all of the walls, dark colors, very masculine and very bachelor. Though, come to think of it, I didn't know if Charles was married or had a family. In fact, I didn't even know if there were other people in the house. I needed to work on my Spidey senses.

But instead, the walls were white and all of the colors were bright. The couch and the chairs Jenny and I slept in were green leather. The coffee table and end tables were tan. A similar color scheme carried throughout the room, highlighted with bright blue pillows and accent pieces. A large, colorful picture of a sunrise hung over the fireplace in a gold frame.

I retrieved my backpack off the couch, pulled out my laptop and sat on one of the chairs by the fireplace. There was another backpack next to Jenny's chair, similar to the one on the floor by me. I wondered what was in them, but tabled the thought for now so I could check out the data.

I powered on the laptop and looked up to see Charles walk in from the kitchen. Jenny returned from the bathroom just then as well.

Charles said, "Breakfast will be ready in a couple of minutes. If you're wondrin' what's in them backpacks, clothes, food, and a few personal items, like toothpaste and a toothbrush, for each of you. I figured you'll need them."

Jenny looked at me, then Charles and said, "Why?"

Charles sighed and sat down on the couch. His bulk sunk deep. "You can't stay here. Eventually, those that killed Bobby and Nick will find you here. Tracked from your car, because of my connection, logic, somethin'."

Aha! "You knew Nick Broxton too?"

Charles nodded. "Same squad." He slapped his knees and stood. "Let's eat."

Same squad? Was someone picking off members of that specific unit? I suddenly felt vulnerable in Charles's house, despite the Fort Knox fortifications.

I locked the laptop, then Jenny and I followed Charles into the kitchen, which was warm because of the cooking. An abundance of white pine cabinets covered the walls. The counter was green granite with copper flakes that reflected the light. The kitchen was spotless, except only those things needed for the morning meal.

Tyler sat obediently on a small rectangular rug. Charles tossed a sausage patty at his feet. Tyler's head tracked the flight of the patty until it landed. Then he just sat there, didn't even look at it.

I got the feeling this wasn't the first such exchange between Charles and Tyler. I raised my eyebrows, impressed. Tyler didn't project anything to me, but I could imagine he was thinking *wait for it, wait for it...*

Then Charles said, "Release!"

Tyler attacked. *Sausagesausagesausage!* In less time it took for him to project his love for sausage to me, it was gone. He immediately moved back to the rug and sat obediently, head pointed straight ahead, eyes glancing between Charles and the sausage, but head still. His eyes shot to me and then locked back on the imaginary target straight ahead. *Charles gives me sausage. You don't give me sausage.*

"I—" I stopped myself this time from answering Tyler directly, instead saying, "If Tyler was even half this good the rest of the time, I'd get him some sausage.

He chuffed.

Charles said, "He seems like a good dog. Reminds me of one I had a long, long time ago. Similar type, Golden Retriever instead of black. Good huntin' dog. Loved that dog."

Charles flipped another sausage patty to Tyler.

Tyler waited patiently.

"Release!"

Tyler chomped. He said, *Charles likes me better than you. He's giving me sausage. You don't have any.*

"That—" Ugh!

Charles and Jenny looked at me.

Tyler grinned.

I said, sheepishly, "That dog sure loves sausage."

Charles said, "Came back from the war, and he was gone. My parents were watchin' him. There wasn't anyone else. My dad said he ran away. He hated animals. No more needs to be said." He clapped his hands once. "Well, enough of that. Si'down and eat!"

There wasn't anything fancy about the breakfast table, but the food seemed fit for a king. And I just remembered I was famished! Pancakes, eggs, sausage, gravy, biscuits, hash browns, orange slices, bananas... My turn to chomp. There was even a bottle of Coke set out for me. And Heinz ketchup. The man was simply brilliant.

Jenny said between mouthfuls, "This is awesome." Mouthful. "I'm so hungry." Mouthful. "You're a good cook." Mouthful. "Are you married?"

So Jenny had been wondering too. That was a sly way to pose the question. Good job. Upon arriving, we'd been segregated to a small portion of what had to be a big house. She and I had not had a chance to talk since, when... since getting out of the car.

"Nope, never married. Just retired from truck driving. Lonely business, that. No time for a wife or family." He looked at Jenny. "What's your age limit for a husband?" He sneer-smiled.

Jenny smiled uneasily.

"I'm just playing, ma'am. And in case y'all're wondrin', there ain't nobody else here but us three. And the dog."

I still didn't get how he did that.

I got seconds on everything, then said, "Why do you have metal shields over the windows and the back door? You have them over all the windows and doors in the house?"

Charles nodded. "Every one. Zombies."

"Zombies?"

"Zombies."

"Zombies." I looked at Jenny and repeated with a slight shrug, "Zombies."

"That's what the secret entrances are for. Among other things. Now I'm not one of them crazy zombie apocalypse doomsayers, but the way I figure it, God's gonna punish us, kinda like them Bible cities Sodom and Gomorra. Except He'll turn miscreants into zombies."

"Zombies."

He nodded. "Zombies. And if the Lord Almighty don't, then that's fine. The protection's also good against peddlers. They're bad in these parts."

I laughed, thankful to have an outlet.

Jenny smiled, still a little uneasily.

Charles said, "Nah, I'm just joshin' ya, son. It's just something fun to me. A hobby. Bob mentioned it one time, said he made tunnels and such, spy games, I thought it'd be fun."

"No zombies?"

"No zombies."

Somehow, now I was a little disappointed.

Tyler said, *I knew that.*"

I gave him a *whatever* look.

Between the three of us, and continued assistance from Tyler, we cleaned our plates, the serving dishes, bowls, pretty much everything.

Charles said, "Getting onto something serious, once you figure out what's in that data, y'all need to leave. The bad guys will be back. You can't hide out here forever. The way y'all eat, I'll go bankrupt in a month."

I smiled.

He said, "I'm going to drop y'all off somewhere, thus the backpacks."

Jenny said, "What? We can't camp out in this weather. We'll freeze!"

"Don't worry, y'all'll be safe."

57

I had visions of bad guys with German accents using us for target practice as we ran through the woods. For some reason, the food didn't taste as good as it did a minute ago.

Chapter Fifteen

I unlocked my laptop and fished in my backpack for the flash drive with the data from Mr. Broxton's computer, hoping in my excessive carelessness over the last day plus that I hadn't lost it. Finding a friend dead, watching another person die, running from killers, shot at, running *over* killers, car chase, drugged… all of this stuff was best experienced in movies, not real life.

I'm just an IT dude with a bad tan.

Which, I've never really understood that expression. How can you have a *bad* tan? You either have a tan, or you don't. There are degrees of darkness for a tan, but they all imply the existence of a tan.

Focus. I popped in the flash drive while listening to the clatter of dishes in the kitchen as Charles and Jenny cleaned. I'm sure Tyler was a willing participant as much as possible.

I tried to open the parent folder containing the data from the hidden directory on Mr. Broxton's computer, but much to my surprise—and dismay—it was encrypted.

PGP encryption, which is typically used for encrypting data exchanged between two or more entities, or data communications such as email messages. This posed a big problem, because the encryption key is randomly generated by the sender's encryption software. A private key is created, and then a public key is created and stored on an online PGP server. That public key is sent to the intended recipient. The recipient then uses his/her private key to decrypt the data or message, allowing access to the content. The algorithms involved in the encryption could take years to crack.

I didn't have years. I also didn't have the key.

Remembering I had set up the second NIC on Mr. Broxton's computer so it could be accessed later, I was thrilled that I planned ahead for once. I love being proactive. Hate being reactive. Much of life is reactive, though.

I powered the mobile broadband card installed on my laptop. This allowed me to connect to the Internet from anywhere, as long as there was cell coverage, without having to be dependent on another source of connectivity, such as DSL, cable, satellite, etc.

I launched Remote Desktop on my computer, created a VPN tunnel to the router I set up on Mr. Broxton's network, and keyed in the static IP address I set up for that second NIC, praying that the bad guys didn't take the computer.

They didn't! I was in!

I opened the PGP encryption app on his computer and got the info Mr. Broxton used to set up the private and public keys and sent it to myself. I could finally take a look at the data in the hidden directory.

I was surprised that Mr. Broxton not only hid the data, but encrypted it as well. He was much more computer savvy than I thought. Which then made me wonder why he needed my assistance…

Speaking of why, why would the killers leave his computer there? They knew the possibility of whatever critical data for their cause existed, or they wouldn't have been demanding such data from Mr. Meredith.

It didn't make sense…

Crap!

I yelled, "We need to go! Now!"

I quickly backed out of Mr. Broxton's computer and network and shut down the broadband card, then powered off the laptop. Unlike a cellphone with GPS, the location of the laptop could not be traced while powered off.

That's the good news.

The bad news is I fell right into their trap.

I'm an idiot.

Being proactive is stupid.

Jenny said, "What's wrong?"

I postponed answering so I could concentrate on gathering my stuff. "Charles, wherever you were going to take us, now is the time. We're going to have company soon!" I began to think I'd never see the data in the files.

Jenny got the message and grabbed her purse and the backpack provided by Charles. "Ellie, what's going on?"

"I'll explain in the car."

She frowned at me. It was a beautiful frown. I hoped nothing ever happened to that frown, save that it turn into a smile.

"Tyler! Come on, boy. Where's Charles?" I increased volume, "Charles?"

Jenny said, "He ran down the hallway when you said we're going to have company."

"Now is not the time for a potty break."

Charles appeared at the end of the hall and motioned for us to follow him, saying, "The garage is over here. Let's go!"

I thought that was a weird location for the garage, which wasn't by the kitchen.

As we hurried toward the garage, we passed another kitchen.

What? I stopped abruptly, causing Jenny to run into me.

"What are you—" She saw me pointing back to the kitchen, then said, "Weird."

We followed Charles into the garage.

A solid black Suburban was aimed at the garage door.

A solid black pistol was aimed at my chest.

Charles owned them both.

He displayed his sneer-smile in all its glory.

I swallowed, my mouth suddenly very dry. I managed to say, "What are you doing?"

"Just get in if'n you don't mind."

"Charles, there's no need for a gun." I really, really hate guns.

"I said get in."

Jenny said, "Why would you do this to us? Was this your plan all along?"

The gun *boomed*.

Jenny screamed.

Tyler barked. A lot.

I instinctively jumped and grabbed my chest, but the bullet travelled between Jenny and I as Charles had adjusted his aim. The gun's report was so loud in the garage I wanted to cover my ears, but my hands were too worried about my chest.

"I said get in the truck!"

Tyler lunged in front of us and growled savagely at Charles. I'd never seen him so wild. Even from my vantage point behind the dog, I could see the exposed teeth under his snarled lips as he moved his head from side to side. His coat quivered in the rage.

I glanced at Charles, hoping he wouldn't shoot Tyler, but I hadn't gathered enough wits at this point to try to talk either of them down. I thought I might have seen a nanosecond of remorse in Charles, but it could very well have been my imagination.

The Suburban idled with the windows down, but even so, there was only a faint smell of exhaust in the closed garage. There must be some form of ventilation system. Or the fumes were drifting into the truck's cabin.

I decided Charles didn't want to shoot us, I didn't yet know why not, or he would have simply aimed and pulled the trigger. So I moved in front of Tyler and opened the door, creating a barrier between the big dog and Charles.

Tyler didn't project anything to me. I told him to jump into the truck, but he didn't obey. He was no longer growling, though he tried to move around the open door.

Jenny moved behind the dog, nudged him, and entered the Suburban.

Tyler then decided to jump into the truck.

I followed.

Charles got into the driver's seat and opened the garage door via remote.

Nighttime.

Nighttime?

We had breakfast just a little while ago. Not in the morning, but at night. I realized my mouth was literally hanging open, so I closed it. None of this made sense.

I looked at Jenny. Her eyes were blank, staring into some inner space.

How long had we been asleep? A day? A day and a night and another day?

What was Charles doing? How did he fit in with the enemy?

None of this was in the script. But the story seemed to be running on rails and I couldn't change tracks.

It was too dark to see outside. The thick tinted windows didn't help.

I tried to open the door next to me, but the door handle did nothing. I looked for a lock and ran my hand across the door, no lock. These doors could only be opened from the outside like police cars. Yes, I have been in police cars.

A metal mesh screen partitioned the front seats and the second row. The third row bench seat behind us was collapsed creating more cargo space.

After some time driving on a small road, Charles turned onto a main road and picked up speed. He switched on the windshield wipers as it started to rain. Blurry miniature balls of light, reflecting headlights of oncoming traffic, danced on the windshield then died when the wipers swept across the glass.

I felt small, insignificant. Like a tiny raindrop, my life would be wiped out.

Charles didn't turn on the truck's heater, so it was cold.

Jenny put on her jacket which she had been holding in her lap.

Our backpacks were behind the seat.

After we'd been driving for a while, I said to Charles, as pleasantly as possible to encourage a response in kind, "Where are we going?"

"Don't talk."

Great.

Jenny had her hands in her lap, balled into fists.

I touched her elbow to get her attention.

61

She looked at me briefly, but didn't say anything or make any other response, then returned to her inner space.

I had to somehow figure out what to do next. We certainly just couldn't jump out of a moving vehicle. Besides, the doors wouldn't open. But was it any better to sit complacently and just let whatever happen, happen?

No. I may not have control over the situation, but I did have control over myself. I wasn't going to sit idly by and just disappear into the night.

"Charles, what's your play in this? Why are you helping them?"

"Don't talk. Trust me, it is better for you if you shut up, stupid kid."

I could see his beady eyes in the rearview mirror boring into me, as if trying to drive home a point.

"Trust you? We did trust you. Look where that got us. I'm not sure if you noticed, but we've been taken hostage at gunpoint by a man we were supposed to trust, who's instead aligned with the enemy!"

I punched the empty passenger seat in front of me.

Jenny woke from her stupor, but she made no effort to look around. We couldn't see anything.

Charles did not respond, but a few seconds later he hit the brakes and turned right. Through the tint, I could see light high in the window next to me. Light poles.

Charles drove slowly and then stopped, turning the truck off. He left the keys in the ignition, got out, shut the door, remembered the keys, opened the door, retrieved them, and then shut the door again. He seemed to be nervous.

I tried my door again, still wouldn't open.

Outside I could hear the deep rumbling of big rig diesel engines. An image flashed in my head of a truck stop, which would make sense considering Charles said he was a retired truck driver. Though it didn't make sense why we'd be here, or what the killers would be doing here.

The rain continued, and without the wipers, we couldn't see out.

I said to Jenny, "Are you okay?"

She shook her head slightly. "I just want this to be over. Whatever they're going to do, just get it over with." A fresh tear streaked her cheek.

I grabbed her hand and turned so that I faced her. "We can't give up. We can *never* give up." I thought for a moment, hedging on what I wanted to say, but said it anyway. "We will get out of this. I promise. Do you understand? We will fight back. Look at me."

She turned her head.

"Promise me you will not give up. *Promise.*"

She nodded, faked a weak smile, and squeezed my hand.

The scars on my arm did not burn in reaction to this newest situation. Strange.

I reached to scratch Tyler's ears, who was on the seat on the other side of Jenny. He wasn't in a talkative mood either, but I knew he would never give up. I knew, in truth, Jenny wouldn't either. But just hours ago, she had watched her father dying on the floor. And we left him there to die.

Things like this weren't supposed to happen in Suburbia.

I prayed. I prayed for strength to not fail Jenny. Or Tyler. Like I had failed my brother and sister. I prayed to the God of the angel armies to send an angel to help. A squadron of angels.

Then I waited.

At some point a door would open. I tried to stay sharp. Whatever opportunity presented itself, I would have to act fast.

I heard voices outside my door and tensed. They seemed to be elevated, but I couldn't pick out the words over the snoring truck engines and the rain.

The back door of the Suburban opened. I whipped around to look, as did Jenny, and Tyler. The sound of truck engines and rain intensified.

Charles stood in the rain, one finger making a quick gesture over his lips to quiet us. He bent to the ground then lifted and rolled a large limp body into the truck.

What the hell?

Blood leaked out of the body's chest.

Before I could say anything, he put a finger over his mouth again. Then he lifted another bleeding body into the truck.

Two?

He grabbed the backpacks and closed the door, restoring the solitude of the truck interior.

A few seconds later he opened my door, motioned again for us to be quiet and gestured for us to follow him.

I froze for a moment, but recognized if we were ever going to get away, it wouldn't be by staying trapped in a truck. I hopped to the ground, reached back for Jenny and called Tyler.

It rained hard. I wished I had my hoodie, but it was stuffed in my backpack.

I could see Charles walk-crawl under the trailer of an eighteen-wheeler to the other side. Even for a big man, he managed to touch the ground with just feet and hands. Jenny and I copied him. Tyler followed with ease.

It felt good to be moving, to be doing *something,* I just hoped the something didn't lead directly to the bad guys.

Again.

We went under two more trailers. Each time Charles got to the other side, I could see his body turn left and right, as if looking for something. Or, maybe he was making sure he *didn't* see something.

After ten or so trailers, I was no longer glad to be doing something. Except for the brief respite of walk-crawling under each trailer, I got pummeled by rain. And colder despite the exercise.

One more trailer and Charles grabbed my arm as I cleared and steered me to the cab. Someone inside held the door open at arm's length.

Again, despite my geekdom, I'm not a small guy. I'm not ever going to be confused with Arnold Schwarzenegger. But even at six-foot, 190 lbs., Charles picked me up, yelled "Duck!" and tossed me into the cabin like a sack of potatoes.

He was gentle with Jenny, but evidently in such a hurry he did not want to wait for us to climb on our own.

Tyler was next. I didn't think he would let Charles pick him up, but it wasn't necessary. Tyler either understood what was happening or didn't want to leave us alone. He jumped up into the cab on his own.

Charles took one last glance around, climbed in, slammed the door, and locked us in. He pressed a button on the dash and all of the windows, including the windshield, went opaque, closing off the outside world.

Chapter Sixteen

We were in a cavernous semi-truck sleeper cab. A curtain separating the driver section and the sleeping quarters was pulled back, opening the entire space. Jenny sat in a chair by a bed. I stood next to her. I didn't even have to bend over. Charles sat in the driver captain's chair. Tyler sat contentedly next to a black man in the passenger captain's chair getting his ears scratched and neck rubbed.

Tyler said, *This is nice. I like it here. I like this man. Who is he? Tell him not to stop.*

That was the first time he'd "talked" to me in quite a while. He didn't seem to want to tear into Charles any more, and he obviously liked the man next to him.

Tyler said, *See how I protected you? I deserve a treat for that. See if he has Cheetos.*

I relaxed. But not completely. "What's going on, Charles? What's happening here? Who were those men you dumped in the Suburban?"

The black man laughed. A deep, musical bass. "C-Man, you really got them *con*-fused!" He chuckled some more, shaking his head slightly.

C-Man?

Charles reached to the side of the driver's seat, pressed a button, then swiveled the chair to face everyone. He sneer-smiled. "Elijah, Jenny, this is Ray Sanders.

Ray smiled—a real smile, radiant, perfect teeth, full of kindness, and no sneer involved. "Hi folks! I'm your *Ray* of sunshine in an otherwise dreary world." He spread his arms wide. He had a wavy intonation in his speech that reminded me of a classic jazz singer. "Consider me your *guard*ian angel, God's appointment." He smiled and chuckled softly, then reached back down to continue Tyler's ear-scratching.

Charles said, "Ray will take care of y'all from here. The fake Feds know who I am now. I'm no longer safe for you so here's where I leave the story."

I said, "I don't understand. You're not with the enemy?"

Ray laughed, a smooth infectious bass, slow and genuine. It made me smile in spite of everything that's happening.

Jenny looked at me, smiling as well.

Maybe God *did* send an angel.

Ray said, fisting his own chest, "C-Man may look like a serial killer, but inside, he's all heart."

Jenny said, "Then what was the point of hijacking us in the Suburban with a gun?"

I said, "Where did you get the Suburban? Is it one of theirs?"

C-Man—I mean Charles—said, "I know y'all have a lot of questions. I understand. But you have to get on the road. Ray knows the story and will explain everything."

"C-Man is right. We only have a few minutes to collect ourselves, then we need to scoot before the enemy catches on. Elijah—I love that name, brother—get the wig out of the backpack C-Man brought for you and put it on."

I opened Charles's backpack, realizing I'd never looked inside. I pulled out a long platinum blonde wig, and laughed. "You want me to wear this?"

Ray said, "Yes, sir. *And* the sweat suit." He chuckled and winked at Jenny.

"What?" I dug into the backpack and lifted a grey and pink velour sweat suit. "No way!"

Jenny and Ray laughed. Even Tyler grinned.

Charles said, "You want to live, son? You don't know nothin' about disguises. There's no point in disguisin' just a little. You want the enemy's eyes to pass right over you without the slightest subconscious flag because of who you are *or* because of the disguise. With that, you'll look like a middle-aged female on a road trip. There's a matching grey beret in there also."

"How did you know my size?"

"It's a sweat suit. Who cares?"

I sighed. I knew he was right. But velour? Grey and pink, no less? Come on. I sighed again, then mumbled something that might have sounded like, "*You* look like a middle-aged woman…"

Jenny was the only one close enough to hear me. She smiled.

Tyler said, *No need to be immature.*

Oh great, the dog heard me. Worse, he's chastising me. A dog. Who knows what *immature* means. I looked at Tyler and said, "I know someone who needs a bath."

Don't be petty.

Ugh!

"Fine. Is there a bathroom here I can use to change?"

Ray said, "No, one of the few things not in this palace on wheels."

"Everybody turn around, then. You too Tyler."

He said, *Whatever.* But he turned his head.

Jenny dug around in the backpack given to her to see her disguise.

I changed into the sweat suit and put on the wig. My black hiking boots looked out of place. "Any shoes?"

Everyone looked at me. And laughed. "Okay, get it over with," I said.

Charles said, "You might wanna stuff your bra. You don't even have mosquito bites worth seeing."

"I don't have a bra."

"Oh yes you do. Look in the pack."

Ugh!

Tyler grinned even wider now, tongue lolling.

"I think we need to disguise Tyler as a poodle."

Tyler quit grinning.

Ray said, "No need, he's not getting out of the truck."

I pulled down the sweat suit far enough to put on the bra. Jenny helped after watching me in amusement struggle to clasp the thing. I rolled some long socks and strategically inserted them.

Charles winked at me and said, "What's your name, honey?"

"Ha ha."

"There are some white Converse at the bottom of the pack."

I removed my boots and put them on. They were too small, but I'd live.

Jenny said, "My turn. Turn around."

I said, "Do I have to?"

"No, not you, Ellie."

"Really?"

"No."

Sadness.

65

A few moments later, Jenny said, "All set."

She had a brown wig in a bob hairstyle, her long hair tucked under the wig, a Texas Rangers baseball cap, her same jeans—not fair—and an oversized dark green winter coat. She smiled at me.

She'd look beautiful wearing a burlap sack.

Charles said, "Nice. Okay, here's the game plan: Despite your whining—" He looked at me—"we've only spent fifteen minutes here. Like Ray said, there's no bathroom aboard this rig. Elijah, you'll go into the truck stop first, don't be rude but don't stop to talk to anyone. Walk a little feminine, falsetto your voice if you have to talk, but not too much, go to the bathroom, then come back. Don't look at anything. Don't buy anything. Don't draw attention to yourself."

"I'll look strange in the men's restroom."

He opened a cabinet under a small sink and handed me a small paper towel. Then said, "Go to the women's restroom. Don't look around, sit down on the toilet. Don't fart too loud. Don't wash your hands." He handed me the paper towel. "Cover your face as you enter and leave the bathroom, as if it stinks to high heaven. Don't mess around. In and out. If anyone looks at you closely, they'll see you're a man."

He looked at Jenny. "When either of you exit or come back to the truck, go under one trailer. If someone sees you, go under another. Act like y'all know what you're doin'. Don't walk straight down the row to this truck. When you return, knock once on the passenger door." He looked at his watch. "We need to be gone in less than fifteen minutes. Go."

I went. Water still fell from the sky, but more of a sprinkle instead of a heavy rain. Light from tall poles in the parking lot reflected off the water droplets and caused thick shadows to gather under the trailers.

I ducked under one of the trailers and moved to the other side, then power walked with a little extra hip sway to the truck stop.

When I reached the double lane in front of the main doors, I was able to see the enormity of the place for the first time. Dozens of eighteen-wheelers, motorhomes, and various other kinds of big trucks occupied long parking lanes. The place was huge.

A huge lighted sign out by the highway stated *TRUCK CITY*.

I've driven by here a few times, but never stopped. Computer geeks and truck drivers typically don't mingle. Truck City is about twenty miles outside of town, and no doubt named by a student from the same creative writing class as the ones who named Fort City and Buy City.

I made sure I wasn't going to be road kill, then crossed the lanes to the truck stop store / diner / gift shop / game arcade / motel / auto parts store / transvestite hangout.

That last bit I told myself hoping not to stick out too much.

A robust gentleman wearing a Harley Davidson leather jacket—I didn't know they made big rigs—opened the door just as I approached and held it open for me.

I let out a high pitched "Thanks" keeping my head down and looked for the men's, I mean women's bathroom. I also looked for bad guys. Not seeing bad guys or bathrooms, I walked the perimeter of the huge market-like interior of the superstructure.

I spotted Hostess apple pies and salivated. A rude voice in my head said *"Don't buy anything."*

Sacrifices.

I located the bathroom sign some five hundred yards away, well, maybe one hundred and fifty, and covered my face with the paper towel as I got near and entered.

66

There were several stalls, a few showers—thankfully unoccupied—and a row of sinks below mirrors. Disposable napkin dispensers adorned the walls. I couldn't help it, I bought one.

The bathroom was clean with baby blue slate tiles on the walls and floor, nickel fixtures, and most importantly, not crowded. There were a few cautious glances from other customers, surely wondering why I held a paper towel to my face, but no one said anything. I selected a stall, did my thing sitting down, and left. No drama.

I took a different route to the truck, ducked under a trailer, and knocked once on the passenger door.

The door opened and I clambered in, fake boobs and all.

Charles said, "Any problems?"

"None."

"Anyone pay any attention to you?"

"Not that I noticed."

"Good. Jenny, your turn."

Jenny left.

I washed my hands using the small sink in the sleeper cab.

A few minutes later, Jenny returned. She was faster than me.

She said, "Beat you."

"Didn't know it was a race."

She gave me a perceptive smile.

Charles stood and clapped his hands once. "All righty, time for me to skedaddle."

I said, "You're leaving?" I really didn't know if that was a good or bad thing, but the scale tipped toward bad.

"I know my actions have messed with your brains. I'm sorry. Ray will explain everything. The enemy will be wondering why their men haven't checked in. I was supposed to be handing y'all over."

I said, "How did—"

He put up a hand to stop me. "No time, Ray will tell you. Y'all have to get out of here. So do I." He stood, nodded at me, looked at Jenny, "Ma'am," and stooped to pat Tyler. "Thanks, Tyler. I'm gonna get me a dog. Take care of them, boy."

Before anyone could say anything else, he was gone.

Ray pressed a button to clear the windows, put the idling rig in gear, and moved out of the parking space to hit the road.

We were pulling a trailer, so I said, "Are we hauling anything?"

"No, we're deadhead right now so we can make good time. I'll catch a load on the way back."

"Deadhead?"

"Means the trailer is empty. You two get comfortable. My place is yours. If you're hungry, there's some canned food in the pantry, and more food in the fridge. You see the microwave."

Now that we were on the highway, I had a mad urge to strip. Jenny helped me take off the bra.

Ray's truck was fascinating. The dark blue curtain partitioning the main space from the front end of the cab was held open by a blue felt rope, like you see in old time movie theaters, only not red. Incandescent xenon lights circled the living quarters of the cab. The place was pristine. The sink was on the other side of the curtain behind the passenger seat, with a mirror above the sink and a microwave above that.

Everything was in blues and greys. Cabinets below the sink, above the microwave and elsewhere were covered in a padded grey leather and blue trim. A pantry and a large pullout fridge drawer were stationed behind the driver's seat. There were two beds along the back wall, similar to bunk beds, with the upper bed folding into the wall when not in use.

Circular windows, or more like portholes, were at the end of each bed. An LED HD flat panel TV covered part of one wall. The opposite wall had more cabinets and drawers for storage. The cab was modern with no wasted space, yet did not feel cramped.

A table rose hydraulically from a cutout in the floor behind the passenger's seat. That chair could be turned 180° to face the table and someone sitting opposite on the bed.

I really liked this truck.

I looked at Jenny who was also taking everything in. "What do you think?"

She said, "It's nice. I'm surprised. Efficient use of space."

I'm not sure why it mattered, but I was pleased she liked it. I wasn't hungry, but I looked at the food options in the pantry. "Hostess apple pies!"

Ray said, "Help yourself! In fact, help me with one too."

I got a couple of crackers for Tyler, who lazed at the foot of the lower bed, grabbed a pie for Ray and myself and climbed into the passenger's seat.

Jenny stretched out on the lower bed, but I'm sure she could hear us talking.

I said to Ray, "Okay, please tell me what's going on."

He chuckled. "No problem, brother. Now, you're going to get mad, but hear me out, all right?"

"Yes."

"You two were sedated for two days."

"Two days!"

Jenny repeated, no longer lying down, "Two days!"

"Well, two and a half days, really."

I threw my arms up. "Why would he do that?"

"That's what I'm trying to get to if you'll let me." He chuckled. "I told you you were going to get mad."

Obviously Ray had a way that just put people at ease.

But I tried to remain angry. "Go on."

"When Charles found you, he didn't know you from Adam. But after hearing your story, he took you in. He said none of his internal alarms alerted him. But he's one paranoid cat, so he sedated you two anyway. That gave him enough time to go through the car and your stuff. He may not look like much, but I've never known anyone smarter than C-Man. Brilliant investigator, strategist."

Ray paused to let that sink in, then continued. "What he found jived with what you told him, so then he sedated you longer with shots."

Now that Ray mentioned that, I noticed my right arm by the shoulder had been itching. I turned to see Jenny; she was looking at her arms trying to find a mark.

Jenny said, "He gave us shots to knock us out? For real?"

I just shook my head. I didn't know what to say any more. This was all just too weird.

Ray said, "Yes, for real."

68

Ray drove in silence for a while. I assumed to let us get over our anger.

The rain had stopped. Trees whipped by as we motored down the highway. I expected the interior of an eighteen-wheeler to be a lot louder, but realized we didn't have to raise our voices to be heard.

Ray continued, "While you were out the next day, C-Man found two bad guys looking at your car in the woods. Actually, his security system alerted him of a perimeter breach."

"Perimeter way out there?"

"Way out there."

"I thought *I* was paranoid."

Ray chuckled. "Well the enemy asked him if he knew who was in the car and where they went. C-Man said he could tell they were desperate, could see it in their eyes and mannerisms, not just their words. He told them he could find you two, that you tore up his woods and he'd be happy to deliver you, but that he didn't have any wheels. That was true too, his truck's in the shop." He said to Jenny, "You sure you don't want anything to eat? There's plenty to drink too."

"I'm fine, thank you."

I looked at Tyler; he napped on the bed. Evidently the story didn't captivate him.

Ray said, "The bad guys tried to get C-Man to just take them to you two. But he refused, saying he didn't want his property messed up any more than it already was. He'd deliver you the next day. All they had to do was leave a vehicle. He said they balked at first, but C-Man can be pretty persuasive.

"He knew there'd be a GPS transponder planted on the truck, so they didn't have to worry about anything happening to it. He also knew the truck would be set up for audio and video as well. He told me that's why he tried to keep y'all from talking."

Jenny said, "That's also why he fired the gun."

I looked at her and nodded.

I said, "We thought he'd gone nuts. Even Tyler wanted to tear into him."

Ray chuckled. "He had to make you think that. Otherwise the enemy would know it was a ruse. They knew where you were. They found you. When they realized you had slipped away, they circled back. It's not hard to find a car-sized hole through the brush in daylight when you're looking for it. C-Man knew he could not get you guys out of there safely. So he hoped if he sold you out, he'd have a way to get you away from the house and make them lose you again. That's real easy to do at a place like Truck City. They'll know that we left from there, but as I'm sure you noticed, there were a lot of potential trucks to get into, and all going to different places. That's where yours truly comes in. Your guardian angel." His smile lit up the cab.

Jenny said, "So Charles killed the two bad guys who came to pick us up?" It was more of a statement than a question.

I said, "He used a silencer, that's why we didn't hear any gunshots over the outside noise."

Ray said, "You got it. Two down. But there will be more. And now they will be mad."

Chapter Seventeen

1:00 AM. I knew I wouldn't be able to go to sleep after being out for two days, but I needed to try and get back to a normal schedule. We paused at a rest stop so all of us could go to the bathroom, including Tyler. Then got back on the road.

I didn't know where we were going. I didn't ask. That's crazy, I know. But I just didn't want to know yet. It would only make it that much harder to sleep, thinking about new cities, new places.

I climbed into the top bed.

Jenny curled into the lower.

Tyler rested at Jenny's feet.

Ray had some Johnny Coltrane going, his head bobbing to the music and swaying to the road, simultaneously.

By my bed, small desk fan hung upside down from the ceiling in a corner. Greatness. But I didn't turn it on yet.

I peered down from the top bunk and said to Jenny, "How are you doing?"

"Tired."

I waited to see if she would elaborate or increase the word output on another subject.

Nope.

I wanted to say something like, "It'll be all right," or, "Keep your chin up" or, something. Instead I said, "Goodnight."

She turned over.

I turned on the fan, rolled onto my back and took a deep breath, exhaling slowly.

Despite my brother and sister dying, I couldn't imagine what Jenny was going through, having just lost her dad. I loved my siblings beyond belief; they were everything to me. But I didn't depend on them. They were not the soul of my support network, as Jenny's dad, and her mom I'm sure, were for her.

Her sense of loss centered on losing her last close relative, a parent: the individual in most people's lives who is the ultimate protector.

When my sister and brother were killed, I lost my last close relatives, and the ones *I* was supposed to protect.

A different feeling. But, I guess the end game is a loss is a loss.

I stared at the ceiling of the cab, which was only about three feet above me. The monotone whir of the fan could not overcome the monotone drone of wheels on pavement. The interior lights cast a soft blue tint over objects, the walls, the ceiling.

Blue is my favorite color. But on that night, the color only increased my melancholy mood.

If I turned my head, I could see the humongous truck GPS on the dash next to Ray, fifteen feet or so away.

I get lost running on an oval track. I needed to get one of those for the *Beast*.

I missed the *Beast*.

No, I missed my sister.

I missed my brother.

I looked back to the ceiling, searching for answers I'd never find to questions that should never have had to be asked. It was definitely going to be a sleepless night.

Since their deaths, I have fought hard during each remembrance of them to not think of those last images, that last scene of their lives. I push back the mental pictures, the screaming... the fear.

I have had a lot of time to practice the discipline. But I've also learned to recognize when I wouldn't be able to capture the thoughts in my rogue brain when it demanded on tormenting me. Sleep abandons me, my mind haunted, until I relive those memories, watching them play in the Movie Theater of my mind.

I have pleaded with God, begged-cried out-*screamed* for Him to take those memories from me.

He has not.

I suffer.

And it kills me every time I remember.

My sister, Chloe, was seven. She had long curly blonde hair, sometimes a little matted because our mom wasn't too concerned about hygiene or how we looked when she was stoned. Chloe had light blue eyes, blue that looked like the sky on a sunny day. It didn't make a difference how dirty we were, her eyes were always that beautiful sky blue.

I think that's why blue is my favorite color. The first time I recognized the striking blue of Chloe's eyes, I can remember thinking they were an amazing color, a color too beautiful for just anyone to have. A color reserved only for that rare, extraordinary person.

A color made for Chloe. And I longed for my eyes to be that same blue, but I wasn't good enough.

Ben, my brother, was nine. He had brown eyes, brown hair, and was darker than Chloe and I. He was a little small for his age. But oh so smart. And wise beyond his years. He was usually the one who came up with the games we played.

We all had deep tans—yes, even me—because we were *always* outside. We lived on the outskirts of town where suburban morphed into full-on rural. This was great for our imaginations as we had a virtually unlimited playground. There were a few neighbors, but they kept to themselves, leaving those Raven kids alone.

School was a different story. Surrounded by houses with fences around their yards, fences that had to be hastily climbed or get beat up.

The house was a wood clapboard four bedroom, two-story, mustard in color. It needed a lot of work which never happened. Though there were various tools, hammers, saws, wooden pencils lying around the house as if in a state of constant readiness, implying the repairs were imminent. Instead the items became permanent decorations.

All of the bedrooms were upstairs. We were never allowed in Allister's room.

The only decorating was baseball. Allister loved the game. In fact, more than anything except drugs. There were baseball pictures, posters, gloves, bats...

Almost every room had a baseball bat. This served a dual purpose: to promote the motif, and be a constant reminder of what he would do to us—or, more effectively—what he would do to a brother or sister if we ever did something he did not like. For example, tell on him.

Where we lived there were lots of trees, dirt, and dead grass. We played cowboys and Indians, cops and robbers, pirates searching for buried treasure, and more exotic settings like a zombie apocalypse on Mars.

That last scenario was fueled by an abandoned cemetery on a hill not too far from the house. Cemeteries for kids are like steroids for the imagination.

We took soap-less baths in a stock pond on a neighbor's property. I would always climb a nearby tree and look for snakes.

Water moccasins love Texas waters. Some people call them cottonmouths. If you're ever unfortunate to see one open its mouth while looking at you, you'll see a bright white, cotton-like mouth. The cottonmouth name I understand. I don't get the moccasin name. They look nothing like shoes.

If the coast was clear, I'd grab my walking stick and wade into the water, slapping it around me on the water's surface to scare off any unseen snakes. Then Chloe and Ben would join me.

Just once did a snake ever sneak up on us. Thankfully, we weren't on his diet plan for the day.

We also played dolls and dress up for Chloe. We didn't mind. She played pirates with us and made a pretty good zombie. It was the least we could do.

We did everything together. We were abused and neglected kids, with the secret knowledge that each day had the potential to bring great physical and emotional pain. And fear.

To quote the philosopher Jon Bon Jovi, "We had each other, and that's a lot for us."

Well, I guess that's not really fair to Mom. At some fathoms-deep level, I think she may have loved us. Maybe just an instinctual feeling, but there just the same. At times she even cared for us.

We did have one neighborhood friend who frequently played with us, Billy.

Billy was a little different, but we didn't care. He was still cool and a lot of fun. He had white hair with black spots, four legs and barked. He liked to wear bandanas and little makeshift cowboy hats. No matter how hard you tried or how fast you ran, you could never get away from ol' Sheriff Billy.

He'd chase us down until we fell, heightened gentleness with Chloe, and then stand on our chests with his forelegs, licking our faces with a perpetual grin.

I imagined he was thinking *Gotcha gotcha gotcha* with each rapid-fire lick. We'd laugh, or giggle in Chloe's case, until we couldn't take it anymore.

He helped save us from losing our sanity, from falling into a hopeless and immutable despair.

He also knew more about our lives than anyone else. Many times when Allister came at us outside, mad about something one of us did, or just mad at the world, if Billy was around he'd growl and bark, keeping Allister away.

Allister would cuss and yell and throw rocks or whatever he could find at the dog. Allister had a great arm and Billy would get hit a lot, but he'd never back down. After a few moments Allister would think we weren't worth the trouble of a beating and just leave.

I don't know where he went. I still don't know if he ever had a job. He never talked about it and I never asked. Though now I know the income came from drug trafficking.

I wished that Billy was our dog and not a neighbor's. He couldn't get into our house.

Many times I'd sneak out at night and talk to him. I don't know if he could hear me, see me, or smell me, but after I'd been outside for a few moments he'd come running over. A large tree by the house had been felled for firewood. I'd sit on the stump facing the house and Billy would sit next to me on the ground, leaning against my legs. I'd talk to him about Mom, about Chloe and Ben, about life, about how someday I would have kids and be an awesome father.

I'd also tell him I wished Allister would die.

He'd listen attentively, never interrupting.

Sometimes I'd get a weird feeling that he said something in response when I paused, but always thought it was just my crazy imagination. Regardless, he was a great therapist.

After ten minutes or so had passed in these sessions, scared of being caught I'd say goodnight to Billy, kiss the top of his head, thank him for spending time with me, and sneak back into the house. I'd look out the window by the front door and see Billy standing there. When he saw me inside he'd run off for home.

I heard Tyler's nails click on the floor so I looked over the side of the bed to see what he was up to. He padded over to Ray, who was eating something I couldn't see. He shared a bit with Tyler who wagged his tail appreciatively.

Content, the dog sniffed around the cab and then jumped back into Jenny's bed.

I yawned and stretched out again, feeling the air from the fan on my face. My eyelids were heavy now, but I still knew I wasn't going to fall asleep until I finished reliving the horrid scene that always haunted me.

It was like a release of sorts. Constant repression of the memories, led to pressure building and building over time until I could no longer hold them in. I begged God...

Each time, after watching the reenactment in my mind, the pressure would die down and I could sleep again. Sometimes I would have a semblance of peace for weeks, maybe even a few months.

I'm hoping Uncle Joe is right. I'm hoping getting this down on paper will have a more lasting remission from the torment.

Hoping.

Chapter Eighteen

I was outside playing fetch with Billy. The air was chilly as winter crept its way into being the prominent season. The sun warmed us with rays unimpeded by clouds and leaves on the trees. A light rain the day before left a soft dampness to the dead leaves on the ground.

Billy liked variety in playing fetch. Sometimes he would simply bring back the ball or stick or whatever and drop it at my feet, looking up at me expectantly, tail swishing happily.

Sometimes he wanted me to chase him. Sometimes he wanted to chase me.

Chloe and Ben were inside the house.

So were Mom and Allister.

I should never have left Chloe and Ben alone. I tried to always be next to them when Allister was home, which, thankfully, was not very often. But just that morning, he had smiled at me. He had a pleasant smile. I'm sure he was rather charming when he wanted to be. The smile shocked me. Though his smile was pleasant, it was never directed at me. It was a big deal. I didn't know what to think, so I went outside to forget about it and avoid any further interaction.

Instead, I should have recognized that nothing good would be born from that smile. He smiled because he knew that he was going to kill Mom that day. Maybe he had planned to kill the rest of us too. Or it might have been a spontaneous decision. I don't know.

He probably had the bad drugs in his pocket when he smiled at me. He knew they would kill her.

He *knew*.

I picked up the blue racquetball Billy dropped at my feet. We didn't have any racquetballs so I don't know where it came from. I guessed it must have been something Billy brought with him from his house. I threw the ball with everything I had. It landed just right on a rock which propelled it impossibly farther than the distance I could throw.

I remember thinking, *Cool...*

Billy was off.

I heard Chloe yell, "Ellie!" from inside the house.

Oh no...

I ran through the front door—

"*Ellie!*"

—and up the stairs.

"Mommy's dead!" Chloe came running down the upstairs hallway from Allister's bedroom. "He killed her!"

Allister chased her out of the room and bellowed in a voice that sounded inhumanly primal, "Get out of here you stupid *slut*!"

I don't know if Mom was really dead. And I don't know if somehow her death did it, or maybe drugs *he* had taken, or alcohol, but something caused Allister to go completely unhinged. I mean he *freaked.*

I fell to my knees in the hallway as I saw Chloe running for me. She wore a frilly yellow dress that waved in her wake.

"Ellie!" She was crying and screaming and hysterical all at once.

As if to cause the greatest damage to my psyche, my mind plays each ensuing half-second frame-by-frame in a maddeningly slow speed.

I opened my arms to catch her...

Chloe's legs pumped furiously…

Allister roared something unintelligible…

I could feel Chloe's fear. Her fear united with my own and seemed to manifest into a separate entity. Powerful. Demon-like. Fear.

Allister reached back and fired a half empty glass beer bottle at Chloe…

The bottle cut through the air like a windmill…

Chloe lunged for me…

I tried to move my hand to block…

The bottle *thwacked* into the back of Chloe's skull…

She let out a muted grunt like some kind of animal, a *wrongness* to the sound that should have been impossible for a spirited little girl…

The force of the impact propelled her into me and I fell onto my back, Chloe landing on top of me…

I smelled beer, thinking it was strange that Chloe smelled like beer…

Allister stood heaving at the other end of the hallway in a white t-shirt and blue jeans. The jeans had holes at the knees. They were unbuttoned. He had on the brown steel-toed boots he always wore. He knew how to kick just hard enough to cause immense pain without breaking bone.

A gun handle sprouted at a peculiar angle from the waistband, not getting enough support from the unbuttoned jeans. His right hand reached for the handle, fingers curling creepily slow.

Index finger, middle, ring, pinky, thumb…He pulled out the gun. He stared at us.

Chloe's head was tucked under my chin…

I should have felt her heavy breathing. I felt nothing.

I hugged her, and said in a sing song voice:

"It's okay, Chloe—"

I knew it was not…

"I've got you—"

I knew she was dead…

I felt a warm liquid roll down my neck. I thought it was lukewarm beer. I slowly moved a hand to my neck, not wanting to wake her even though a part of my mind knew she wasn't asleep. I tried to wipe off the liquid.

My hand was covered in the red beer… No, that's not possible.

Covered in blood.

The hallway was void of sound. As quiet as an undisturbed, ancient crypt. I smelled dust and cobwebs and spiders.

Then I heard multiple creatures shrieking in laughter like a pack of wild hyenas. Vertigo hit me and the walls and ceiling spun clockwise, ceiling, wall, floor, wall, ceiling... I blinked repeatedly to try to restore lucidity, to keep madness from consuming me. I felt tingly all over, then realized I was covered in the spiders—no, not spiders, just tingly. I banged the back of my head on the floor—*thump thump thump*—trying madly to regain rationality. Red and white spots popped in and out of my field of view. I squeezed my eyes shut, then opened them and after a few brief moments, they locked onto Allister.

He swayed left and right, seeming to fall off balance just standing, but then right himself gracefully. There was something wrong about his movements, like he was dancing to music only he could hear. He leveled the gun on us. It was steady.

I rolled Chloe to the side. Her limp arms plopped softly to the floor. Her shoes thudded on the wood. The back of her head was split open. I could see a jagged line of cracked white. Bone.

I stood—

Ben came out of his room. He'd been hiding and appeared when it got quiet.

I screamed, "Ben! Get—"

The gun *boomed*.

I saw Ben's little body lifted up and fly back into his room from the force of the shot hitting him in the chest.

He didn't make a sound. One second he was there in the hallway… and then he was gone.

The gun's report was deafening in the closed space, causing a high-pitched ringing in my ears.

The air smelled burned.

I looked at Chloe; she had not moved. *She's dead*, I told myself again.

Allister turned back to me. His face was stoic. I didn't know what a madman should look like, but I thought there should at least be some form of emotion. Anger, amusement, sorrow, giddiness… something.

The revolver seemed huge. I'd never seen it before. Either it had been hidden, or Allister recently acquired it.

I wondered if Mom was really dead. Maybe she would get up and save me.

Then I turned and ran.

I tried to jump to the stairs to get out of sight more quickly.

The gun boomed.

My right leg landed awkwardly on the second step, twisting my ankle, and then I bounced-rolled down the rest of the stairs.

I didn't cry. I didn't scream. I seemed paralyzed. No, I could move my arms. I tried to stand, pushing up with my right leg. The pain caused me to drop back down to hands and knees.

I looked up at the top of the stairs. Allister stood on the landing. He swayed.

I tried to get up again, but I was too weak. So incredibly scared.

Allister descended. A silent monster.

A demon.

His steps were irregular. There was no rhythmic cadence normally seen when someone goes down stairs. One leg went out, hung there, then down, jolting his body. The next leg swung out, slightly to the side, down, jolt.

I froze. The movements were intimidating as hell. Inhuman. He looked to be moving in slow motion, but he covered a lot of space with each step, like he was going down two steps at a time.

Leg swung out, land, jolt.

I started crawling to the front door. I'd left it open when I ran into the house. Leaving the door open was something that always earned us a beating. Right then I didn't care about the freaking door. I seemed to be moving in slow motion myself. It was only fifteen feet away.

It felt like fifty.

A crash behind me. I instinctively looked. Allister had fallen to the floor. The revolver slid away from him along the wooden floor. How did that happen?

The emotionless visage became enraged. He roared. No words, just *roared*.

I crawled to the door again, picking up my pace. With my hurt leg, I knew I wouldn't be able to outrun him. A baseball bat leaned against the wall by the front door. If I could get to the bat and get a lucky swing…

Allister moved inhumanly fast, caught me by the neck of my shirt, and spun me on my back. He'd twisted his huge fist in my shirt, tightening the fabric, choking me.

I tried to pry his hand away, but it was behind my neck and I had little strength at that angle. Even if I had full strength, he was way stronger than me. I looked up at him.

His nostrils flared. A visible vein in his temple pulsed impossibly fast. He was biting his tongue. A thin line of blood trailed down his chin. A drop fell into my open my mouth. I reflexively tried to recoil, but I couldn't move. Hot blasts of fetid breath buffeted my face as he exhaled forcefully.

His feral eyes swung up from me and his head snapped from side to side as if urgently looking for someone in a crowd. Sweat fell from his head into my eyes. It stung, but I didn't want to close my eyes. I *couldn't* close my eyes. I ignored the pain.

His eyes settled on a small table within arm's reach. He grabbed a hacksaw, raised it over his head, roared, then brought it down on me.

I blocked the blow with my left arm. Thankfully the thin blade gave some, but it still sliced my flesh to the bone. My arm lit up with the abrupt awareness of fire-hot flame. My scream came out as a hoarse exhale. I tried hopelessly to kick at his legs with my one good leg.

He brought the hacksaw down on me again.

And again.

And again.

Blackness flowed over my vision as my consciousness began slipping away. I couldn't breathe. I no longer felt the pain of the hacksaw cutting into me. I no longer felt anything.

I heard a vicious wolf-like snarl behind me, it seemed way off in the distance, then saw a flash of white. My body was pulled roughly forward and then thrown. I slid a few feet across the floor on my stomach.

Billy had run through the front door and launched himself at Allister's chest. The force caused Allister to fall backward, bringing me with him as his hand had caught in my shirt.

Stars floated in my vision. My hearing was muffled, as if someone covered my ears. I could only hear faint ringing. I felt dizzy. My brain shutting down from a lack of oxygen.

Then my surroundings rushed at me as if I fell head first from a ten story building. The world snapped into place.

Blood pooled quickly under my left arm. My neck hurt and I couldn't swallow.

Billy growled and snarled as he tried to get at Allister's throat, who was lying on his back with his arms desperately fighting to keep Billy away.

A shiny object on the floor caught my eye. I had landed close to Allister's gun.

I heard a yelp and saw Billy fly across the room.

Allister had gotten his legs under the dog and was able to kick him away. He scrambled to his feet.

I scrambled to the gun.

He'd either forgotten about me and the gun, or wasn't concerned. He probably didn't think I had the guts to use a gun.

Billy growled ferociously and barked at Allister from a distance.

I picked up the gun and made it to my feet. I'd never held a gun before. The metal was surprisingly heavy, and warm. I had to use both hands to make sure it didn't slip out of my bloody grip. I couldn't squeeze with my left hand, but I could use it to help steady. I could see chunks of raw flesh cut up on my arm, but the pain hadn't returned yet. I didn't know if that was good or bad. But I was relieved for the time being.

Allister had picked up the baseball hat.

Billy backed up a few feet and stopped to growl violently. He was in a low stance, ready to launch at Allister again. Then he looked at me, stood, turned slightly and backed up another couple of feet, away from the door, and resumed growling. Billy was leading Allister away from me.

Allister waggled the bat as if readying for a pitch and stepped toward the vicious dog. His eyes were mad with rage. Not of this world. His arms were bleeding badly, and he had scratch marks on his face.

He remembered me and turned to see where I was.

Billy barked wildly to regain Allister's attention.

Allister turned back to Billy.

I moved to a spot a few feet directly behind Allister, so that he would have to completely turn around to see me. I wanted to shoot him in the back. I *needed* to shoot him in the back.

I wish I would have.

Billy looked at me—no, stared *through* me. I knew he was going to give his life for me.

I heard someone yell inside my head at a volume so loud I jerked, *ELLIE! RUN!*

Then there was an ear-piercing yelp as Allister swung true on Billy's skull.

Allister turned to face me.

I brought up the gun and pointed at him, hoping maybe I'd get lucky with a shot and slow him down so I could do my best to run away.

Boom!

Boom!

Boom!

Boom!

Click, click, click, click, click.

Once I started I couldn't stop. I fired the remaining four shots of the six-shooter and tried to keep shooting.

Allister was on the floor. A large red circle grew in the middle of his stomach. Blood poured out of a hole in his throat.

My first shot miraculously hit him in the torso. The gun recoiled up, I fired again, striking the neck. Both hits were beyond my ability to make. My aim was guided somehow. It didn't make sense.

After each shot, I didn't know to bring the gun back down again. My next two shots went over his head. I could see bullet holes in the ceiling.

Billy lied motionless on the floor. The top of his head was deformed.

He had *knowingly* and *willingly* sacrificed his life for me. Giving up his life so I could escape the monster named Allister Raven.

78

I shuffled numbly to the front door. I didn't bother going upstairs. I knew Chloe was dead. I knew Ben was dead. I knew Mom was dead.

I wished I was dead.

But then a small feeling rose within me, little more than a suggestion, that maybe I was saved for a purpose.

I limped outside.

Billy's blue racquetball was on the ground a few yards away.

I limped up to it and stared down at the ball. I squatted, dropped the gun, and picked up the ball. I could still see a small spot of moisture leftover from Billy carrying it in his mouth, returning for another game of fetch.

I cried.

Chapter Nineteen

I sobbed silently, tears streaming down my cheeks, my body convulsing in short, quick shudders. I faced the back wall of Ray's cab and tried my hardest to be quiet.

Tyler sensed something was wrong. I heard him jump off Jenny's bed below me and then stand, placing his front paws over the top of my bed.

Because my fold-up bed was only halfway up the rear wall of the cab, it was easy for him to do. He said, *Ellie.*

It was the first time he'd ever called me Ellie.

I wiped the tears off my face with the sheets and rolled over.

He looked at me, mouth closed, in intense concentration.

I was glad it was Tyler and not Ray or Jenny staring at me, or I'd have been embarrassed. Even in the low light, I'm sure it was easy to see I'd been crying.

I'd never thought about whether dogs or other animals understood the significance of crying in humans. I have no doubt dogs can sense emotional strife in us. Maybe even cats too. I'd heard people tell stories about times when they were upset and their dog jumped up next to them on a couch or in bed to provide comfort. Maybe it's just imagination, but I don't think so.

After Billy died, I've never been close to another animal.

But I still believe it to be true. Billy knew when I was upset.

Tyler could have easily jumped onto my bed. But I'm not sure the extra 90lbs would have been good for it. Jenny might get a painful surprise.

I think he sensed that as well, because he made no attempt to jump onto the bed.

I scratched behind his ears and said, "Thanks."

He said, *Want some Cheetos?*

I smiled and nodded. "Yes."

Tomorrow. I'll get you Cheetos.

He dropped and returned to Jenny's bed.

Drained, I closed my eyes. And slept.

"Ellie. Elllllllieeeeee, time to wake up."

Someone shook my shoulder gently. I opened my eyes and snapped them shut to protect them from the evil sun. I hate mornings. I gingerly opened my eyes to slits, allowing them to adjust to the harsh light.

Sunlight gushed through the windshield of the cab. It wasn't directly burning my retinas, but still bright enough to hurt until I was accustomed.

Jenny stood in front of me. When I opened my eyes, she smiled and said, "Hi."

It was a very surreal experience. Here was the true girl of my dreams—not some short-term fantasy—standing two feet away from me while I was lying in bed, smiling. Wow.

I tried to say hi back, but instead said, "*Hhf,*" my mouth dry and uncooperative. I'm sure my breath smelled like I'd been chewing on three-weeks dead opossum too. I hate mornings. I did not make another attempt to speak.

Jenny kept smiling at me. She was a vision in the truest sense of the word.

The sunlight behind her highlighted strands of her hair. Wow. She kept smiling at me, expectantly. I eventually caught on that I was supposed to react in a certain way to a certain something, though I didn't have a clue as to what.

I took a quick peek: Thank God, she had on clothes.

She lifted a bag of Cheetos above the edge of the bed so I could see.

I laughed and quickly covered my mouth with my hand. Carcass breath! Toothpaste. I needed toothpaste. Mission critical.

I leaned over and saw Tyler sitting on the floor looking up, grinning, his tail swishing enthusiastically.

How did he...?

I sat up, smiled, plopped onto the floor, and muffled, "Let me brush my teeth."

Taking advantage of the sink in the cab under the microwave, I then felt human. Or at least my mouth tasted like I was human.

Jenny gave me a hug, a real hug, then handed me the Cheetos bag. "I cooked breakfast."

I got two Cokes from the small fridge.

Jenny opened the bag, poured a few Cheetos on a paper plate for Tyler and we all ate breakfast.

I said, "Where's Ray?"

"He went into the truck stop to take a short nap. He said this place is nice and has clean beds, long enough for even him. He said truckers stop here to catch some Z's. Dogs on a leash are allowed in the store. You'd be surprised how big it is in there. So Tyler and I went hunting for breakfast. He got all excited when he saw the Cheetos bag."

He projected to me, *Told you I'd get you Cheetos.*

Good dog.

I had a flurry of questions I asked Jenny between bites:

"What time is it?"

"11:00."

"Where are we?"

"Amarillo."

"Why are we here?"

"Ask Ray."

"How long have we been here?"

"Forty-five minutes."

"What's next?"

"Ask Ray."

"More Cheetos?"

She smiled and poured some more, also for Tyler.

Tyler said, *I like her. You should marry her. She's a great cook.*

I laughed, drawing a weird look from Jenny.

"Why are you laughing?"

"Tyler thinks you're a good cook." Oops.

She smiled. "He does, huh? How do you know?"

"Um, because uh... he thinks whatever I think. Yeah."

"Is that right?"

"Um, yeah." I looked at the Cheetos bag. "He also thinks you're beautiful." Only by eating Cheetos with a Coke for breakfast in the parking lot of a truck stop in Amarillo could I be so bold as to say something like that. The perfect storm. Still, I could feel my cheeks flush.

Tyler said, *What? No offense, Ellie, but she's not my type.*

I backhanded him on the side.

After a pause, Jenny said, "Well, your pickup lines are getting better. Using the dog is a nice touch."

I was suddenly warm in my long-sleeved shirt.

She gave me Perceptive Smile catalogued as #9, then said, "You have Cheeto dust on the side of your mouth."

I stood, looked in the mirror by the small sink, wiped the food from my mouth, then said, "Did you sleep okay last night?"

She pushed her lips out as if in thought and said, "Yeah, I slept well." She thought for a moment, seemingly trying to make a decision, then said, "I heard you crying."

Oh. Great.

"Were you having a nightmare?"

"A nightmare, yes." Thanks for the save, I thought. "I had a bad nightmare."

She looked as if she wanted to say more, but decided not to, leaving it up to me if I wanted to continue.

Nope.

She didn't need to hear about my past, anyway. She just lost her dad. Then I remembered some people receive healing by helping others. Jenny was definitely somebody that looked out for the welfare of others. It was evident in the way she treated customers at Buy City. It was evident in the way she treated me.

I took a deep breath and let it out slowly. I couldn't' talk about it. I'm sorry. I'm selfish.

I said, "Did Ray say anything about using the showers in the truck stop?"

"I asked, he said they were clean if we wanted to use them. From what I saw of the store, it does look like a nice place."

"Good. I need a shower. But you go first. Take your time. I'll go when you return."

"All right." She grabbed her backpack and left.

I sighed, wondering why I had to be such a dweeb. I almost felt like Jenny was starting to like me, for more than a friend. I reminded myself that was exactly what I wanted to happen more than anything, and yet my self disagreed, didn't want me to get close to anyone. Stupid self.

Well, speaking of self, it was good to have some minutes by myself for a while, Tyler notwithstanding. I get antsy when I've been around other people too long.

Tyler relaxed on the floor, keeping his thoughts to himself. Then he said, *I need to pee.*

So much for solitude. I stood to connect his collar to the leash and take him outside. "I'm going to get you diapers."

If you ever try that your gonads will be mine.

"What!"

The hero said that in a movie once. He kicked butt.

"You watch movies?"

Of course. Don't you? Action movies are the best.

"Figures. Aren't you done yet?"

If you'd give me some privacy.

"Oh brother."

I let Tyler draw out the rope in the retractable leash. He found a suitable trailer wheel on a neighboring eighteen-wheeler and did his business. I felt bad letting him urinate on the trucker's wheel, but I'm sure it's seen far worse.

Returning to the cab, Tyler picked up where he left off and napped.

Because of my gift-curse I'd never owned a dog, but I was sure I was going to have to get him outside to an open space sometime soon so he could run around and get some exercise. He'd been cooped up for a couple of days.

The hydraulic table rose with a slight airy sound, delighting my inner child. I placed my laptop on the table, smiling. I had to get a hydraulic table for my apartment.

Apartment... Uncle Joe... I still hadn't talked to him since all of this started. I had to find a way to contact him soon.

I fished for the flash drive with the data from Mr. Broxton's computer. I started to wonder if something yet again, some sort of crisis, was going to keep me from looking at the data, but quickly averted my thoughts, not wanting to jinx the opportunity.

Chapter Twenty

I decrypted the drive and accessed the data. I opened the folder named *Recipes* and perused through the list of subfolders: *Chicken Marsala, Fettuccine Alfredo, Veal Parmesan...* I started with a folder titled *Miscellaneous* because it was not named after a food, even though it still sounded innocent enough. I'd work my way through all the other folders if there were no clues in *Miscellaneous.*

It felt good to use a computer again. To be is to compute.

The only subfolder was named *Briarstone.* Interesting. I knew Mr. Broxton was on the board of directors for a financial company called Briarstone, possibly the chair. I didn't know a lot about Briarstone, other than it was a Goldman Sachs level firm, only because Mr. Broxton had told me.

Inside the folder *Briarstone* were additional folders labeled with the names of people, ten in all. *Nick Broxton* and *Bob Meredith* were two of the names. The rest were people I'd never heard of, which made sense considering I knew little about Mr. Broxton's work. I did know there were ten directors on the board, again because he told me. So my immediate assumption was these were the ten.

I let out a whistle. I could only imagine the money and power this small number of people possessed. What, maybe in the top 5% of American wealth? Top 1%? I wasn't good at that kind of thing.

Mr. Broxton once told me, speaking while watching me work on his computer, "As you progress through your adult life, succeeding—for I have every expectation you will—do not succumb to pursuing a position of executive leadership for a financial company, or a seat on the board. Money is ultimate power. Money can be evil. And to control the money of tens of thousands of lives is to control them. Power obtained from money creates a constant temptation to become corrupt. It changes. It captivates. It consumes. There are ten individuals on my board. I trust only two. And sometimes that number is halved, not trusting even myself."

He said this with great conviction, his tone grave. I turned to glance at him briefly, he wasn't looking at me, but staring at something in his mind I couldn't see.

He continued, "Elijah, there is something I need to tell you, something in which I could use your help in trying to investigate. I should have sought your assistance some time ago, but I made a poor choice—his cellphone rang. "One moment." He answered, then quickly left the room. He never finished confiding in me. He did not bring it up again. I did not ask, not wanting to infringe. That was a few months ago.

Now I'll never know.

Yet, the memory of that odd interaction seemed to be an omen for this moment. So far, two people had lost their lives for the data on that drive.

The sunlight filtering into the cab darkened significantly. Concerned, I got up to peer skyward through the windshield and saw a large cloud moving in front of the sun, casting a shadow over my small part of the world.

I opened Mr. Broxton's folder. There were some spreadsheets containing formulas and figures I didn't understand, plans, documents that looked like meeting minutes, goals... nothing real exciting.

I figured that if my hunch was right, and there was some bad mojo about the board members save one other person, I'd bet Mr. Meredith's folder wouldn't be exciting either. I looked anyway, anticipating Jenny asking me.

There was more of the same: strategic plans, spreadsheets, etc... There were also multiple lists of investors, but no investment numbers.

I looked around to see if anyone was watching me. Tyler napped. No one watched me. My scars didn't burn, but my "warning system" didn't work that way, considering I didn't seem to be in danger. I was just paranoid... and procrastinating. I was afraid of what I might find in the other folders. Both dreading what might be in there, and dreading what might *not* be in there, as in nothing, as in losing my one good lead so far as to why all of this was happening.

My heart was in exercise mode even though I sat unmoving in a chair.

I took another look around. Nothing. I opened the first folder, named *Aaron Lynch*. There were a few subdirectories, all labeled with dates and years. I opened one of them. My heart went from beating too fast, to stopping. There were dozens of pictures. The files had simple names, like *001, 002*, etc. but I could tell from the file extensions they were pictures. There were no images or thumbnails, just the file names. I could change the settings to display images.

I was afraid to. They may have been nothing more than someone's vacation pictures.

Yet I doubted it. And I felt unclean just sitting there.

I opened a picture. A second. A third. I closed the folder. The name Aaron Lynch still highlighted. A tear slid down my right cheek and fell onto the table, splattering into remnants.

The pictures were of a grown man and a little blonde girl, she couldn't have been more than twelve. Someone had blurred the portions of the pictures, but it was obvious the pictures portrayed sexual acts. In each of the three pictures, the girl's mouth was open in a scream I couldn't hear.

But I could feel it.

Bile crept up my esophagus, burning, like a volcano about to erupt. I tried to swallow the acid and force it back down. And again.

My God.

I stood, staggered to the sink and splashed water on my face, and just stayed there, hunched, my breathing trivial, my head leaning on the sink. I did not want to look at myself in the mirror.

That little girl, that poor little girl in the pictures... her life, ruined. Emotionally, socially, psychologically, painfully...

I had seen kids like her in the system. Some abused before they were placed in children's homes, some after, some both. There is a filter in our brains, even as children, telling us that this is wrong. It is meant to be a barrier to guard our minds, and our bodies, from being violated. But when some perpetrator breaks that barrier, tears it to shreds, and forces himself, or herself, on that child, the psyche is ruined. There are so many wrong messages that are sent and believed, the brain telling you *you're* ruined.

This is not to say there is no hope for sexually abused children. There is. And we must *fight* for that hope. We must *fight* for them. We must do everything we can to help them recover, and have a "normal" life, even a good life. But that place in their brains where they were broken, in many ways, will be something they will have to deal with the rest of their lives. In the good times, the bad times, all of the time. It never goes away.

85

I felt my jaw begin to ache as I clenched my teeth. I felt a massive pressure inside my chest. With it, a wave of anger coursed through me, through each arm and leg, through my head. My body began to shake, shake with anger, with rage. With something darker than rage.

I shook my head in disgust. Rage replaced my nausea. I wanted to break something, to scream and yell and... to kill something. No, to kill someone.

I wanted to kill Aaron Lynch.

I knew that was fallout from my own upbringing. From exposure to the violence that Allister so embraced. Such hate.

Maybe what I believed was wrong, maybe I should let God seek vengeance. If I was honest with myself, I would not debate whether I was right or wrong. I'd know that God would indeed take vengeance.

But this was one of the areas that I really didn't want to be honest with myself. I believed there should be a death penalty for repeat sexual offenders. Child molesters, rapists... Death penalty. No second chances, or third... No rehabilitation.

I promised myself if I ever caught someone raping a child, or an adult, I would kill them. And deal with God later.

I raged.

This doesn't mean that I'm some vigilante. It just means they deserve to die. Worthless piece of—

Jenny opened the door and entered the cab, her backpack slung over one shoulder. "Hi the—" She stopped in mid step. "What's wrong?"

I was standing in the middle of the floor, mouth curled in a snarl, fists clenched, shaking. I'm sure I looked like some kind of maniac.

I *was*.

She pulled the door shut behind her and walked closer to me, but kept her distance.

I could see fear in her eyes. She was afraid of me. That stung.

I closed my eyes and kept them closed, trying to take slow, deep breaths. My heart was still hammering. I worked to bring myself down, to calm the storm.

"Ellie, what's wrong?"

I knew if I talked, my anger would only escalate. So I pointed at the laptop.

She looked bewildered, but took the cue, put her backpack on the floor and sat down at the table, facing the laptop.

Tyler woke up when Jenny entered the truck. He padded over to her, seeking affection. But he sensed something wasn't quite right. He either did not talk to me, or in my angered state, I could not hear him.

I heard a few clicks of the trackpad buttons on the laptop, then Jenny said, "Oh God."

There were some more clicks from the laptop, then Jenny repeated grimly, "Oh God. Those poor children."

Children? I thought. As in more than one? The extreme effort I undertook to calm myself was failing.

Jenny closed the laptop lid, stood, and walked over to me.

My body rebelled against my brain's direction to be calm. Fury, adrenaline pulsed through me.

If she was still scared of me, she covered it. Instead, she took each of my hands in hers, turning them so that the backs of my hands were visible. I resisted at first, but she gently, yet

86

firmly, pulled on me. She massaged them with her thumbs, not making eye contact. Then she stepped closer and hugged me.

Again, I resisted at first.

She said, "Breathe. I'm here."

I took a deep breath and exhaled, closing my eyes again and just standing there. I had to think, concentrate. It took force of thought—ironically—but I could feel myself relaxing, letting Jenny calm me. It felt wonderful. The affection, the concern, the understanding. She didn't really know about my past, the abuse, the terror, but she did know I had grown up in the system. Maybe she put things together.

Under normal circumstances, I'd have been elated. Supremely elated. But with the polar opposite emotions surging through me, her actions merely helped me back off from the cliff. Which was still a good thing.

After a few minutes of standing there, embracing, I was finally able to speak. "The girl in the pictures," I had to stop to regain control of my voice. "She looks just like my sister, only older."

Chapter Twenty-One

Jenny didn't know I had a sister, or a brother. Outside of counselors who would never remember me, and Uncle Joe, saying something to Jenny was the first time I'd divulged such information to another human. I didn't even tell the various children's home workers and foster care workers. I didn't trust any of them at first. Some never.

I'm sure many of the workers had been briefed to a degree about my past, which would include a statistical rendition of my immediate family and their deaths. A few tried to inquire. I did not get angry with them. Despite my childhood, I like people. I did not inherently assume each one only asked because they were careless and deceitful. Or, at least I tried not to make the assumption. Regardless, I just shook my head politely when asked about my family or past indicating that part of my life was off limits. Even when other kids asked.

My memories of Chloe and Ben were sacred. I felt in some way the memories would become diluted if I mentioned them to anyone, maybe even tainted, like my memory of that final day.

To Jenny's credit, she held on to her curiosity and did not let it out. She did not try to draw information from me. She just stood there, hugging me.

The fury, the rage… the storm quieted.

She hugged me. She cared. She cared about *me*.

I don't want to sound like a hermit. I have a few friends. And of course, I have Uncle Joe. And God.

I also don't want anyone's pity. In fact, the *last* thing I want is pity. It is not possible to pity without judging. The two cannot be separated. To pity is to compare your current state to the state of someone less fortunate, to assess the differences and place yourself in a higher position.

Show empathy, or sympathy if you cannot identify with a less fortunate person. Have mercy if it is full of grace. *Honor* them.

But never pity.

The girl I loved, the girl I didn't deserve was hugging me. I had a hard time reconciling all of these conflicting emotions.

After some minutes, we both simultaneously decided to break the embrace, our timing in sync with one another. My eyes watered. I swiped at them quickly. Stupid eyes.

I no longer shook; the rage racing through me had died down. Yet I knew the rage was only in remission, waiting in a dormant state, anticipating my release of control.

I hoped that would never happen.

And then part of me hoped it would.

I said, "I can't look at any of the other folders. The only one I saw was Aaron Lynch. I need you to see if the other people have similar material.

She stepped back and looked me in the eyes.

I'm not going to pretend I knew what she was thinking and what she did or did not feel for me. But I don't believe it was my imagination that *something* had happened. Something passed between us. There was a clarity in her look, an earnestness as she looked at me I had not seen before. I did not know what it meant.

Maybe it was an expression of her feelings for me. I tried not to speculate.

She nodded. "Okay."

"We need to find them," I said.

She sat in front of the laptop again.

I grabbed my backpack. "I'm going to go take a shower."

"I'm sure I'll need another one after looking through these folders." She smiled to show she was only half-joking.

She had such great control. I could not sit in that chair in front of that laptop, knowing what was in at least one of those folders, so calmly. My sanity would be weakened.

"Do you want anything from the store?"

She tapped her bottom lip, pondering. "Chocolate is always good. You might get some things to replenish what we've used of Ray's. Maybe some extra."

"Chocolate. Extra food. Got it." I opened the door, but turned and said, "Jenny…"

She looked at me.

"Thanks."

She smiled.

As I walked across the parking lot to the truck stop, I turned around a few times, scanning for black Suburbans. I didn't see any.

The truck stop was bright and shiny and smelled like tire rubber. Several banks of fluorescent lights covered the ceiling, casting a bright-white on everything. The top half of the walls were covered in white slate tiles, the bottom half in grey slate, separated by a six-inch brushed nickel strip. It looked expensive.

I always envisioned truck stops as poorly lit, nasty-dirty places. Ray was right; this stop was far from it.

Row after row offered an impressive variety of goods for the travelling trucker or family. And ten feet right in front of me on an end-cap, center stage, calling out to me, a display of Hostess apple pies. My brain performed Handel's "Hallelujah Chorus," in HD stereo.

You could also buy iPads, cellphones, TV's, t-shirts, and antifreeze. It was still a truck stop, after all. Tires lined the long back wall. There was even a place to mail things.

I own zero credit cards. Which was good because I didn't want to pop up on some fake Fed's computer screen because I have an apple pie fetish.

Over to the right were a few workstations with computers. Nice. My latent brilliance arrived. I paused to savor the moment; it was a rare occasion.

At this point, I had no idea whether the bad guys knew about Uncle Joe. I had to assume yes. They seemed to have extensive resources. At minimum, wisdom suggested Uncle Joe's phones were tapped. Calling him would potentially place him at risk, as well as Jenny and I. Even if I bought a reusable cellphone, or called from a payphone, I couldn't conceal Uncle Joe's end. The line would be traced back to the origin and location of the caller: me.

Email? Just as bad.

But old-fashioned letter delivered via courier? Seemed rather unlikely the enemy watched Uncle Joe's front porch.

Was the idea paranoid? Certainly. It's not whether you're paranoid, it's whether you're paranoid enough. The deaths of Mr. Broxton and Mr. Meredith proved there was strong reason to be overtly paranoid.

Uncle Joe was my last living relative. I was taking no chances.

A plan in place, I headed to the bathroom to shower and think about what I was going to say in the letter to Uncle Joe. Then I bought a cellphone, activated the anonymous short term service, and went to one of the computers. I found a web service in which I could use an online form to write the letter and have it couriered to Uncle Joe next day. I included the number of the temporary cellphone in the letter so he could call me. I advised him to use a payphone.

I was stoked to have a cellphone again. Reconnected to the world. I could even use it to check the time. Technology.

Then I went shopping for Dr Peppers, Cokes, hot dogs, buns, Cheetos, real dog food, two bowls, plus various other foodstuffs. And Hostess apple pies. I looked left and right to make sure nobody was going to try to steal my apple pies and paid cash.

Chapter Twenty-Two

When I returned to Ray's truck, the engine was idling and all of the windows were opaque. The door was locked, so I knocked once.

Jenny opened the door and took some plastic bags from me as I climbed in.

Ray was hunched low in the driver seat, his back to everyone, talking quietly on a cellphone. The sweet notes of jazz drifted throughout the cabin, making it impossible to hear Ray. Probably intentional.

Jenny started pulling things out of the bags.

Tyler vigorously sniffed the various items that were placed on the table and counter, his tail swishing eagerly. *What did you get? What is this? What is that? Did you get me anything? What did you get me?*

Jenny pulled out the Cheetos bag and set it on the table.

Tyler stood on his hind legs to see the bag. He said, *Mine*, snatched it, and padded to the bed, jumping on top.

I said, "Uh, no. But nice try," and walked to the bed to return the Cheetos.

I picked up the bowl that would serve as Tyler's dog bowl and poured some dog food for him.

Tyler sniffed happily, then said, *Real food! Wait, can I have Cheetos first?*

"No."

Bugger. He ate.

I had stashed a Godiva chocolate bar in my back pocket instead of leaving it in one of the shopping bags. It was cold enough outside that it wouldn't melt. I said, "Hey, what's this? Cool, look what I found." I showed her the chocolate.

She smiled, it made her look like a goddess. No, not like... she was a goddess. She said, "Have I ever told you that you're my favorite Elijah Raven in the whole wide world?"

I feigned deep thinking for a second, then said, "Um, no, don't believe so."

"Well, it's true." She took the bar and opened it. "Godiva, chocolate of the gods." She took a bite. She was a goddess eating Godiva chocolate of the gods. There were a lot of god-things happening here. She offered the chocolate and said, "Want some?"

I won't repeat the first thing that came to my mind.

She seemed to realize the suggestiveness of her question and her cheeks reddened. Then she favored me with Perceptive Smile #1, which was the most frequent smile she gave me.

A flash of insight gave way to a flash of horror. Was I that easy to read? Probably.

I got Tyler some water and asked Jenny, "What's Ray doing?"

"I'm not sure. He came back after resting, I told him about the pictures and he—"

"There were more?"

"Yes." Jenny looked away so I couldn't see her eyes. "Every one of the people listed except Dad and Mr. Broxton."

I felt lightheaded and sat down. Anger's flame flicked on again. I snuffed it and promised myself there would be a time.

Jenny said, "Ray looked at the names on the folders, but didn't say anything. He breathed heavily, not like he'd been running, but slowly and loudly inhaling and exhaling through his nose. He turned away, started the truck, turned on the music, darkened the windows, and has been talking quietly on the phone since."

I nodded. "We have to do something."

Jenny said, "What? What can we do? How are we going to find these people? And even if we did, what could we do about it? These are some of the richest people in the world. We need to tell the FBI, or at least the police."

"FBI imposters are already chasing us. We can't go to them. Someone inside must be helping them. They have to be for Mr. Broxton to be fooled. Their credentials must be legit. We can't go to the police either. If Feds are involved, seems likely some local police could be getting their hands dirty. If we go to the locals, someone could run it up the chain, then it's game over. Not only would it do nothing to bring justice, but it would send the hellhounds on us, and they would know where we are."

"Okay fine, if we can't contact the authorities… we can't do this on our own, Ellie."

I sighed. "I know. You're right. But there's no other choice." I smiled. "Maybe our guardian angel can help," and nodded toward Ray.

She lifted her eyebrows.

As if on cue, Ray got up from the driver's seat and walked over to us. "All right, folks, it's time to roll."

"Where are we going?"

"Denver, Colorado, Rocky Mountains, my home, *God's* country." He favored us with a big smile; his bright white teeth looked crazy white compared to his dark skin. "We should—"

Jenny said, "—why are we going to your house?"

I said, "—why are we going to Denver?"

Tyler said, *I love Colorado.*

I looked at Tyler and wanted to ask him how he would know anything about Colorado, but figured asking the dog such a thing in front of Jenny and Ray would only heighten concerns about my stability.

Ray chuckled at the questions, surely expecting them. "Oh, we won't be going to my house, we'll be going to my *home*. The Rockies are home for me. We have some friends who are going to help us out. What God can do, it can blow... your... mind."

I hadn't noticed how tall Ray was. Until then, I hadn't seen him stand. I had to tilt my head up to look at Ray, who must have been more like 6'6", a good half-foot taller than me. I said, "I hope so."

Ray smiled, staring intently at me and said, "Elijah, there is no need to hope, when one has *faith*."

I'm sure it was just my imagination, but when he said 'Elijah,' the name seemed to echo faintly. I shook my head as if breaking a spell.

Ray patted me on the shoulder, his hand large, and warm, and firm. He looked at the things we'd bought from the store. "Wolf brand chili. I love Wolf brand chili. 'When's the last time you had a hot, steaming bowl of Wolf brand chili?'"

Remembering the TV commercial of old, I said, "Well that's too long!"

Ray laughed heartily, slapping me more on the shoulder. "That's right! That's right! Well thank you two for your kindness. Let's get going. Buckle up. God can blow your mind, and I have something to tell you as proof."

Chapter Twenty-Three

Ray shifted the big rig into gear and looked left and right multiple times as we pulled out of the long parking space and onto the service road feeding Highway 287. The big truck lurched and growled, slowly gaining speed.

Although the truck was solid, you could still feel the immense power of the rig vibrating in the cabin. It seemed right that someone as powerful as Ray drove the semi, leading us to the next phase of our quest.

What *didn't* seem right was the fact we were on this quest to begin with—in fact, well underway—and until now I hadn't even realized it.

I sat in the passenger seat watching the world go by on the other side of the window. The terrain was mainly wild grass and flat, with a few brown hills that seemed out of place. We passed a few sections of farmland with huge water irrigators that sprayed on the crops and were as long as half a football field.

Jenny reclined on the lower bed reading a paperback, I couldn't see what. Tyler was at her feet, content.

I wondered what would happen to him when all of this was over. He didn't have a home anymore. For that matter, neither did Jenny. She still had the house, but would she want to keep living there now that both of her parents had died? I'm sure it was paid for, but still.

Since that day when I was ten, when I walked out my front door and found Billy's racquetball, I never stepped inside the house again. All of my things, Ben's things, Chloe's, my parents'... I just left them there. Everything.

I walked away and never looked back.

I'm sure I was in shock. I had nothing with me, except Billy's racquetball. I couldn't eat a racquetball. How did I expect to survive? I suppose deep down I didn't expect I would. At least I hadn't planned on it. Those next few days...

I turned to look at Tyler.

Noticing the attention, he raised his head and smiled in a doggy pant, his tail wagged.

I smiled and turned back to the open road. A road I had never been on before, a road far away from home, much farther than I'd ever dreamed.

A new road.

Ray had put on some smooth jazz in the cab's surround system. It wasn't quite the same as Sinatra's *Strangers in the Night*, especially since it was daytime, but it would work.

I'd been watching the scenery go by, my thoughts wandering aimlessly, when I recognized a familiar tune on the sound system: Dean Martin's *Everybody Loves Somebody*.

I looked at Ray, who was smiling, of course. He was always smiling. And one big eye was eyeing me from the side. I said, "You like Dean Martin?"

"He's all right. I don't like him as much as you do."

Huh? "How did you know I like Dean Martin?"

Ray chuckled. "I'm your guardian angel, remember? I know *everything* about you."

"That's not spooky."

He laughed.

I'd been waiting for Ray to continue telling us what he started back at the truck stop, what he said was going to 'blow our minds,' but he hadn't volunteered further details as we drove up the highway toward Colorado. Wanting to change the subject from his supposed knowledge of my inner secrets, I prodded, "Don't you think we've been hanging over the cliff long enough?"

Jenny put the book down and moved to a closer seat.

Ray turned and said, "Hi Jenny, come join us." As he looked back to the road, he continued in his deep, mellifluous bass, "I need an audience with flexible minds. Minds capable of faith, of believing in what cannot be seen." He paused to see if we were willing participants in the audience.

Ray turned to glance at each of us. He looked up at the sky, seemingly searching for something, then nodded. "What I'm about to tell you, you have to keep to yourselves. People's lives depend on the secrecy. *Your* lives depend on the secrecy. Trust me." He flicked glances at each of us again. "There are a few dozen of us, we call ourselves—unofficially—the Network. Officially, we have no name. C-Man, myself... we're a part of the Network." He paused. "As were Bob Meredith and Nick Broxton."

Jenny said, "What? What is this network?" A touch of scorn in her voice. "Dad never said anything about it. I've never heard of it."

Neither had I.

Ray's voice took on a serious tone. "We're a group of people with the common goal to help those who have been abused. Men, women, and children. And to make things right. We don't always play by the book. The government, politicians, law enforcement agencies, they all have laws that regulate how they operate. Some of them pay no heed to these laws, of course. But if we were known to them, our activities would be severely impeded."

Ray paused as he concentrated on maneuvering the eighteen-wheeler within unexpected congestion on the highway.

He continued, "Great timing for that little traffic jam." He chuckled. "Perfect illustration for what our lives would be like in the Network if we had to deal with bureaucracy and its attempts to deadlock us, all in the name of protecting civil rights for the criminally sane."

I said, "What do you mean?"

"The ACLU and other like-minded groups and activists fight hard to protect the rights of rapists and abusers. Now, by that I don't mean they specifically target serial rapists and do what they can to keep them free, but they do make concerted efforts to thwart the labors of watchdog groups like the Network. And then, there are the crooked politicians, the crooked law agents, who care more about money than protecting the innocent. Some of these crooks have a lot of influence, and can make decisions or promote laws impacting large numbers of people, all under the guise of making America a better place for the common folk. The end result is rapists get to keep on raping, abusers keep on abusing. It keeps us from doing our work and bringing the criminals to justice. So, we bring justice to them." Ray smiled at us.

"I don't want to say we're above the law," he continued. "We're not. There's a fine line there. But, I'll say we *bend* the law, work around... okay, sometimes we *do* break the law. But we bring justice. I can own that."

He lapsed into a long period of silence, just watching the road as he drove.

I glanced at Jenny; neither one of us said anything. We just watched the road ahead as well. I felt like this was some type of interview, like an interview for a job. I focused on what Ray just shared with us: the opportunity to bring rapists and abusers to justice.

I have a passion to help kids… But there is not much I can do on my own. But this group, the Network, would be an outlet for that passion.

Would I be willing to circumvent the law, even break it to help others?

Hell yes.

"I'm in."

Both Ray and Jenny looked at me.

Jenny said, "In what?"

"The Network. I'm in."

Ray chuckled. "Not so fast, Elijah. I appreciate your fervor, but this isn't a recruiting effort."

"Bull crap. You wouldn't be telling me—" I looked at Jenny "—*us*, if you didn't want us to help."

Ray stayed silent for another long stretch. In fact, I worried he wouldn't respond, that I was indeed wrong, and he was just providing a little information. And now wishing he hadn't said anything to us.

Finally, Ray said, "This is the part that's going to blow your mind. Are you ready?" He looked at each of us. "You discovered the evidence Nick had found. He told you to grab that evidence before the enemy took it. You went to Bob's house; the bad guys were already there. Both Nick and Bob were part of the Network. You escaped from three armed men. And during the escape, you two just *happened* to drive into the woods on C-Man's property? Also a member of the Network. There is *no* such thing as a coincidence. That is divine intervention, my friends." He looked at both of us again.

Tyler said, *He's right.*

I glanced at Tyler. I hadn't considered before whether animals had a belief, or were capable of belief, in God.

Ray asked, "You follow?"

I paused to make sure I didn't miss some hidden message, then answered, "Yes. You're saying that Jenny and I didn't end up in Charles's woods by accident, but that God had orchestrated those events."

Ray smiled. "Close. I'm not saying He directed *all* of the events that led to you driving through his woods. But I *am* saying it was no accident you ended up there. God has big plans for you two. Big plans."

"I don't consider myself a puppet." Jenny said. "I am me. I make decisions for myself."

"And I agree," Ray replied. "You're not a puppet. But that doesn't mean you can't be influenced. Tell me this, what were you thinking when you swerved into the woods? Did you think about the possible ramifications, plan the potential outcomes? Or did you 'just do it'?" Ray made quote signs around the phrase.

"Well, with something like that, you don't plan it out. It's a reaction. We were getting chased. I suddenly thought of that as a possibility for getting away."

Ray smiled. "So you think it's impossible for you to have been influenced to make that decision?"

Jenny thought for a minute. I mean she actually thought for a full minute. "I didn't feel anything influencing me. Certainly didn't feel anything inside my head."

"Where did the idea come from? Where do *any* ideas come from?" Ray spread out his arms as if to imply all of the ideas in the world.

Jenny said, "I don't know. They can't *all* be from God. Why would he be making decisions for me if he is?"

Ray smiled. "Something to think about, isn't it?"

I said, "This hurts my head."

Ray said, "But! Tis so sweet—" Ray sang the words in his deep bass, "—to trust in Jesus; Just to take Him at His Word."

The man could sing. Wow.

"Just to rest upon His Promise. And to know, thus saith the Lord."

I clapped.

Jenny smiled a little. "My mother used to sing that to me when I was a child... Before cancer took her. I loved it when she sang to me. God didn't make her any promises."

Ray's smile vanished. "Oh, but you're wrong, dear Jenny. You're wrong."

Her face was expressionless.

"But methinks now is not the time to talk about it. You and I will have a nice little visit sometime."

Wanting to break the awkwardness, I asked Ray, "Can you sing *Swing Low, Sweet Chariot*? I love the way that song sounds in the lower registers. I like to sing it, but I can't hit the low notes."

"Do you know what that song means, Brother Elijah?"

"It's about slavery, right?"

"Well, it was written during that time, but it's actually referring to the prophet Elijah's ascension, when a chariot from Heaven came down and gave him the ride of his life—or end of life." Ray laughed heartily.

Jenny and I laughed too. You couldn't help it. If you heard Ray laugh, you were going to laugh. No choice.

"Really?" I said. "It's about Elijah?"

"That's right!"

"Cool."

We rode down the highway, Ray singing *Swing Low, Sweet Chariot,* nailing the low notes, making the cabin rumble as if he were a diesel engine.

Chapter Twenty-Four

We made it to Denver that night after stopping once for lunch and bathroom breaks. Ray pulled the rig and trailer into a warehouse. A lighted sign outside stated International Distribution and Holding Center.

Ray powered the driver's side window down and yelled, "Hi, Honey, I'm home!"

Some people hurried to the truck and unhooked the trailer after cranking down the legs. We were in a huge, four-story warehouse with tan painted cinder block walls and a concrete roof. The building looked to be about four hundred yards long and another one hundred wide. The length was hard to determine because the entire warehouse was not lit at that time. Our section was very bright and made the grey-painted concrete floor shine. Catwalks ran the length of the building with intersecting pathways. The truck's idling engine echoed loudly in the cavernous space. A man gave Ray a thumbs up, then Ray pulled the truck forward and parked it in an open bay.

Three-story office space overlooked the nearer end of the warehouse. These rooms were topped by a mezzanine with a bright yellow railing.

Ray, Jenny, and I hopped out of the truck, Tyler jumped.

Large heaters hung from the ceiling overhead, providing background noise as well as warmth. But it was still chilly. I didn't know what the outside temperature was, but I imagined it had to be colder here than it was back home. I was wearing a long-sleeved t-shirt—black, of course—but the chill felt good to me.

Jenny wrapped up in her jacket.

A half-dozen men and women stood semicircle around us wearing sweatshirts or coats. Some were smiling at us.

Ray stood next to us, beaming. "Everyone, meet my new friends: my brother Elijah Raven, Jenny Meredith, and Tyler." He indicated each of us with a hand, and stooped to pat Tyler, who wagged his tail.

Ray looked at us and spread an arm towards the semicircle, "These are members of the Network."

A white man wearing a blue Air Force sweatshirt and cap said, "Are you sure it's safe to talk about the Network in front of them?" He didn't seem to be upset, just cautious.

Ray nodded. "Absolutely. In fact, they are new recruits. At least Brother Elijah is."

Jenny stepped forward spontaneously and said, "Oh, I'm in!" Then she stepped back self-consciously, embarrassed. I'd never seen her embarrassed before.

Ray chuckled. "There you have it. Meet two new recruits." He smiled at us with genuine pride. He said, "This is Diana Roca, Jason Christian, Chris Fraher, Cheryl Smith, Toby Hinshaw, and Merle Gornick." They each stepped forward and shook our hands when named.

Jason was the one wearing the Air Force sweatshirt. He said, "Welcome to the team."

I nodded and said, "Thanks."

Diana said, "Nice dog."

Tyler said, *I like her already. You can tell she's smarter than all the rest. Maybe combined.*

I smiled and tried not to laugh.

Diana knelt to the floor and cooed Tyler. The big dog immediately went to her, rolled onto his back, and solicited a tummy rub. Diana complied.

Cheryl was a small black woman and wore a large dark green coat, which looked to be two sizes too big for her. She hugged herself in the big coat and said, "It's cold out here. How about some hot cocoa?"

Toby, wearing a black zip-up hoodie, said, "It's always time for hot cocoa." Gesturing for us to follow him, he said, "C'mon guys, let's get inside the office."

Ray said, "Toby, why don't you show Brother Elijah and Jenny the operations."

Toby said, "Sure thing."

Tyler, still getting a tummy rub from Diana, said, *I'll stay here, thanks.*

I said, "Come on, Tyler, let's get inside."

Tyler sat up partially and said, *Really?*

I fought the urge to reply with a yes, instead saying to Diana, "Looks like you have a new friend."

She said, "I'll take him." But stopped petting him so he would get up.

"Come on," I repeated to Tyler.

Tyler stood and looked at Diana. He said, *Thanks.* But he knew she couldn't understand his projected thought.

But, she nodded as if to say you're welcome, and as if she *did* understand him.

I've never known anyone else with my gift. Coincidence? I didn't know, but I'd have to follow up later. Right now, in front of all of these other people, would not be good. I certainly did not want to reveal my secret to everyone, even if they were in Ray's Network.

We followed Toby through a door into the offices.

We were in a reception area. The space was bright, clean, and modern. Paintings of various forms of transportation hung on the walls. Security cameras watched from two separate corners. We walked through this space to one of two doors. Toby held a card to a badge reader and the door popped open. We followed him down a hallway and were stopped by Ray at an intersection.

Ray said, "Toby, when you take them to the Slush Pit, ask Jason to show them how— never mind, I'll ask Jason myself."

Jason approached from yet another hallway, his face red and jaw clenched.

Ray said, "What's wrong?"

Jason closed the gap between us before saying anything else, then came to an abrupt stop. He swallowed. "C-Man is dead."

Chapter Twenty-Five

Jenny gasped.

I whispered, "No…"

Ray said, "Oh Lord," then leaned against a wall. "Oh Lord…" He buried his head in one massive hand. After a few moments, he looked up and said, "Wilkerson?"

Jason said, "Correct. Charles missed his last check-in, so Wilks went to investigate. Found him outside the house. They…" Jason took in a deep breath. "They removed his eyes and tied him to a tree, then tied his arms to branches like a mock scarecrow."

Ray's nostrils flared. He balled his hands into gigantic fists. I felt sorry for anyone that ever felt those knuckles. Even if he deserved it. That was the first time I'd seen Ray angry. I was scared.

He said, "Send a containment team. Try to sanitize the house and property as much as possible. Even if they tortured C-Man, he wouldn't tell them anything. But they might find something at the property if given enough time."

Jason said, "Already done."

Ray replied, "Good. Now take Elijah and Jenny to the Slush Pit. Give them the assignment."

Jason shook his head as if trying to break an illusion. "What? They haven't even been trained—"

Ray interrupted, "I said give them the assignment. Now." His deep voice echoed in the hallway though he wasn't yelling.

Jason looked at him, not in defiance, but in concern. He looked at me, then Jenny.

Ray said, "I will escort them and watch them. But C-Man sacrificed his life for these two."

Tyler said, *And me.*

Ray looked at us, then focused back on Jason. "They are in it now whether they like it or not. This is in honor of C-Man." He looked at me.

I nodded, though I didn't really know what I was nodding about. It just felt like the right thing to do.

Jason said, "Understood. I apologize for doubt—"

Ray said, "No, you are right to doubt."

Jason exhaled slowly, then said to Jenny and me, "Follow me."

Toby said, "I will inform the others," and walked off in another direction.

Jenny, Tyler, and I followed Jason down the hallway and to some stairs leading down.

The stairs emptied into another hallway. We were on the basement level. Double doors, open, were to the left. The floor in the room was a couple of steps lower than the hallway. Can spotlights illuminated small sections, while the rest of the space was in relative darkness.

A large curved desk faced the left corner of the room. A bank of eight monitors, four on top of four, rose from the left side of the desk. There were two chairs at the desk. The right side had several reference manuals and multiple high-tech phones. A large flat panel monitor was positioned about four feet up on the wall to the left. Another large flat panel hung from the ceiling in the right corner. Two spotlights lit up huge floor-to-ceiling maps of the Americas and

99

of Eurasia/Africa/Australia. A small table with chairs was centered in the room. Security cameras were high in the corners by the door.

Jason said, "This is the Slush Pit, the command center of the Network. It's similar to a police dispatch."

Jenny said, "Why's it called the Slush Pit?"

Jason said, "Good question. Seems strange, doesn't it? Well, there's no real nice way to explain. A lot of terrible images, scenes, news items come up on these monitors. There are hundreds of news feeds that connect into the Pit as well as Network members connecting who are out on assignment. Considering what we do, who we're trying to protect, you can imagine it's almost always bad news. Disturbing news. After you've taken a shift in the Pit, you feel like you're emerging from slush, trying to break through the surface. The shifts are always short and there are always at least two people in the room when we're monitoring. It can get really depressing."

Jason paused, and seemed to be trying to think of what to say next. "Well, anyway, we can talk about that later." He clapped his hands together and rubbed vigorously, as if trying to start a fire. Then he said, "All right! Let's get started!"

Jason sat in front of one of the workstations and logged in. He looked back at us over his shoulder and said, "You're going to like this…" He opened a directory the Network had on Aaron Lynch, dug deeper into the folder and opened multiple windows. He looked at us and gestured with his chin to look at the large screen to the left on the wall, a slight smile on his face. He grouped the separate windows on the smaller screen in front of him, and flicked them with the mouse to the large screen. The separate windows were automatically resized and positioned so that they could all be seen on the large screen.

"Cool," I said. "I want one of those."

Jenny said, "Yeah… that would be a hot item at the EC."

Jason smiled. "This is a custom set up. It costs maybe…" he pursed his lips and tilted his head left and right, "around twenty grand."

"Oh," I said. "Never mind."

Jenny said, "Yikes."

Jason stood and stepped in front of the large monitor. One of the windows had a picture of Lynch and a short bio and business profile. There were eight satellite images, eight street maps, weather conditions for the different locations, company profiles and business news, personal financial information…

Jason touched one of the satellite images with his right hand, then used his left hand to drag the corners of the image in opposite directions, expanding the size of the window.

"It's touchscreen too?" I blurted.

Jason nodded, mimicking a bobblehead doll. "Yep. Pretty cool, huh?"

"Totally," I said. "This is obviously way out of the league of what you can get at Buy City. Where did you get it? I assume the vendor also did the custom set up."

"Yep," said Jason, smiling. "Me."

"You?"

"Really?" said Jenny.

Jason mimicked a bobblehead again. "Yep."

I said, "Wow, that's really impressive."

"Thanks. Ray says you're into IT stuff also. I'll show you how I set it all up sometime."

"Thanks!"

Tyler said, *He's better than you.*

He didn't get me that time. I ignored him. I can outwit the dog every once in a while.

Jason said, "This is a satellite image of what's suspected to be Lynch's most prominent residence. With someone like him, of course, he'll have multiple houses. And also multiple companies, some that don't even exist. These additional images peer in at some of the other locations known to have a strong association with Lynch. We don't have the resources to follow him wherever he goes, or any other suspect, for that matter. But especially in Lynch's case, he *does* have the resources to cause trouble if he found out about us. That's why Ray said we had to get a containment crew to C-Man's house. It's highly probable the goons that had been chasing you two work for Lynch."

Jenny said, "Those fake feds? How could a single person pull off something like that?"

"Easy," said Jason. "Millions of dollars can accomplish quite a few things, if used right. And he doesn't have to operate on his own. He can hire/bribe/coerce people into doing work for him.

"At any rate, he caught onto Broxton and your dad, Jenny. We don't know how. But if he figures out there's a group of people trying to stop him, and others in his line of business, then he could cripple us. We have to remove him as quickly as possible."

"Remove?" I said.

Bobblehead nodding. "Remove. Take him out of the picture, make him disappear, however you want to phrase it."

"Kill him?" said Jenny.

"Well, let's not phrase it quite like that. But that's the assignment for you two."

"Whoa! What? We're not contract killers, or *removers* or whatever you guys want to call it. There's no way we can do something like that."

Jason smiled. "You're right. Thankfully you don't have to." He brought another window to the front and expanded it, then zoomed in. "The goal of this assignment is fact finding only. To get information on Lynch we can use to come down hard on him. We take the evidence and get it in the hands of the right people who can make something happen. Sometimes that's us, as in other people in the Network. Sometimes it's anonymously given to someone or someone plural outside of the Network."

Jason pointed to the image of the zoomed high-rise. "We have strong reason to believe Lynch is using this facility for a child prostitution ring behind the scenes. None of us have gone there to investigate yet. That's what you will be doing, with Ray's supervision." He stopped to let us think.

Jenny and I shared a look. I was sure we were thinking the same thing.

I said, "We want to help, of course, but, as you said so yourself, we haven't been trained for anything like this. We don't know what we're doing."

"I agree," said Jason. "But I don't call the shots. Ray does. He said it's a go. So, guess what, it's a go. You can refuse, of course. But from what Ray's already told me about you two, I doubt that's going to happen."

"No," I said. "That's not going to happen."

I looked at Jenny; she nodded in agreement.

"Okay, so what do we need to know?"

Jason smiled, then clapped his hands again and rubbed enthusiastically.

101

He spent the next hour briefing us on what we needed to know, or at least what the Network knew of the location and Lynch's operation to this point.

Jenny said, "How could he get away with something like that, especially right there in the city?"

"Oh, it's easy. Some establishment that doesn't stick out. A lot of traffic that seems ordinary. Detroit's economy is suffering, so this brings a lot of money into the city. There are those who don't care about where the money comes from, just as long as it's there."

"Sick," said Jenny.

Jason gave a single nod and said with a humorless smile, "Welcome to humanity."

I looked over at Tyler to see if he had any sort of reaction. If he did, he didn't share with me. Instead he just kept his head on the floor, resting. I'm sure he already knew just how depraved humans were.

Jason said, "And yet, the potential exists for redemption in everyone. Even those committed to pure evil, just for the sake of evil. I did not always believe that. It's something Ray taught me. That doesn't mean everyone will change sides, so to speak, evil for good. And that doesn't mean we can hang tight, and hope they come around someday, see the Light, if you will. We, the Network, strive to bring about redemption for the children. We're not perfect. God saves us. With His help, we'll save the children. And others who have fallen into that life. So, tomorrow, you two will be going with Ray to Detroit."

Tyler popped his head up. That got a rise out of him. *And me?*

I said, "What about Tyler?"

"On this one, Tyler will need to stay with someone. Remember, Lynch's whole operation is organized around not sticking out. We can't stick out in any way either. Tyler would stick out."

We wrapped up the intel session and followed Jason upstairs to eat. We were in a large room decorated like an old hometown diner. There were enough tables to seat forty, but there were only a dozen of us sitting at one long table. It was nine o'clock. I knew I was starving, probably most everyone else too.

The food was *amazing*. Chicken fried steak, cream gravy. Mashed potatoes, cream gravy. Chicken fried chicken, cream gravy. Green beans, no cream gravy, buttered corn, brown sugared carrots, fried okra, macaroni and cheese, squash casserole, biscuits… Served family style: on large platters and bowls. You got what you wanted and as much as you wanted.

Jenny looked at me and said, "Wow."

I said, "Can you cook like this?"

She said, "Are you kidding? There's a reason there are a hundred cans of food in my pantry."

I looked at Tyler, who noisily enjoyed a plate of his own.

"Better than Cheetos?"

He said, *Yep.*

Heinz ketchup bottles sat on the tables. I got some weird looks using a combo dip of cream gravy and ketchup for my chicken fried steak. Those people just didn't have a palette as sophisticated as mine.

Jenny said, "But I can cook better than mixing ketchup and gravy."

"Hmph."

I took in everyone at the table. People were smiling, laughing, enjoying the food.

Ray came up and sat at the empty spot across the table from me. "Like the food?"

"Oh good grief, yes," I said with a mouth half full of mashed potatoes, breaking my own rule. "Incredible!"

"It's happy food. In the South it's called comfort food. Food is actually something that can create great enjoyment. It can make you happy. We deal with such heartache here, we try to do all of the little things that can make people happy. Of course, it's still mainly a choice by the individual. He or she has to make the decision to be happy. But we try to help with the little things."

I said, "I agree, happiness is not a circumstance. It's a choice."

Ray smiled, "Right on, Brother Elijah." He looked to his left toward the kitchen.

A plump black woman walked through the doorway into the dining room, smiling broadly with evident pride in the delight on everyone's faces. Above the doorway was a sign: NEVER TRUST A SKINNY COOK.

Ray said, "There's our real life Aunt Jemima."

I said, "What do you mean? Because she's a good cook?"

"That's obvious. Her name really is Jemima. We all call her Aunt Jemima."

She walked over to us. "Nice to meet you, Elijah," she extended her hand to me, "and Jenny," still smiling broadly.

You can identify the personalities of some people very quickly. Jemima had the matronly persona of someone you could go to with all of your problems she'd make you feel like you didn't have a care in the world.

We both replied with, "Nice to meet you."

"Are you enjoying the food?"

"Oh yes," I said.

She smiled that broad smile again. "I see you like ketchup with the gravy. My husband—Lord Bless him—he used to like that too. For years I banned him to use it on my cooking. But then I finally gave up. He said he wasn't trying to mask the flavor, he was just getting lycopene." She laughed wholeheartedly, her shoulders hopping up and down.

Jenny said, "I can't believe how good this is. I'd gain two hundred pounds if I ate like this every day."

"Oh no, no, Honey, plenty of exercise, it's all right. See?" She stood sideways to present her figure. "It takes a lot of hard work to keep a body like this."

Ray laughed. She slapped him on the back as he did so, with a mock look of reprimand.

I said to Jemima, "Aren't you going to eat?"

"No, I've been sampling as I cooked. I'm all right."

"Well, thank you for making this incredible meal."

"Aren't you sweet? You're quite welcome, Sweetie. I'd better go get dessert out here."

"Dessert?" I patted my stomach. "Oy."

Ray said, "After you've experienced the life-changing experience of eating Aunt Jemima's banana pudding—"

"Boy, you're laying it on thick!" said Jemima.

"—you'll never want to leave the table!"

Aunt Jemima left and returned with large bowls of banana pudding.

Jenny said, "Do you want some ketchup with that?" While offering me the bottle.

"Ha ha," I said.

We ate banana pudding (fantastic!), then Ray said, "We'd better get some sleep. Trouble waits for us in Detroit tomorrow."

I said, "How are we getting there?"

"Ol' *Neb*," said Ray, enigmatically.

I put on my best blank look, which comes naturally.

Ray obliged. "The *Nebuchadnezzar*."

How does one increase the level of blankness in their expression? I tried it anyway, and added a sound effect: "Huh?"

Jenny said, "Your truck, right?"

Ray smiled. "That's right."

"Oh," I said. "I knew that. Just wanted to give you a chance to answer."

I don't know how she does it, but Jenny can combine a *whatever* look with a smile. Of course, full of perception. That was Perceptive Smile #4.

That night I dreamed of Heinz ketchup bottles smiling at me, spraying ketchup everywhere. The liquid changed to blood as it slid down the walls to the floor.

Chapter Twenty-Six

"So, I realized over the past couple of days, that I know very little about you," said Jenny.

We were in Ray's truck, the *Nebuchadnezzar,* driving through Nebraska, Ray's head bobbing to some jazz as he drove. It still wasn't Dean Martin or Frank Sinatra, but it was all right. Tyler napped, I was teaching Jenny how to play Cribbage, which I learned from Uncle Joe, a master of the game. Jenny didn't seem to be very good with card games, but it was something to pass the time.

I said, "I don't like to talk about myself. Besides, speaking of talking, you're one to talk."

"There's a difference."

"How?"

"You haven't asked."

"Oh. Well, technically, you haven't either."

Perceptive Smile #0. I know 0 can't really be used to number a smile. But this smile was unclassified—I didn't know what it meant.

She made some sort of a growl, then said, "So, Elijah Raven, tell me about yourself."

"Still not a question."

She said, "*Ellie…*" with rattlesnake warning in her tone… but without the rattle. Which was good; that would have just been freaky.

"Hmm?" I said, feigning ignorance to her meaning, or hearing loss, or both.

She sighed. "Will you please tell me about yourself? About your past?"

Here was this girl—scratch that—here was *the* girl of my dreams interested in me, or at least about me… In fact, if I were into idol worship, I would have a wooden statue of Jenny in my apartment, bowing before it every day, praying, burning sacrifices—toast, for instance—to the Jenny Goddess. And, I would probably have the statue with me on the road if it wouldn't have been weird for Wooden Statue Jenny and Real Life Jenny to be at the same place at the same time… and yet I *still* didn't want to talk about me.

I know I'm not the only person who doesn't like to talk about him/herself. And maybe for some of them, reluctance doesn't stem from modesty or embarrassment, but from a genuine, almost *fear,* in talking about yourself. If so, those people would understand.

Outside of my love for my brother and sister, there is nothing worth remembering from my past.

And yet, Uncle Joe, disagrees. He and I have debated this—multiple times—when he kept pushing me to write. He wants people to see how I've overcome my past.

But, I haven't overcome my past. I've just accepted it.

"Jenny, do you remember, it seems weeks ago, when I ran up to your car on the street by your house, and got you to back up out of sight?"

She pushed out her lips as if in deep thought, not necessarily trying to remember, but trying to figure out where I was going with this. Finally, she said, "Yes."

"And remember the first thing I blurted out when I jumped into your car?"

More lip pushing. She had not mentioned it since my mouth and brain stumbled all over themselves, neither had I, so I didn't know if this time she was actually trying to remember, but then she smiled, somewhat embarrassed.

"It was easier for me to blurt 'I love you,' than to talk about my past."

105

She laughed, looking thankful for the opportunity to release her embarrassment. "But that was a mistake. You didn't mean it."

Whoa, oh yes I did. But what I didn't know was whether she was giving me the opportunity to save face, or if she really believed I didn't mean it.

Okay, maybe telling her I loved her *wouldn't* be easier… I turned so I could see Tyler on the bed. I needed his advice. I needed *anyone's* advice. Ugh.

She grabbed my hand. "Look, I'll make it easy on you. We'll talk about that moment some other time. For now, I don't want to know about your feelings. There was a lot of stress and chaos right then. I want to hear about *you*."

"You don't give up, do you?"

She smiled, a defiant smile.

I hadn't started cataloging defiant smiles.

"I am nosey and I am persistent." Her face softened. "I know I'm prying, but I think it would be good for you to tell me. Who knows what horrors we're going to find in Detroit. I know you have lived horrors of your own, Ellie. You've already told me about them."

"What!"

"Well, not me directly, but that night you had the nightmare, you talked in your sleep." She swallowed. "A lot."

I sat back in the chair, my body slumped. "Oh."

"How about this: I'm not going to force you. If you don't want to tell me, you don't have to." She pointed to the Cribbage peg board, on which I held a substantial lead. "But if I win this game, you have to tell me what happened. If you win, you can tell me all about the Rat Pack."

"Ooo, really?" I perked up.

"Yes."

I looked at the board, evaluating my decision on whether to accept the bet. I was winning 80-40. No way could I lose. I felt bad accepting the bet, knowing she didn't really understand the game. But if it meant I didn't have to tell her about my past *and* I could tell her about real music… I couldn't decline. "I am going to change your life forever."

We finished the game.

And of course, I lost. Unbelievable. She hustled me. I just know it. And, just in case I didn't know which one of us was the victor, she drove the point home when she drove the peg into the final score: "Booyah!"

Ray turned to look at us, smiling.

Tyler repeated, *Booyah!*

Oy.

She was not a graceful winner.

"I need some time to think about this. We'll talk after dinner."

She got up from the chair, stood next to me as I still sat in the chair (shocked) and hugged me.

Ray said "Anyone hungry?"

Tyler said, *I am.*

Chapter Twenty-Seven

We dined at a Cracker Barrel. I love the Barrel.

The food was good, but my dread over talking to Jenny about my life tempered my enjoyment. Watching Ray in amazement as he ate all three dinners he ordered helped a little, but not enough. So I tried to push another dread to the forefront in my mind as a replacement. "Ray, so what are we going to do if we find Aaron Lynch?"

Ray had been smiling as he ate, savoring his food, but the smile disappeared at my question. "There is no if, we will find him. And we will stop his child prostitution business."

Jenny said, "How?"

"By any means necessary." He repeated for emphasis, "*Any* means. We may not be able to stop him on this trip. I'm concerned about getting either of you in too much danger. We will scope the business, environment, and people. We'll gather enough information and evidence to provide local and/or federal authorities to break him. It won't be easy. Lynch is a master at covering himself, his businesses, and his clients. So we may have to send in a second team to break him."

I said, "What do you mean, break him?"

Ray took another bite, grabbed a butter knife and with tremendous force, etched a line down the middle of the empty plate. My mouth dropped.

I glanced at Jenny, she had stopped chewing and her eyes were wide.

Ray swallowed the bite, then pressed the edge of the knife *hard* into the etched line. His teeth clenched and you could see muscles on the sides of his face bulge.

There was a sharp crack and a hard knock. The plate split in two and the knife *thunked* into the table. Other dishes on the table bounced.

He leaned in and stared at me. His eyes full of anger, hatred. Malice. Forearm muscles rippled as he squeezed the knife.

I became unnerved and pushed back from the table.

He said, in a nearly inaudible growl, "We *break* him."

I involuntary whispered, "Oh my God."

Jenny looked like she wanted to flee in terror.

Neither one of us said anything.

The restaurant was full and busy, with lots of chattering voices and clanking silverware. No one except us heard the noise from Ray's power display.

Ray saw our waitress approaching, sat up and smiled as if nothing had happened.

The waitress asked if we wanted refills.

Jenny and I were still too dumbfounded to answer.

The waitress didn't notice as she was captured by Ray's smile.

He nodded affirmative for Jenny and I, then said, "It seems I may have cut too hard on this plate."

The waitress then noticed the two broken halves of the plate in front of him. "Oh my stars! How could that happen? I'm so sorry! Are you hurt?"

"No, not at all, ma'am. And it's my fault, actually. I'm the one who should apologize."

She said, "Nonsense! You can't cut the plate in half!" She carefully picked up the pieces, "Heavens to Betsy," and placed them on her serving tray. "Would you like anything else? On the house."

Ray shook his head, smiling, "No, no, I'm good, thanks. And I would like to pay for that plate."

She said again, "Nonsense," then looked at Jenny and me to ask if we wanted anything. We both shook our heads.

She left the ticket, apologized again and virtually begged us to let her know if we wanted anything else, no charge, then walked away.

Ray looked at us and said, "Want dessert?"

Jenny and I just shook our heads again.

I had never seen such an awesome display of strength. And how could he withstand the immense pain the knife handle must have caused to his palm as he bore down on the plate?

I wasn't hungry any more.

Jenny didn't seem to have an appetite either.

Ray's plates were all clean. He said, "All right, then." He grabbed the ticket for the cashier, left a Benjamin Franklin for the tip, and got up to leave.

After returning to ol' *Neb*, I gave Tyler some leftovers, which he greedily enjoyed.

I had to admit, Ray's plate breaking demonstration momentarily made me forget about my talk with Jenny.

I looked at her and pointed to the Cribbage board. "Two out of three?"

She shook her head.

It had turned dark outside while we were in the Barrel. That was good. It made me feel less conspicuous, with fewer eyeballs trying to peer into my past.

I looked at Tyler, who stretched on the bed to nap again. A thought occurred to me, and it was a true concern, not just another stall technique: Tyler needed exercise. He'd been cooped up for most of the past few days. Okay, maybe it wasn't completely altruistic, but he needed exercise just the same.

"I need to take Tyler outside for some exercise. He's going to get weak and atrophy from being so stagnant."

Jenny smiled, a perceptive quality associated with the smile, of course. "The dog is not going to get fat by not exercising tonight."

"Oh, I hadn't even thought of that. His self-image is at stake."

Tyler said, *I would like a steak, medium rare, but that has nothing to do with my self-image.*

I said, "Not that kind of steak."

Jenny looked at me quizzically. "What?"

Ugh. "Never mind."

Tyler, though laying on his side, wagged his tail, smiling at me. *Got you.*

I ignored him.

Jenny said, "Besides, it's *freezing* outside."

I peered through the windshield. "Um, no it's not."

She looked at me as if I had just tried to convince her that pimples were the new look.

Okay, fine, she deserved to look at me that way. We were in Nebraska. In December.

108

She opened a weather app on her phone, got the local report and showed me the big fat *0* for the temperature. As in 0 degrees.

I shrugged. "So it's a little cold."

"A bet's a bet. You lost. You're not getting out of it."

"Don't you have any sympathy? No compassion?"

"I've never been confused with Mother Theresa."

"Okay, let me get a drink of water." I stood—

"Ellie. Sit."

I sat.

Tyler said, *Hey, good boy. I'm proud of you.*

I ignored him.

Despite her claim, she reached out and took my hand.

I was sweating. Yeah, 0 degrees outside and I was sweating. And no, I wasn't wrapped up in blankets and Ray hadn't converted the cabin into a furnace.

There's no point in repeating word for word what's already been put down on paper. Abridged version: I told Jenny about that singular day that has plagued my waking and sleeping hours since. I told her about Allister smiling at me, about the bad drugs given to my mother, about Chloe dying in my arms, about Ben getting blown away… I told her about Allister coming after me, and about Billy saving my life. I described how I killed Allister.

I did *not* tell her that Billy projected his thoughts to me and that I picked up on those thoughts.

I don't know if our friendship will mature into a love relationship. Obviously, it's my dream that it will. But there's no doubt she will not look at me the same when she finds out about my gift.

I impressed myself in that I got through the whole story without crying. My voice cracked a couple of times, and my eyes may have watered, but that's it.

"Oh, Ellie, I'm so, so sorry." She stood and stepped over to hug me. Fiercely.

Okay, full disclosure: a stray tear slid down my face. I wiped it before Jenny could step back and notice, fearful I was breaking the man code. But then I glanced over at Ray. I could only see the back of his head, and with the music playing, I don't know how he could have heard me telling the story, but I saw him first try to wipe his eyes with the back of his hand, then changed strategy and grabbed a nearby napkin.

I wondered, because I'm weird like that, with Ray being twice my size, bigger eyeballs, bigger cheeks for tears to slide on, if his actual tears were bigger than mine.

I guess part of my wonder was a distraction my brain created because I didn't really know how to react to Jenny hugging me so intently. Part amazement. Part euphoria. Part embarrassment.

Eventually, after what seemed like a long time, and yet strangely not long enough, Jenny released me. I felt awkward at that moment as well.

Uncle Joe hugged me. But I wasn't really in the hug business, especially emotional, heart-felt embraces like the one Jenny just gave me. I guess some of the reluctance comes from the duality of my mother. She would hug me, then let Allister beat the crap out of me.

Jenny wiped her eyes on her sleeve. She said, "So what did you do next? After you picked up Billy's racquetball, where did you go?"

109

I tried to think back to that time. Unlike the events beforehand, images that were seared into my brain, I don't remember much about what happened after that. I was in a fugue.

"It's hard to remember. I'm sure I was in shock. I knew it was cold outside, but I didn't feel it. I didn't feel anything. Just numb. I remember shaking, but I think that was from the adrenaline crash. I walked down our dirt driveway to the street and started walking toward town. Dazed.

"After some time—I don't know how long—a car stopped and someone started calling my name. I hadn't noticed the headlights but after hearing my name, I emerged somewhat from my daze and noticed then it was dark. I must have been walking for a few hours. I'm sure I looked like something straight out of a weird horror flick: my left arm shredded, blood all over my clothes and a blue racquetball in my hand.

"A lady got out of the car and stepped toward me, then stopped and backed up a little when she saw the blood. 'Oh my God. Are you hurt? Elijah?' I recognized her, Mrs. Carter. She was a neighbor a little farther down the street. She had three kids close to our ages. She wasn't mean to us, but she wouldn't let her kids play with us. She was a dedicated member in the Stay Away From Those Raven Kids Club. 'Elijah?' she repeated. I didn't mean to ignore her. I didn't try to be defiant or anything. I just couldn't speak. My brain needed a reboot. She moved closer to me, but not close enough to touch me or vice versa. I don't blame her, really.

"She took another tentative step toward me and said, 'Elijah, what's wrong? Is that blood? Are you hurt?' She was dealing with her own shock. I still couldn't speak, but I pointed back in the direction of my house, which was a few miles away. She said, 'Something bad happened at your house?' This time I managed a nod.

"Cellphones weren't nearly as popular back then as they are now, especially in rural areas, so she couldn't call 911. She opened the back door of her car and said, 'Elijah, let's get you some help. I'll take you to the hospital.' Minute-by-minute my brain emerged from its near catatonic state. I managed to say 'Not hurt.' Looking at my arm and the blood covering my clothes, I could tell she didn't know what to think about my statement. Finally, she said, 'Well, let's go to a hospital anyway. They'll fix whatever's going on.' Maybe she said that as much for her own benefit as for mine, but I knew they were never going to be able to fix what happened.

"Yet I saw no point in telling her otherwise. I noticed she didn't offer to take me back to my house. Obviously, she knew at this point something terrible had happened. She probably didn't think that four people were dead—and that I had killed one of them— which was good, or she may have just freaked out altogether and left me.

"Mrs. Carter took me to the hospital and explained she found me on the road. I was attacked, well-meaning, but attacked nonetheless with questions. Most of which I couldn't think of words to use for answers. Someone said call the police. My mind retreated back down a long hallway to a room far, far away."

I'd been talking for quite a while. Though I tried to be light-hearted at times and infuse humor, talking about this was emotionally exhausting. I'd hit a wall.

I said, "Many of my memories in the hospital are blurry. I'm tired. I don't want to talk about this anymore." I stood.

Jenny hugged me again. "You did really great, Ellie."

I tried to smile. I brushed my teeth and got in bed. I wondered if I was going to have a hard time falling asleep. I don't remember anything else after that.

Chapter Twenty-Eight

I woke up when I felt the truck stop. We were at a rest stop. Evidently Ray needed a bathroom break.

I ran and did my thing, then went back to get Tyler so he could do his. Jenny slept through the stop.

It was still dark outside. And cold. A clock on the dash stated 3:22AM.

Ray said, "How you doing?"

"Tired. How are you?"

"Wonderful." He gave me a *huge* smile. Even his eyes twinkled.

I don't know how anyone could be cheery at three in the morning. Ridiculous.

I went back to bed.

I woke to the crinkling sound of a paper wrapper. Daylight accosted my eyes. I closed them. The crinkling stopped. I attempted to view the world again.

Jenny stood by my bed, smiling.

You know, I could wake up like this every day for the rest of my life and be the happiest man alive. There are, I concede, certain situations that would add to said happiness...

Jenny held up a Hostess apple pie.

Jenny got me a Hostess apple pie!

She said, "I cooked breakfast again!"

I started to think this whole human thing she put on was a façade. She's actually one of the Heavenly Host.

She said, "Sleep well?"

I nodded, got up, brushed my teeth, and said, "Where are we?"

"Just outside Detroit."

"You mean, we're here?"

She gave me perceptive smile #6. "Well, *here* is relative. We're always *here* because it's impossible to be *there.*"

"That's so weird it makes sense."

"Of course it does."

I commanded my eyeballs to not roll. "Where's Tyler?"

"Ray took him outside to play, get some exercise."

"Cool. So what's the game plan?"

"That's a Ray question."

As if summoned, Ray opened the truck door. Frigid air rushed in, howling a war cry, invading the warm cab. Tyler jumped into the truck and Ray followed.

"Good morning, Elijah!" Ray's hearty smile warmed the cab again.

Ray said, "I heard you two talking about me."

I glanced at Jenny, then back to Ray. "No way, you couldn't hear us out there."

Ray continued beaming. "Did you mention my name?"

Jenny said, "Yes."

"Then I heard you."

I didn't know how to respond.

"It's okay, Brother Elijah, there is a lot about me you don't understand."

He put an arm around me, said, "And some day you never will," then laughed. He squeezed me hard around the shoulders and shook me side to side, jostling me as if I were a hollow mannequin. "I'm just messing with you." He winked at Jenny.

Ray let go of me and stepped back. "I imagine you two want to know what's next."

I said, "Bingo."

"We'll be leaving *Nebuchadnezzar* with a friend who manages a distribution center here in town. We'll change over to an SUV, something more acceptable to the clientele. We'll also change into appropriate clothing."

"I'd really prefer not to be dressed like an old woman again."

Ray smiled. "Don't worry, Brother Elijah, I've got you covered. When we get there, follow my lead. Do not answer any questions or respond unless specifically addressed by someone. The cover business is an advertising firm. I will present some mock business projects, one of which we've discovered is the key to admittance as clientele. The only way for us to be able to gain access to the inside is as clients."

Ray's smile faded. "This most likely won't be pleasant. You two will have to steel yourselves for seeing and/or hearing crimes against the kids. Again, follow my lead. If we blow our own cover, I doubt we make it out alive, or worse, unchanged."

I swallowed. "What do you mean, unchanged?"

"We've heard rumors that Lynch uses mind manipulation through neurochemistry drugs. Probably to enhance the client's experience, as well as—and far darker—changing the emotions of the children, making them easier to control."

"Oh my God," said Jenny.

Ray said, "I'm not exaggerating, or trying to be overly protective, when I say this is not going to be easy. That's why we *do not* engage. I don't care what horrors you see or hear, *do not* get involved. We are here to gather evidence. Evidence only. Another team will neutralize Lynch if the authorities do not. We, as in you two and myself on this trip, are not equipped to deal directly with Lynch's security team. Got it?"

Jenny and I both nodded. But I didn't think if I could stay detached if I saw something. But I understood Ray's point of view. Jenny and I were not prepared to combat them, if it came to that. We wouldn't survive. Sacrifice one to save many?

A horrible concept.

But true.

We went to designated rooms to change, where Ray's friend already had our clothes set out. Whoever picked mine out was a genius. Waiting for me was a bright blue dress shirt and a shiny grey suit. It looked like something Mr. Broxton would have worn. I hoped I got to keep the suit.

After changing, we met in the lobby. Jenny wore a fitted green blouse and a black miniskirt with black high heels. Her long auburn hair was tied up in some sort of bun, a style I couldn't name.

Regardless, she looked *amazing.*

Her name should be Venus.

I wondered if she'd mind if I called her Venny instead of Jenny.

She did a quick twirl around and said, "Do you like it?"

I opened my mouth to say something, closed it, tried again, then gave up and just nodded. She smiled, Perceptive #9. "You don't look so bad yourself, Mr. Raven."

I still had nothing. So I just stared at her.

Ray wore a sharp beige suit and carried a burgundy leather portfolio.

We got into a silver Mercedes G-Class SUV, and Ray drove us into downtown Detroit. Tyler stayed with Ray's friend at the distribution center. I never did meet or see this friend. I didn't know if that was the idea or just coincidence.

Ray mentioned in the future we could have Tyler act as a service dog. But because of the location, atmosphere, and purpose of this visit, Ray did not want any of us to be under pressure to perform as if we required a service dog. There were people in the Network who were blind or paralyzed who would not have to act.

When we left, I had a sudden fear that I'd never see Tyler again.

We entered the underground parking of one humongous skyscraper, and rode the elevator up to ground level.

My heart beat as if I ran up the stairs instead. We hadn't even entered the lobby of the skyscraper yet, let alone the advertising business. I tried to calm myself, but I was unbelievably scared. I'm sure some of the fear stemmed from worry about our safety. But I was more scared about what I was about to see. I didn't know if we'd actually see any children, but my fear didn't care about that.

The elevator doors opened into an alcove. The walls were made of green granite. There were ten banks of elevators. Each elevator was flanked by brass columns. I'm sure additional service and private elevators existed elsewhere. The alcove led to a massive atrium that rose from the center of the building as high as I could see. Large trees grew out of plant beds. The noise created by an eight-foot waterfall dominated the background sounds. The floor was white granite, with flecks of red and yellow. The first four floors were walled with glass. Sunlight highlighted leaves on the trees. Balconies circled the atrium on each floor above, which led to various businesses.

A large circular security desk faced the alcove. A wrap-around green granite counter surrounded the desk. I could see four men sitting/standing in the desk area. One of them acknowledged us with a smile and asked if we needed assistance.

Approaching the desk I noticed a wide kiosk with two sections. One listed the names of the businesses—there were dozens of them—and the other displayed a map to help locate the desired business.

I wondered if anyone in these other businesses knew what was really going on in this building. Surely not. I imagined they were oblivious to the outside world, which started as soon as they walked out the door of their respective office.

The men at the desk were all wearing blue blazers and had earpieces with a wire dangling out of their ears. No doubt they had concealed weapons under their jackets. Detroit wasn't the most crime-free city in the US.

Ray said, "We're looking for Hanes and Lincoln Advertising Agency," to the guard who had acknowledged us. The other men gave us cursory glances then continued what they were doing.

The guard said, "Yes, do you have a Confidence Badge?"

I thought, great, we're already screwed. What the heck was a Confidence Badge?

But Ray just smiled, opened his wallet, and handed a card to the guard.

The guard said, "Thank you," then swiped the card in an unseen machine on the other side of the counter. I saw a green light reflect off his face, then he returned the card. He said, "Take the P1 elevator to the 40th floor," and pointed to a different alcove.

As we walked to the new elevator alcove, I asked Ray about the card, or Confidence Badge, he gave to the guard. Ray looked down at me from his higher vantage point, and smiled. "A friend." I thought he was going to abstain from sharing anything else, but he said, "Hanes and Lincoln is a very private, very confidential advertising agency. The people and businesses who seek the agency's assistance, do not want the rest of the world to know. High profile, upper echelon individuals and businesses enjoy complete anonymity while using the agency's services. *Any* service. This includes the use of private elevators. Clients can access the agency's premises with *confidence* their privacy is protected."

"Confidence Badge."

"Confidence Badge." He looked at us and said, "From this point forward, act as if everything you say is heard—because it is. Likewise, trust that your every move is being monitored." He nodded, then continued leading us to the private elevators.

There were four elevators in this alcove, which looked similar to the public elevators. We entered the elevator marked P1. There were buttons for 40 stories, and a few that descended lower than ground level. A clock displayed 12:05.

With 40 buttons, our destination must be the penthouse. I thought that was cool, despite my trepidation about what we might see. Ray inserted the Confidence Badge in a slot and was rewarded by the button for the 40th floor lighting up. He pressed it.

None of us said anything, nor did we look at each other. Ray had his eyes closed, I assumed in prayer.

I thought that was a good idea, so I did the same.

The doors slid open. The clock displayed 12:05. Fast elevator.

We emptied the elevator into a small hallway. Directly in front of us were large mahogany doors with a simple nameplate stating *Hanes & Lincoln*. There were no windows. The hallway ended twenty feet in both directions. There was no other way to get here except by using this elevator.

The elevator doors closed.

A camera above the agency doors watched us, as did cameras on both sides of the hallway.

Mahogany wainscoting covered the lower half of the walls. The upper half was painted tan, bare otherwise. There was no door handle, no doorbell, no intercom, and no window to get anyone's attention. I wondered if we were supposed to do something with the Confidence Badge, but there wasn't any type of card slot.

I tried my best to not look like I didn't belong there. I glanced at Jenny; she was doing a better job of it than me.

Ray just stood, looking at the wood doors.

We stood there a long time. Nothing happened. I thought maybe we missed something. Then I wondered if the German dude was going to ride up the elevator with the Goon Brothers and finish what they started. I couldn't help it, I glanced over my shoulder at the elevator. A call button beckoned to be pressed, but nothing else.

I left the button alone.

We stood some more. Still nothing happened. I wondered if grey hairs were growing in my raven black hair yet. I wished there was a mirror.

Not that I'm vain like that, it's just how my brain works.

We stood.

I recalled again Ray's directive to follow his lead, no matter what happens. Leading by example, he stood. So I followed his standing, though since we weren't moving, I can't really say I followed him.

We stood.

I was beginning to get thirsty. Oh, and hungry.

Maybe they were out to lunch.

I wondered if it was now dark outside.

I wondered if a zombie apocalypse finally went down, and we were the last three humans alive. What if Ray had secretly been infected and he turned into a zombie? I was pretty sure I could outrun Jenny, but with only twenty feet of hallway on either side of us, it wouldn't do me much good.

Besides, I couldn't do that to Jenny.

If I did, I had no doubt she would save a particularly horrid zombie attack just for me if I did abandon her. Even if she was a zombie Venus.

The mahogany doors opened.

We entered.

Chapter Twenty-Nine

We were in a waiting area (gee, great, more waiting). No one greeted us. No receptionist, no receptionist desk. Everything was in black and white, a study in contrast. Two black leather couches sat on a white marble floor, facing each other. Various black framed art adorned the marble walls, which had threads of black, weaved throughout. A black clock with a white digital readout displayed 12:12.

What?

Just five minutes elapsed while we waited in the hallway?

Nuh uh. They had to be screwing with the space-time continuum.

A black coffee table held only a single white ashtray. A small black wet bar was against the wall to the right. The liquor inside the various bottles provided the only color in the room.

A tinted glass door opposite the entrance led to another room or hallway. This door also had no visible way to open it.

I wondered who or what opened the mahogany doors for us to enter.

Ray gestured to the couches, indicating to Jenny and me to sit. He continued to stand, facing the tinted glass door.

There were no magazines, books, TV's, or anything else to occupy oneself while waiting in this first room. So I looked more closely at the art on the walls. It seemed to me to be nothing more than black scribbles on white canvas. I'm sure it was priceless.

The glass door slid open, revealing a poorly lit hallway. No one was in sight.

Ray said, "Let's go."

We followed him into the hallway. The glass door behind us closed.

This hallway had black marble floors, fifty feet long. Lighted sconces on the walls every five feet illuminated the hall. Another door, similar to the one we just entered, waited for us at the end of this hallway. The low light glimmered off the tinted glass. The side walls were bare except the sconces. No doors, windows, or even priceless scribble art.

It was incredibly quiet and still. I felt like I was in a modern catacomb. None of us talked. The only noise came from the *click clack* of Jenny's heels on the marble floor.

Click clack.

Click clack.

Click clack.

The sound took on an ominous tone.

Click clack.

My rogue mind conjured an image of a dead man swinging from a noose, the popping of the strained rope making a *click clack* as the body swung like a pendulum.

Click clack.

Impossibly, the sound of Jenny's shoes seemed to slow and deepen in pitch, like a dying phonograph.

Click...

Clack...

The lights dimmed.

The scars on my arm burned lightly. That... wasn't my imagination.

We were only ten feet from the next door. I debated on whether I should break protocol and warn Ray and Jenny about the pending danger. But it would take a while to explain the whole scar-burning thing. They probably wouldn't believe me. Yet to do nothing and let us walk into a trap was worse.

Screw protocol.

I reached for Ray to get his attention—

The glass door opened and a naked girl with blood smeared on her legs and hands shot through.

Ray took a step back, but kept his balance.

Jenny screamed.

I stumbled backward and fell down.

I am not a jumpy person. Living through the violence I've experienced, and living in various homes where boys' only goal in life is to scare one another, I very, rarely, get startled.

But this was different. This scene wasn't *right*. She scared the crap out of me. She seemed possessed. Her face was painted white, like a porcelain doll. She had black eyelids and very heavy mascara, which, on her pale skin, made her look deranged. She had on thick, bright red lipstick. But the worst part was the wide, toothy smile. The expression was a paradox to her condition.

I could not comprehend the scene. I sat. Stunned.

I know this is not the behavior of an action hero. But remember, I'm not an action hero. Or any other kind of hero.

Why would she be smiling?

The tinted glass door in front of me had closed. I could see my faint reflection in the glass.

My brain slowly attempted to cooperate with my will. I turned to see Jenny race after the girl, heels left in the hallway.

Ray ran after Jenny.

I saw all three disappear into the waiting room.

So much for keeping a low profile. And not engaging.

I couldn't think.

My scars still burned.

I started to get up, then the door in front of me opened again.

A young girl with blond hair in a yellow frilly dress ran out.

Chloe!

She stumbled and fell, landing on top of me.

A deep male voice yelled, "Hey!"

I felt a sting on my thigh, but ignored it.

She breathed heavily, tears streamed down her cheeks. She wasn't wearing the heavy makeup like the other girl.

I hugged her tight, trying to calm her, whispering, "Oh, Chloe, you're back. I've missed you *so* much. It's okay, I've got you, it's okay. We're together again."

I couldn't *believe* I had Chloe back. My sister! Was here. In my arms. Alive!

And then, from a calm, small room deep in my mind, *Reason* reached out to me, telling me that this little girl could not be Chloe. Reason was cruel. It told me Chloe was dead. It told

118

me she died with a fractured skull. She died in a pool of her own blood. And then Reason flashed those images into my conscious.

I flinched.

And it worked.

My right mind told me to get up. Run! Save the girl!

I felt another sting in my thigh.

The girl started sobbing heavily, her body convulsing—then abruptly stopped.

I pushed her up to tell her we had to leave. Now!

Then her face did something it wasn't supposed to do: it *melted*. Her cheeks stretched, the skin morphing into long strings, and just slowly slid down. Her nose oozed over her mouth and to her chin... Then her eyes popped out, dangling in midair, tethered to optical nerves, leaving black holes for eye sockets, deep pits straight into Hell. Her lips parted and dissolved, revealing shiny white teeth smiling in a death grin while her skull bobbed up and down, yet slowly moving closer to me, Hell reaching out to me through the black, eyeless holes.

A quick, inescapable terror consumed me—fear seized my very soul—as I watched her skin pool to drop on top of me like acid. I *knew* if I fell into those pits, Allister would be waiting for me, greeting me with *his* smile. And a hacksaw.

I rolled to the side and scampered away from her. My back jammed against the wall in the hallway as far as I could go, pressing against the sheetrock but still I kept kicking, pushing back.

Then... the wall opposite me, started melting too, flowing down. My hands pushed on the floor, which should have been solid, providing resistance to my touch. But the floor was soft. My hand travelled into it, deeper, deeper, to my elbow, and then I pulled it back.

Giant roaches with fangs swarmed on the walls, the floor, the ceiling. I yelled.

From that same small room in my mind, Reason called—calling out to me. This was not possible. Skin did not melt off little girls. Walls did not slide down to the floor. Floors did not turn into pudding.

One sting. Two stings. In my thigh. They were needles. Drugs. Hallucinogens.

I closed my eyes, squeezing them shut. Concentrating on reality.

The floor felt solid again. I pushed against it. Then it softened.

I opened my eyes and saw the tallest man I'd ever seen looming over me. He was ten feet tall, dressed in white, and couldn't have been more than one hundred pounds. He reached down from on high with arms too long even for his ten-foot body and grabbed my wrist.

I tried to hang onto a tiny fragment of reality. I cried out, calling for Ray or Jenny to help me, but my tongue was too thick, heavy, immovable. The words were no more than garbled sounds. "Thhhway fffp mm."

The skyscraper man reached for my other wrist. I flailed my arms, a useless effort to keep him from grabbing me. I swung my arms anyway. My knuckles smacked the wall, the floor, and the wall again. Repeatedly. I kicked but only made contact with the floor.

Another man, even taller than the first, came down the hallway with giant wheels. I thought the wheels would run over me, slicing my legs off.

One man hauled me to my feet. Standing, I thrashed again, making contact a few times with objects other than walls or floor, but it was impossible to put any force behind the punches. The second man put a jacket on me backwards, way too easily. I felt straps tighten against my chest and then I could no longer move my arms. They pushed me down to sit in the thing with the giant wheels. I glided across the floor.

I tried to ask them where they were taking me. But only grunts escaped my mouth.

I felt a pinch on my neck. Then darkness oozed over my eyes like melting skin.

Chapter Thirty

For a long time, an interval beyond my awareness to measure, I couldn't tell if I was awake or asleep. It might have been hours. It might have been days. I was on top of a bed. I tried to move my left arm to scratch an itch on my head, but couldn't. I looked at the arm to see what the trouble was and discovered the arm was strapped to the bed. The same with my other arm. And legs. This did not make sense to me. Not to mention it was going to make scratching the itch rather difficult. Ditto going to the bathroom, which I had the sneaking suspicion would be a need in the not-so-distant future.

I was wearing a white pullover shirt and white pants. They looked like pajamas. Someone had changed me out of my regular clothes into these. My scars were exposed.

Thankfully I could still move my head and look around. I was in a room that looked like it belonged in a hospital. There was one bed, the one restraining me. I did not like the bed. It was not nice. A track on the ceiling curved around the end of the bed, with a curtain pushed to one side. White walls, white ceiling, and white floor. There were no windows. There was a dresser attached to one wall, but no mirror. This too was all white. It certainly smelled like a typical hospital. Antiseptics, cleaners, the minor scent of ammonia…

Two posters displaying the brain at different angles hung from one wall. The brains were sliced into sections with lines presumably identifying those sections. They were too far away for me to read. Various art depicting a cat or cats also covered the walls. It was all elegant, not like a felt picture of bulldogs with stogies playing poker. There were even three small sculptures of cats.

One door led to, I supposed, a bathroom. A second door, wide enough for a hospital bed, probably led to a hallway. There were no monitors, no nurse call button, no not-so-fancy remote to make the bed rise.

The walls, the ceiling, nothing melted and roaches no longer swarmed any surface. Whatever drug the darts contained that caused the hallucinations had worn off.

I wondered what had happened to the two girls that made them run in fear and panic. And how they'd even gotten that far. Why was the one girl smiling? No way was it a real smile. What happened to them after I left? Did they somehow get away, were they captured? I wondered if Ray and Jenny were here in other rooms, I wondered if I'd ever see them again. I wondered how long I'd been in the room, about what would happen next, and how I was going to get out of there. All I could do was wonder.

There wasn't sufficient information for me to answer any of the questions bouncing around in my head. I had two choices: think or sleep.

I slept.

I woke when I heard the door open. A male orderly or nurse, impossible for me to tell if it was one of the skyscraper men I punched before—the word *punch* just seems more manly than *slap*—entered, pushing a cart.

Followed by a cat.

A cat. Really. I instinctively looked at the three cat sculptures to see if they were still there. Yes.

I looked at other objects and surfaces to make sure I wasn't hallucinating. The cat was two-toned, grey on top and white on the lower half. He jumped onto the bed and looked at me with greenish-brown eyes.

I looked back to the male orderly/nurse. So, of all of the questions I *could* have asked, you know, trivial things like, 'Where am I?' 'What am I doing here?' 'Why am I strapped to the bed?' 'What are you going to do to me?' etc. Instead, I ask, "Are you an orderly or a nurse?" Really, it was important for me to know. If I was going to die, I wanted it to be at the hands of a nurse. Not an orderly. It just didn't seem right. I mean, you don't ever hear stories about evil orderlies. Only evil nurses. After all, Nurse Ratched wasn't Orderly Ratched.

I needed help. More ways than one.

Some people have an abstract fear of clowns.

I fear orderlies.

The orderly/nurse did not respond to my question. He lifted a chrome lid, exposing a tray that held a small plastic cup with pills and a hypodermic syringe.

For a brief moment my mind yelled, *Food!* I realized then, I was starving.

I realized something else, and said, "Can I go to the bathroom?" My early premonition about needing to go to the bathroom had come true. My prognostication skills were still pretty good.

Again, maybe not the most important thing to ask within the grand scheme of things, but the situation did have the greatest criticality for the immediate future.

The… I'll just call him *Man*, ignored me. Man waved his hand palm up over the tray, indicating I had a choice between the pills or the shot.

I said, "What is it?"

Evidently, Man grew tired of my incessant questioning. He picked up the shot, swabbed my right upper arm with alcohol, and not worrying about being gentle, buried the needle and pushed the clear fluid into me.

Um, ow!

Then he turned the cart around and walked out of the room.

The cat stayed. We stared at each other for a while.

I said, "I don't suppose you can get these straps off me, can you? And, are you edible?"

I let out a little giggle, then erupted into laughter. I knew what I said wasn't funny, and it certainly wasn't calming my bladder, but I couldn't help it. I was *happy!* Tears gathered in my eyes, then slid down my cheeks to the bed. One tear tickled my left ear on the way. I laughed enthusiastically.

The cat wasn't impressed. Why was he even there? *How* was he there?

Two men entered the room. In my exuberance, my fear abated, I couldn't care less whether they were orderlies or nurses. One held a small black device with two metal prongs. It looked cool. He pushed a button, and blue current like miniature lightning bolts arced between the prongs. Way cool! It was probably meant to be a threat.

I thought it was funny. I laughed.

The other one unlocked the door to the bathroom. It was locked? Now *that* was hilarious. I laughed even more. I looked at the two guys, neither of them were laughing. Nor was the cat. That's okay, I had enough joy for all of us.

That same little room, Reason Room, opened its door and this cute little entity, Reason, popped its head out. It tried to get my attention to tell me nothing was funny and that something was wrong with the way I was acting.

Ah. Drugs. I burst out loud, "Happy hypo! Happy happy hypo!" And laughed. Oh how I laughed.

Reason slammed the door.

Ouch.

I laughed anyway.

One dude—now they were dudes instead of orderlies or nurses—unstrapped me.

"Thanks, dude."

He gestured toward the bathroom. I noticed the people around here don't talk much. Oh well. I gave the dude a thumbs up and flashed a winning smile. I didn't know how long it had been since I'd gone to the bathroom, but wow, did it take a long time to empty my bladder! That made me snicker.

Fun!

I used my foot to flush the toilet, because even while drugged I was still a germaphobe, washed my hands and went back into the room.

One dude locked the bathroom door. Both dudes left. The cat was gone. I was still hungry, but I was too happy to worry about it.

But then the door opened again and a different dude pushed in a cart. The same grey and white cat followed him in. The dude lifted the cover: FOOD! Omigosh! I was *elated*! I wanted to give him a big hug, but the dude quickly pulled out one of those shocky thingies and stepped back. I said, "Just a little thank you hug?"

He looked at me, expression blank, then pressed the button, creating a sizzle noise.

Okay, he didn't want a hug. But that's all right. I had food! A banana, an apple, and an orange! And they were *deeelightful*. At some point while I ate, the dude left. I didn't even get to say thank you.

The cat stayed behind, eyeing me. I offered a piece of banana.

I heard, *No thank you.*

Whoa! The cat talked!

Oh, wait, he projected that to me.

I'd forgotten about the whole animal communication thing.

I tried to listen to Reason (Ha! Listen to Reason). I almost started laughing again, but I squeezed my mind, like squeezing my fist, exerting self-control. It seemed to help.

Maybe I could get some information from the cat if he'd cooperate.

Cats—animals—don't usually choose a party line and side with the bad guys. They can be trained. And they can even be manipulated to express malice. But an animal is not a "bad guy." An animal may kill, but survival and protection are not the same as killing because they're evil, vengeful, envious, lustful, greedy, etc. It is the virus of human corruption that taints animals.

Go us.

I figured that even if I was under audio/video surveillance and I talked to the cat, those monitoring would think I was crazy because of the drugs, or just naturally crazy. They wouldn't be able to hear the cat respond, if he chose to.

I eyed the cat and took a bite of the apple. After swallowing, I said, "What is your name?"

The cat said, *Winchester, sir.*

Despite my sincere effort, I couldn't help it. I laughed. "Winchester? Sir?"

The cat repeated, *Indeed. Winchester, sir.* He actually had an aristocratic, British accent. I've rarely encountered an animal with sufficient intelligence for sophisticated communication. Tyler was above average. But it's rarer still to communicate with one that had an accent. I can't even pretend to explain how that's possible.

I continued laughing and continued to try to stop, which only made it worse, as is usually the case. "Winchester! That's great!" I used my shirt to wipe the tears from my eyes. I said, as gravely as I could manage, "I'm terribly sorry, I mean no offense."

Winchester just looked at me with a stoic expression.

Finally composing myself, I said, "Really, I'm sorry."

Winchester's expression did not change.

Great, I thought, I'd offended the cat.

Winchester said, *The gentlemen dressed in white will be back soon to get your tray. They will make you go to sleep. Then another time they will interview you, and you them. His Grace, my master's preferred name, takes great pride in this institution.*

I said, "What is this place?"

His Grace will explain. Afterward, you will never be the same. You do not want to be here, sir. I humbly suggest you leave.

Of course I wanted to leave! But I didn't say for fear of scaring off my one chance to get help, Winchester.

All of the humor, drug-induced or not, died. I took a deep breath, then said, "Can you help me?"

The door to my room opened and two men entered, one pushing another cart.

Winchester jumped to the floor and trotted to the door. *I cannot. Do not take the pills.* He left.

I wanted to throw something at the cat. But I didn't have anything. Besides, I didn't want to be strapped down again. They may do so anyway, but little doubt they would upon seeing me act out in anger.

As before, one of the men lifted a chrome lid, revealing a tray with a hypodermic syringe and a tiny cup of pills. He waved a hand over the items, waiting for me to choose. Don't take the pills, so says Winchester. I pointed to the syringe.

The man grabbed the shot, swabbed my arm with alcohol, and plunged the needle.

Ouch.

I wondered if this was Winchester's way of getting even with me for laughing at him. No. Tyler was mischievous, but truly getting even with someone was a human response. Winchester gave me a message, even if it seemed weak. What did I expect? He's a cat. It was my job to figure it out.

The man covered the tray and placed my food tray on the cart. They left.

Thankfully, even though I'd finished the food, they did not strap me to the bed.

And then I discovered why. The shot was a tranquilizer. I wondered what the pills were. Same thing?

I slumped and my upper body felt heavy. I stretched on the bed to take the pressure off. This time, I needed to think. I needed to decipher. I needed to plan.

I slept.

Chapter Thirty-One

I woke up the next day. Or was it? I didn't know. No clock and no day/night cycles to observe equals no idea what time or day it was. My biological clock could have helped, but I'd been sleeping, tranquilized, and eating at different intervals.

I was hungry and thirsty, and needed to go to the bathroom again. So it had to have been a few hours, at least.

I checked the bathroom door, still locked. Even though I knew the answer, I checked the hallway door, and received a shock. The door shocked me. Not static. A true jolt.

I felt like I was in a Pavlov experiment. Just to be defiant, I touched the doorknob again. Ow.

I looked around the room. Maybe I really was an experiment. I assumed rooms like mine neighbored both sides.

In my current state, I was completely dependent on the evil orderlies for food, drink, and toileting. Maybe they wanted to see how I'd react. How long before I lost it and went berserk. Or how long before I just gave up and accepted my new life.

Fun times.

I got back onto the bed and despair fell upon me like someone spreading a blanket.

Was this really my new life? How long would it take before my musculature weakened from inactivity? I did a few jumping jacks and some pushups.

How long could I endure the monotony of being in the same place, doing the same things, day after day after day? How long before I went insane?

What about the kids here? What kind of life were *they* living?

Worse. They were being used for sex.

God help them.

I closed my eyes. Images from my past, things that I have seen tormented me. They gave me a sick understanding of what they were going through.

God help them.

God help me.

I looked at my hands. And then the scars on my left arm, turning the arm over. The skin had deep grooves. In other places it was raised and in various colors, white, red, and tan. Some sections looked especially stretched as attempts were made to stitch the numerous patches and slices of skin back together.

Uncle Joe offered to pay for plastic surgery. But by then I'd lived with the scarring for so long, it was just as much a part of me as the arm itself.

I had been through worse than this. I had lived through darker, seemingly hopeless days. Yet I had persevered.

Those kids, they didn't even know it. But I was most likely their best chance for escaping.

I had survived. I would survive again. And I would do everything I could to help them survive.

I'm not a hero. But that's not going to stop me from doing my best impersonation.

I may fail. No, considering my circumstances, I probably *would* fail. But failing to do something—anything—was worse than unforgiveable.

126

Based on the smiling naked girl, who knows what kind of psychological damage had already been inflicted.

The door opened and two of the guys in white entered, but this time, they were accompanied by a third man, this one in a black suit, a stark contrast to the two in white. As usual, the orderlies/nurses did not speak.

Maybe that was why the suit joined them. He said, "Hello, Mr. Raven. His Grace would like to speak with you. You may go with us peacefully, or we can *influence* you to be peaceful. We would prefer you to be lucid for this conversation." One side of his mouth twitched up.

My brain stopped on 'His Grace.' Who in this age really wanted to be called His Grace? "Uh, I'm sorry, can you repeat that?"

The Suit looked at me evenly.

I saw Winchester the cat walk by in the hallway. He did not enter, nor did he look into the room.

I stammered, trying to recall the rest of what he said. My eyes flicked between the three men. "Yeah, um, yes, peacefully. I'll go peacefully. Who are you?"

"Who I am is not important. This way." He extended his arm to the doorway.

I stood, then the orderlies displayed in unison their wares for me to see. In one hand, they each held a Taser. In the other, *huge* hypodermic syringes.

Hell's bells, screw up now and I'd be a vegetable.

The Suit led the way into the hallway. The evil orderlies followed. I tried to see as much as I could, and memorize the layout of the building as we weaved through hallways. From what I could see, the rest of the place also looked like a hospital, though without some of the things you'd expect to see. Like IV stands, monitors, wheeled hospital beds or gurneys in the hallways, or staff, except for the two following me. What I *did* see were a few more cats. There were several rooms, but the door to each was closed. I could hear indistinct noises coming from some of the rooms.

We took an elevator up. The hallway meeting us was strikingly different. Floor to ceiling mahogany paneling, green-shaded light fixtures mounted on the walls, thick, burgundy carpeting… The space looked like it belonged to Fortune 500 executives, not a hospital.

We walked down the long hallway to the door at the end. The Suit opened the door, holding it for the rest of us to enter. We were in what was probably supposed to be a receptionist area, but was instead more like an antechamber. Really. It looked straight out of a castle. Stone floor and columns, huge tapestries hung from the walls, gold trimmed furniture… Instead of a receptionist's desk, there was a long wooden table. The coffered ceiling had a large oval shaped area in which a battle scene was painted, angels versus demons.

The Suit walked to the table and pressed a button, then two French doors slid open, revealing another room. A Throne Room. Complete with throne, although it was empty. And instead of stairs that led to a raised seating area for the throne, there was a ramp.

An executive desk was off to the right side of the room, next to a large fireplace. A man who looked to be in his 40's sat behind the desk, eating something. Standing to his right was one of the Goon Brothers that tried to kill Jenny and me at her house. The German leader of that group sat in a chair at a small table a few feet away.

The man eating at the desk looked up as we entered. "Ah, Mr. Raven. A pleasure. Do come closer so that I may have a good look at you." He had a German accent, but not nearly as strong as that of the goon leader. His brown hair was thinning on top, and he had a round, portly face. There was an excess amount of skin under the chin that rolled into a thick neck. I could not see his body behind the desk, but the sight of his face and pudgy fingers suggested he was obese.

I turned to see if my personal escorts were still with me. Affirmative. The goon behind the fat man glowered at me. I imagined he was internally begging for me to try something idiotic. Though… he may not have actually thought the word *idiotic*—too many syllables. *Dumb* was more likely.

I noted the absence of Goon Brother.

Having a shortage of good choices at that moment, I approached the desk as directed.

The fat man indicated the goon and said, "That is Boris. I'm sure you remember his brother, Moris, who is no longer with us."

"Oops," I thought. And said.

The goon—Boris—looked at me in a way that gave me the impression he was visualizing doing really mean things to me, like snapping every bone in my body, one at a time, then pulling each individual broken bone out with unsanitized clamps, after first, of course, cutting open the skin with a Sawzall (also unsanitized) to gain easy access, then rearranging the bones in places they weren't supposed to go.

The fat man waved toward the goon leader and said, "I believe you are already acquainted with Wilhelm Hecter."

Hecter gave me a slanted smile and inclined his head slightly.

I wanted to say something smart like, 'What, are you supposed to be, some sort of Hannibal Lecter wannabe?' But I was lacking in appropriate Jedi Knight skills. And what I wanted to say would have surely been classified by Boris as belonging in the "Dumb" category. Though he wouldn't have thought *classified*. Or *category* for that matter. He would have simply thought, *Smash*.

So I said it anyway. And added, "If so, you suck at it. Hannibal is way cooler. And better looking."

He maintained his slanted smile, but his face reddened a shade or two.

Boris made no response. I guess I gave him too much credit. Or he agreed with me that Hecter was a sucky Hannibal.

The fat man laughed. "Such impudence from the little duck!" He beat his palm on the desk and laughed again.

I turned to see if I was about to get zapped by a Taser. The Suit had snuck out of the room. The evil orderlies might as well have had sheetrock for faces.

The fat man worked to regain his composure. He used a handkerchief to wipe his eyes and his forehead, then said, "Please, please sit down," and pointed to a heavy-looking leather wingback chair facing opposite him on the other side of the desk.

As I walked toward the chair and sat, he pressed a button on the right arm of his chair, and then a stick popped up. He maneuvered the joystick and glided around the desk. He was in a wheelchair. He moved up to me and said, "You'll forgive me for not standing," he waved his arms at the wheelchair. "It is a difficult proposition for me. I, am Aaron Lynch." His bushy eyebrows waggled and I noticed he was very expressive with mouth and eyebrows as he spoke.

Upon announcing his name, the goon, goon leader, and evil orderlies all bowed.

Seriously.

I did not hide my disgust.

The fat man, or Lynch, suddenly grabbed my jaw in his right hand across his body. He struck so fast and unexpectedly I didn't even have time to flinch. His grip was unbelievably strong.

I put my hands on his wrist to push his arm away, but Hecter swiftly struck both wrists with a metal cosh, right on top of the radius.

"*OWWGHT!*" Holy *crap* that hurt! Sharp pain shot up both arms to my shoulders. I jerked my arms back to my chest to protect them. My fingers numbed and didn't want to move. I couldn't tell if my wrists were broken.

Lynch continued to squeeze the sides of my face, putting tremendous pressure on my jaw. My cheeks pressed against my teeth and my lips pushed out. I tasted blood. His grip a vise. I tested moving my head, he only squeezed harder. Instinct told me to fight back, but I was powerless to do anything. I couldn't move my head, I couldn't feel my hands, and the only thing I could kick was the wheel of his chair.

He forced my head to the left and right, as if appraising me. "A fine specimen, little duck. A fine specimen indeed." He released me and rolled back behind his desk.

Hecter sat back in his chair. The orderlies had left. The Goon was smiling at me. I think he just got a joke he heard yesterday.

A person's normal reaction to pain is to rub the offended body part, but my fingers were still numb. Red knots grew on top of each wrist.

Pain—severe pain—had been a frequent companion of mine. That certainly didn't mean I sought its companionship, but with relationship came knowledge. Just like knowing how a friend will react to you.

I pushed back the throbbing in my wrists and face, focusing on each part individually at first, then mentally I grouped the separate pains, shoved them into a room in my mind and shut the door, fighting against it as a separate entity, a foreign substance in my body.

Allister had a cosh, a weighted lead ball at the end of a leather baton. He thought it was cool. Hecter could have easily cracked my skull if he'd hit my head instead. They were a popular weapon of choice for Nazi Germany Gestapo.

When in some years of your life pain is a daily, inevitable yet unwelcome visitor, you either learn to deal with it or you accept the suffering. I refuse to accept suffering.

This is, of course, nothing but a mind trick, a charlatan's bogus con to make pain go away. In truth, it doesn't leave. The pain is still there. The suffering is, at times, constant. But I'm not going to let myself believe that.

I forced my fingers to move, slowly tightening my hand to a fist, then releasing. I clenched my jaw and then opened slightly, sliding side to side.

I did not then rub my face. I did not want to give Lynch the satisfaction of knowing he hurt me.

Some people would say that's being passive aggressive. I prefer passive defiance.

Aggressive defiance would come later. I hoped.

Lynch's eyes looked upon me, appraising. I do not know how I scored, nor did I know the scoring system. I'm sure my cheeks were red. I could still taste blood in my mouth, but my tongue didn't find it on my lips. Good.

After a few moments of scrutiny, he nodded. Then he poured a brown liquid out of a crystal decanter into two crystal goblets. It looked like tea. He pushed one of the goblets across the desk to me.

I glanced at the offering and then ignored it.

He smiled and said, "Oh, come now, Mr. Raven." He took a sip from his goblet. "You act as if it is poison. If I wanted to kill you…" He opened a drawer and removed a gun, "I would simply…" He cocked the hammer, aimed for my head, "Shoot," and pulled the trigger.

Chapter Thirty-Two

I'm still alive.

I flinched hard enough to make the wingback chair stand on its back legs. The force of the bullet just over my right shoulder helped.

Lynch thought my reaction was funny, he was busy laughing.

I attempted to discover if I sat in a warm puddle, without actually using my hand to detect moisture. It's trickier than you might think.

Lynch finished laughing, then grasped the goblet nearest him, lifted in a toast and took another sip.

This time, I *did* try to hide my disgust because I had a sudden idea. If I could somehow win his favor, I might be extended certain privileges. With privileges might come opportunities, opportunities might lead to escape.

Again, without Jedi skills, or even a handy dandy lightsaber, I was no match for these people. Taking them on would be pure, unadulterated stupidity.

I didn't pretend that I could rescue everyone, however many kids that might be. But if I could get away, I could bring back help. Maybe Ray and Jenny were already doing that. Or, maybe they were trapped like me.

Maybe they were dead.

Only Boris stood. The rest of us sat. Hecter was over my right shoulder about ten feet away.

Lynch snapped his fingers, and then Hecter brought over a tray of food that had been on the table next to him, setting the tray on Lynch's desk. Lynch appeared to sniff at the items presented before him. I couldn't hear a sniffing noise, but his nostrils danced and his head bobbed slightly. He smiled.

Little cakes, crackers, scones, and tarts were displayed in arcs across the tray. There were four different spreads, each with its own elegant knife.

Lynch looked at me, seemed to make a decision about something and then nodded. He pointed at the tray with his right index finger and moved it around as if it were a divining rod. The finger settled on a scone. He nimbly plucked the treat with his fat fingers, then spread clotted cream with the flare of an artist. He placed the scone on a saucer and pushed it across the desk to me. "Enjoy, Mr. Raven. I'm sure you will find the scone delightful. You will be *rapt* with pleasure."

I looked at him and blinked. Psycho.

He prepared a scone for himself and ate the thing in three bites before I could take my first. And he didn't make a single crumb. He dabbed at his mouth with a velvet napkin that appeared out of nowhere, though there was nothing on his mouth. Neat freak psycho.

I took a bite of mine, smearing some of the cream on my upper lip, and watched two crumbs fall in my lap. My jaw still hurt, but I pushed through it. Lynch was right, it was really good. I don't know about the rapt pleasure part, but it was indeed delightful.

Lynch said, "You like?"

I nodded yes after a second bite, and felt another crumb brush my chin. Despite myself, I really enjoyed the scone and cream. I wondered if the cream contained some form of mood elevating drug.

Lynch smiled, pleased. He said, "This is but a simple pleasure, and yet, still a pleasure. But consider this: I can give you a *lasting* pleasure, one that will be constant, one that will remain, one that will not ebb." He looked at me, one eyebrow raised.

The scone no longer tasted good. I didn't know what Lynch was getting at, but I was *certain* I would not find it delightful.

He continued, "As in with the taste of this treat, you have had but just a taste of how I can make you feel. Do you recall how happy you were in your room? It was the greatest place on Earth, yes? Even though you were locked in a confined space, no windows, nothing to do, nothing to entertain you, monotony day in and day out. You *loved* it!"

Wait, *day* in and *day* out? "Um, how many days have I been here?"

Lynch once again found humor in my reaction. He reminded me of Santa Claus, but there was nothing jolly in the laugh. It was empty of mirth. Lifeless. "You have been here for five days, my new friend."

Five days! How could I have been there for five days? Five *days*. I sank back into the chair. Then the questions pounced: Why hadn't Ray and Jenny gotten me out of here? What happened to them? Or the rest of the Network?

I was hesitant to ask Lynch about them. But surely he had to know I wasn't the only one that came here. "Where are the two people that were with me?"

Lynch picked up a tart, it looked to be raspberry, sniffed, and then bit it in half. He chewed slowly with his eyes closed. He did the same with the other half. After a long time, five or six times longer than it would normally take to eat the tart, he inhaled deeply and exhaled. "Life is short, Elijah—may I call you Elijah? Things must be enjoyed while you are able to enjoy them. As you can see, I enjoy food." He waved his hands presenting his immense torso followed by another mirthless laugh.

"But food is not my sole enjoyment. No, no, *no*." He seemed to purr as he said the words slowly, lasciviously. "I take pleasure in slaves. In boys and girls, young men, women." He licked his lips. "And they take *pleasure* in me." He closed his eyes again and tilted his head back, reliving some sick memory. "*Yessss*."

The clotted cream rose in my throat, mixed with the bitter, acidic taste of bile.

He opened his eyes, returning to the present. "Yet, I believe I have not answered your question. Your friends: Ray Sanders and Jenny Meredith. They are here, do not worry. Unchanged. At least for now. I do not know what I'm going to do with Mr. Sanders. He is of no use to me. But Miss Meredith, I have great plans for her, magnificent plans. A delightful creature, yes, yes." He wiped his mouth with the velvet napkin.

I was at a loss for words. Rage, anger, shock, helplessness, fear, all fought to dominate my mind.

Lynched looked at the expression on my face and abruptly broke into laughter.

That gave me time to try and create order in my head. I needed information. I was only feeding Lynch what he wanted by asking questions. He owned the game, the chess board, and all of the pieces save one: me, a pawn. I had no choice. I had to play his game. "Where are we?"

He smiled. "We are in a private psychiatric hospital in the Upper Peninsula of Michigan."

I caught the shock too late, giving Lynch another opportunity to delight in my expression.

He said, "It is easy to move someone when they are heavily sedated. We transported you, and others, here in specially prepared moving vans. You were clueless. Just think of the experiments I can perform on you while under general anesthesia. I can probe, cut, make changes

132

in your brain, remove a kidney. I can amputate a leg. You have no control. You have no knowledge of what's happening to you. Nor do you have any… cares… *That* is the extreme power of mind manipulating medication. And that's just anesthesia.

"I can make you sleep for years. I can make you sad. I can make you jump for joy every time you see me. I can make you claw out your own eyes. I can make you kneel before me. I can make you *worship* me. I. Am. God."

Hecter and the Goon both bowed deeply.

Lynch gestured to both of them with a hand, as if I hadn't seen what just happened. He repeated, "I. Am. God."

They both bowed again.

I had never seen anything like this in real life. Movies could not accurately portray the pure creepiness of this scene. Nor could a movie do any justice in representing the pure wickedness that was Lynch. The man was a monstrous predator of complete corruption. And a megalomaniac to an infinite degree. He seemed to be too aware of the immediate reality to be insane, but maybe he was just highly capable of hiding his insanity.

Lynch held up a syringe. "And this is all I need. I can make you dream, fantasize. I can make those fantasies come true. Delightfully so with no hesitation, no inhibitions. I can remove your every care, your every concern. I can make all of your fears go away. Total bliss, Elijah. Total bliss. Heaven."

"That is not Heaven. *That* is Hell. No!"

Hecter stood.

I glanced at him, fearing another strike from the cosh. I tried to regain my composure.

Lynch waved Hecter back. "Now now, little duck, you can choose to be calm. Or I can calm you." He waited for me to relax, then said, "Good. Choice is a funny thing, is it not? I offer you a choice, yet regardless of your choice, I get what I want.

"Nevertheless, you should take advantage of your freedom to choose. These moments, will be going away soon. I want to talk to you while you still have the intellect to understand me. A pity, but this opportunity does not present itself to me as often as I would like."

"What do you mean?"

Lynch ignored me. "Back to your previous question, we are in a private psychiatric hospital used for testing emotional rehabilitation and drug therapy. We have tremendous success with children and early adults. There is a high demand, but we have sources for keeping a strong supply of test subjects, some of which are funded by your tax dollars. They are *always* happy. When, on the rare occasion, our methods are investigated, the patients talk about how happy they are. They have been programed with answers to all of the questions. We keep certain officials happy with treats. It is a wonderful scenario for *everyone* involved."

I said, "By treats, you mean the subjects—these kids and adults—are used as sex toys."

Lynch laughed. "That is *exactly* what I mean! It is a real life fantasy! Everyone is happy! And it is big business, oh yes." Lynch tapped his fingertips together, as if clapping with only his fingertips, smiling. "The income is reinvested into the program. You do not understand, this institution requires a substantial amount of capital."

"You are a monster." I spat the word monster. Special privileges be damned.

"Indeed," Lynch replied, still smiling. "I. Am. God."

The others bowed.

The way he kept saying the phrase like that and the reactions of Hecter and Goon had to be some sort of program. Monster wasn't a strong enough term for Lynch. I had seen a lot of evil in my life. Allister was downright demonic. But his capacity for evil paled in comparison to this monster. Lynch was Evil, capital *E*, on a grand scale. Allister was abusive, even a murderer, but as far as I knew, only malevolent to his family. A family flu.

Lynch was a plague.

I had no way of knowing how far reaching his infection spread. All of these test subjects, or kids, and probably even the adults, had been *altered.* They were no longer themselves, programmed to do whatever Lynch commanded.

Not just intrinsic aspects like losing their virginity, dignity, or control of their bodies. Although those things are huge, they did not make a person who he or she is. The very essence that makes them, *them,* had been taken away. The intimate elements that make us unique: thoughts, emotions, desires… free will.

The things that make us human, created in the image of the real God.

All stolen by Lynch.

He was right. He was a god with a forced following that literally worshipped him.

And I knew it.

"You're telling me all of this because you want to glory in your kingdom. How can you have full glory when no one knows about your conquests?"

"You are sharp, little duck. Yes, yes, go on, go on."

"You're telling me because you have no fear. That's what you meant by my freedom of choice, or more accurately, my freedom to *live*, going away soon." It hit me like another strike from the cosh. "You've disclosed everything to me only because you know my mind will be programmed to provide no resistance. I will be altered in such a way that I will have no acknowledgement of what was really going on. And I'll be *happy* about it."

Lynch sat straight and clapped. "Right you are! Bravo! Bravo!"

That's why the naked girl was smiling even though she had blood on her. She wasn't actually happy.

She was no longer human.

I felt sick.

Lynch ate another tart. "A treat?"

I swallowed bile.

Chapter Thirty-Three

Lynch said, "Surely you have more questions. You are a bright little duck. Intelligence begets curiosity." He gave me that expectant look again.

I stared at him. I wanted to pour on the hate and tell him how *disgusted* he made me. Though it would get me nowhere, and probably what he expected. He would find pleasure in my disgust, remembering my emotions during my pre-altered state, reveling later when I was "happy" while used as someone's treat.

I had no doubt this scene was being recorded. He would watch it *ad nauseam*.

Lynch still waited for me to talk, to ask questions.

I did need information, but I didn't see how I would ever be in a position to do anything about it. Regardless, I knew he would voluntarily tell me more. He couldn't help himself. He wanted glory.

The wait was brief.

"Really, little duck, this is more fun if you ask questions. But I am undeterred!" He looked at his watch. "Oh, how time flies... It is lunch!" He pressed a button on a raised panel.

One of the orderlies entered through the double French doors carrying a small leather portfolio and approached Lynch. He bowed and said, "Yes, His Grace?"

Winchester the cat also walked in behind the orderly. He jumped onto Lynch's desk and sat in a corner. He seemed uninterested in the food on the tray. Instead, staring at me.

Lynch stroked the cat, and after pondering a moment, said, "I believe I will have the special today." He looked at me. "Oh, what a delight!" Looking back to the orderly, he said, "Yes, excellent choice, I must say. The special."

The orderly bowed and left. Winchester remained.

Lynch said, "Where were we? Ah, yes. You were being a stubborn little duck. Not to worry. Your next question to me will be: how did you get here? I mentioned the moving vans. But of course, you mean how did you enter an office building in Detroit and end up in a psychiatric hospital in northern Michigan?"

I imagined Lynch frequently engaged in question/answer by himself.

"We really do operate in advertising there in Detroit. It itself is a lucrative business. But we also engage in much more enjoyable activities. Secretly. It would be difficult to attract the right clientele, and keep them anonymous, in hosting those activities in a hospital in the Upper Peninsula. Think of this as our training center. This is where the subjects learn to act, talk, and perform. The office... that is where they perform."

By *learn* he actually meant *program*.

"The office is set up for private sessions with clients. Advertising *and* activities. Very secretive. Everyone respects the privacy, the secretive nature, even those who are not involved with the activities. They, of course, know nothing of the scale. That is, everyone until you and your friends visited." He glowered at me for a brief moment.

He continued, "Next you will ask me, what I am going to do with you, and your friends? I have decided that you, and the lovely creature with you, will be used. You both will procure handsome fees. It will take time, of course. Programming adults is more difficult than children, and far more expensive. The black man will be kept alive, at least for now. I have not yet had the opportunity to test on an adult of his size. I have no other use for him. He will scare people."

Winchester continued to stare at me.

Another orderly entered the room pushing a cart with a familiar chrome lid covering a tray. A second orderly followed, also pushing a cart. The first wheeled the cart next to Lynch, the second next to me.

Winchester turned to see the orderly next to him, then looked back at me. That orderly lifted the lid and placed a tray of food in front of Lynch. It looked to be duck.

Lynch bobbed his head, sniffing, smiling appreciatively.

I've never had duck, but I've seen pictures. It's one of those things I want to try someday… Or, that is, if I'm not turned into an automaton.

The orderly next to me left the tray covered.

Lynch eyed me, then said, "You have no further questions. I have enjoyed our visit. I'd say, please come back again, but you will not be *you!*" Then, not exhibiting his normal neat freak etiquette, grabbed a duck leg and ripped it off the cooked duck. Tissue and juice flew in a miniature explosion from the torn carcass.

Winchester seemed undisturbed, still sitting in a corner on the desk.

Since I'd been at the hospital, at least while conscious, the scars on my left arm had burned slightly but constantly, an ever-present warning. Because it had been constant, I discounted the warning as an effect of this place.

When my scars burn, there is no intelligence to the burning. There's no psychic link instructing me, *Incoming baseball bat behind you!* It's just a general warning of potential danger. It makes me wary, but I have to figure out the source of the danger.

When entering Lynch's office, the burning intensified marginally, but again stayed constant. I thought it was Lynch's malign presence.

Lynch tore into the duck leg, growling, shaking his head side-to-side like a dog trying to break a rabbit's neck. Grease rolled down his chin along with bits of meat. The scene was a stark contrast to his gracefulness before. He glared at me, and yelled while feasting, "I'm going to eat you, little duck! Impudent little duck! *Eat you!*"

My scars flared.

I glanced to see who was behind me: no one.

Lynch threw the desecrated duck leg at my head.

I jerked to the side as the leg struck the chair to my left, leaving a greasy smear spot, then bounced to the floor.

My scars still burned, though I didn't think the thrown duck leg was a real danger.

Then the orderly swiftly lifted the lid off the tray on the cart next to me as I recoiled from the flying duck leg. I had time to see a syringe, but before I could react, it was in my shoulder.

Lynch shouted, "Eat you, little duck! You are *MINE!*"

I heard a soft voice in my head, as Winchester projected, *Elijah, do not take the pills.*

Then nothing.

136

Chapter Thirty-Four

I woke up in my room. Once again, I had no idea how long I had been there. Which, as I thought about it, was a good thing, because that meant I wasn't stoned, or reprogrammed.

I wasn't strapped to the bed either. Though not stoned, that fact did make me quite happy. Knowing my brain was scheduled to be turned into Windows 3.1, having the freedom to both think and move around was an immense relief, even if only mock freedom.

In other words, there was still hope.

Now, what to do about it?

One thing I knew, I'd been here long enough to need to go to the bathroom.

And, as before, the stupid door was locked. Why would the bathroom door be locked? Did they think I was going to drown myself in the toilet?

I sat on the bed and did my best Winnie the Pooh impersonation. *Think think think.* Pooh Bear was an uber genius compared to what I was to become. Then I did as much praying as I did thinking.

Even though much of the time I considered my gift a curse, I knew without doubt the gift was given for me to help people. This time, I hoped *people* was me.

I knew Winchester was my way out of here. Aha! Maybe he had a lightsaber.

Yeah, probably not.

The cat kept telling me to not take the pills. Not quite sure how I had much *choice* about that. Unless... there *was* a choice between the pills and the shots. Each time an evil orderly brought meds to me, they offered a choice between pills or syringe. It seemed too easy to try to *cheek* the pills. That's a trick you quickly learn in kids' homes where you push the pill to the side of your mouth, hiding it between cheek and gum. When requested to open your mouth to prove you've swallowed the pill, unsuspecting houseparents believe the pill to be in your tummy when they don't see it in your mouth or under your tongue.

The really careful ones would take a tongue suppressor and a flashlight and investigate the sides of your mouth.

But I had an additional talent for subterfuge. Well, if you call bone structure a talent. On the floor of my mouth where the tongue rests, there is a bump, or tiny shelf, of bone on each side just underneath the teeth. A dentist told me it's called torus mandibularis, or tori plural. It doesn't bother me except when the dentist puts those x-ray plates in my mouth. If I live long enough to get dentures, the bone will cause problems with denture fabrication.

The bone is large enough for me to hide a pill. While not especially rare, it is uncommon enough for even the most thorough youth care workers to not think about looking *under* the bone shelf under the tongue. Once I figured that out, I never again took a pill I didn't want.

What I believed Winchester was telling me, was to choose the pills, and fake it. The degree of difficulty is, um, slightly higher in faking the injection of a shot. Winchester couldn't have known about my ninja skills with hiding pills. Maybe he'd seen previous victims try to cheek the pills. Surely they were not successful.

Maybe he was just a deranged cat with a fetish about pill avoidance.

No, I had another theory, one that I believed to be truth. I think Winchester was simply a secret agent for relaying a message from a Creator Who knew me better than any other being in the universe.

I am thick-headed, stubborn, and dense. I am human.

The 'mobile' connection to my head had probably been ringing off the hook. That is, if said connection really ringed, and there was a hook for the line to be on or off... If I knew how to check the voicemail, there might be an important message.

Wouldn't that be cool? To get a voicemail from God?

Message one: "Hello, Elijah. This is God. Today you are going to be tempted to [insert vice here]. Don't."

Message two: "Hello, Elijah. This is God again. I heard what you said about the man who cut you off in traffic. His mother had nothing to do with that."

Okay, maybe not so great to get voicemail from God. But again, a loving Father would not be all about admonishing.

I believe God is constantly trying to communicate with us. We're just not in a mindset or mood to hear Him most of the time. The line is fuzzy because of interference on our end. Or many times we don't recognize His voice.

Animals don't have the problems with static that we do. They also don't have the intellect, which, of course, is why the line is crystal clear.

Why doesn't God just take the interference away so I have a crystal clear connection too? That whole free will thing. And that whole faith thing.

But of course, who am I kidding? I don't have the answer to this or things like why God allows bad things to happen to good people. Why did Chloe die? Why did Ben? Or Billy? Why was I abused? Why this? Why that?

I learned I would never be smart enough to know the answers.

The door opened and an orderly entered pushing a cart, followed by a second orderly, Taser held at the ready. A chrome lid covered some goody for me. I leaned so I could see around their feet and was relieved when Winchester came in as well. I'm not necessarily sure why I was relieved. Did I expect Winchester to really smuggle in a lightsaber for me? Or maybe he'd slice the jugular open on each orderly with his killer kitty claws.

He jumped onto the bed.

The first orderly lifted the lid, exposing a pill cup and a syringe. He waved a hand over them, waiting for me to choose.

I didn't know what kind of sick satisfaction Lynch got out of presenting a *choice* of administration.

Winchester said, *Don't take the pills.* He looked at me and winked. Or that may have been my imagination.

I pointed to the pills.

The orderly opened a drawer on the cart and handed me a miniature bottle of water.

I took the two white pills, pressed them into their hiding spots in my mouth and quickly took a drink of water, throwing my head back as if swallowing something difficult.

The pills were surrounded by skin-covered bone, so they were not in danger of being absorbed like nitrogen pills placed under the tongue. But I did not want to take a chance of them dissolving even a little. I didn't know if these pills were supposed to make me happy or sleep.

I opened my mouth before being asked, and the first orderly prodded in my mouth with a stick and a flashlight. He did not care about being gentle. He did not say anything, as usual—I wondered if the orderlies were moot—but he had a look of distaste. Either because he was a germaphobe like me and knew that mouths were demon spawn for germs, or because he much preferred to stab me with the syringe.

He probably told Lynch he was being stupid with the pills vs. shot thing. Lynch probably ripped the orderly's tongue out with his fat fingers.

Satisfied, he stood, turned the cart around and left with the second orderly.

Winchester stayed.

I retrieved the hidden pills and spit both to the floor. *Thwoop. Thwoop.*

I stepped on the pills, crushing them with my heel, and then kicked them to spread the powder.

Winchester said, *Excellent.*

I said, sarcastically, "I'm glad my actions meet your approval."

Child.

Oh, another thing about animals. Most of them love to insult me.

"Rodent licker."

Showing maturity I did not possess, Winchester ignored me. He said, *Shortly, they will bring you dinner and more medication. Too bad it will not be leg of rodent. Tonight, one of them will return, believing you to be asleep.*

I nodded to show Winchester I understood him.

He will give you a shot to force sleep. Tomorrow morning, another sleep shot and then they change you.

"How do you know this?"

I have seen it. Hundreds of times. Same routine each time. You have one chance tonight. Good luck. My time with you is over. He jumped off the bed and walked to the door.

I said, "What do you mean? Forever?"

The door opened and an orderly hurried in, only one this time, and opened the bathroom door. He pointed impatiently.

I imagined he was the Orderly of Bathrooms, running around to each room, unlocking the loo. I wondered how happy *he* was.

Winchester left the room.

Chapter Thirty-Five

As Winchester described, orderlies brought food—meatloaf, which could have been rodent—and medicine for dinner. I ninja skilled the pills and spit them out. Again I didn't know if they were supposed to make me happy or sleepy. I guessed the latter and feigned sleepiness.

Winchester did not accompany the orderlies.

The Orderly of Bathrooms did his thing so I could do mine, then I went to bed.

I had no way of accurately tracking time, but I knew I'd been in bed for quite a while. Despite the lengthy period of inactivity, I was too wired to sleep. From what Winchester described, I had one chance to get out of here. But I did not know how, when, or where I could take that chance.

My mind raced with possibilities. But with so much unknown, the only conclusion I came to was that I was nervous. Which helped me figure out nothing.

The door opened and adrenaline instantly replaced anxiety.

I lay on my side on top of the sheets facing the door. My light was off, but light from the hallway wandered in, casting a figure in silhouette. I expected to see a second figure, but only one appeared. It approached without hesitation, holding a syringe at the side.

Every adult I had seen in this place had been male. I hoped this one was also male. Not that I had a moral challenge hitting a woman who wanted to reprogram me.

I knew it was likely that most every adult working here had been programmed. They were not themselves. But I could not allow myself to follow that train of thought because then I would be unable to act when needed to secure my freedom. I had to act without compunction, leaving no room for regret. If I worried about, for example, whether evil orderly was programmed to give me sedatives, I would become the next evil orderly.

Or sex toy.

Besides, and maybe I was inaccurately passing moral judgment, but most—probably all—of the adults there deserved to die.

Anyway, the reason I hoped a male entered the room was because I planned to plant the top side of my foot as far into the man's groin as was anatomically possible, with extreme force. While a severe kick to that region would also be painful for a female, it would not be as debilitating an event as it would be for a male.

I needed to strike with enough force to not only debilitate, but drive the air out of the person so that he or she could not cry out. My leg had been resting in a ready position for so long I was afraid it might cramp. I did not want anyone to see me move to get into a position to kick.

The figure walked up to me and extended the arm holding the syringe.

I kicked. *Hard.*

I was rewarded with a male's breathless, "*Hoomf.*" He dropped the syringe and fell to the floor.

I had but only a few seconds to react before he recovered sufficiently for movement or voiced a cry for help, or before someone saw us.

I could see the syringe's needle glinting in the light from the hallway. I stabbed the man's upper arm and plunged the shot into him. "Take that."

He was either going to sleep for a long time, or be happy enough to ask me to kick him again.

I searched his pockets and found four more shots, some keys, a pack of cigarettes and a lighter, and gum. There wasn't enough light for me to see if the keys were labeled, but I got lucky with the third one, and unlocked the bathroom door.

Since the room door locked from the outside, I left it open and prayed no one would walk by.

I dragged the downed man to the bathroom and shut the door. The bathroom had no nightlight so the blackness was perfect. I felt for a wall switch and risked turning on the light.

Which stung.

The orderly snored on the floor with his mouth open. I had not seen him before. Since none of the orderlies ever talked, out of morbid curiosity, I angled his head to the light so I could see whether he had a tongue. He did.

He was about my same size, maybe a little shorter. I removed his clothes, which consisted of what you'd expect an orderly to wear: white shirt and pants, t-shirt, and tennis shoes. Thanks to my germophobia, I almost wigged out when I put on the t-shirt, but the t-shirt's absence could easily be noted because of the V-neck in the outer shirt. Anyone seeing me up close would recognize I obviously did not belong. But I hoped to only be seen from a distance, if at all. Even though I had not been provided underwear, I could not consider wearing this man's. I went commando.

The shoes were a tight fit, otherwise all was well… except for the slight body odor I detected on the shirt. Happy thoughts. Happy thoughts. Happy thoughts. I dampened my feather duster hair and did my best to paste it to my head.

I pocketed the shots, keys, and lighter, left the cancer sticks and gum, turned off the light and exited the bathroom.

Another figure waited for me in the gloom.

But, thank God, this one had four legs.

Winchester said, *Follow me.*

Chapter Thirty-Six

I said, "Where are Jenny and Ray?"

Winchester replied, *They are not here.*

I frowned. "Lynch said they were."

He lied to kill your hope.

On a previous occasion in which I briefly roamed the halls, escorted, I tried to memorize the layout. I was glad I had the feline guide, because I would certainly get lost in the maze of hallways filled with closed doors. Bright, shiny floors reflected the overhead fluorescent lighting. Hallway after hallway looked identical in crème colored walls. There were signs pointing to specific points in the hospital and room numbers by the doors, but they had no meaning for me. There were exit signs as well, though I was sure they would sound an alarm if opened.

Winchester seemed to know that as well, because he did not lead me to any of them as we hustled down the halls. Being faster than me, and far quieter than I would have been if I sprinted, the cat ran to the next intersection, waited for me to catch up, then led in the new direction.

Tyler led me through the culverts—what seemed ages ago—but hurriedly following Winchester down hallways in near silence in a seemingly vacant hospital had a definite dreamlike quality.

The place was dead. I didn't know if there was a fully staffed nightshift, or just a skeleton crew, but I only saw one person. He sat at a desk with his head buried in a magazine.

But then it only made sense. If everyone was drugged to sleep, the hospital would seem to be dead.

We ran down a descending hallway that ended in frosted glass double doors. This area was different than every other section we'd been in.

Winchester said, *Open the door.*

I complied.

We entered this new area and stepped onto plush, red carpeting. Mahogany covered the walls.

Behind us, the door automatically closed. There were no door handles, buttons, or any other method that I could see to open the doors from this side.

I whispered, "Is this where Lynch lives?"

Winchester said, *Yes. Now be quiet.*

Bossy, aristocratic, saving-my-life cat.

I was sure Lynch came and went as he pleased. So he had to have a separate entrance into the building. This exit was where I assumed Winchester was taking me.

Even though he was a cat, and by nature as silent as cottonwood seeds floating in the air, Winchester walked slowly, creeping down the hallway.

Even though I can be as dull as a cinder block, I registered Winchester's caution and engaged stealth mode.

We passed a door, and I could hear Lynch's unmistakable mirthless laugh.

I stopped and listened intently. If he was laughing, there was little doubt some atrocity was occurring.

Winchester said, *What are you doing? Come on.*

I gestured with my head toward the door. The laughing on the other side could easily be heard.

Winchester said, *Are you crazy? Come on.*

I looked at the doorknob. Maybe I *was* crazy, but I couldn't help it. I was compelled to act. To my surprise, my scars had not burned throughout this escapade, including when I kicked the orderly. I had not been in danger.

Now, as I stared at the doorknob, the burning flared.

I kept staring.

Winchester said, *Elijah, come on.*

Of my paranormal talents, telekinesis is not one of them. Though that would definitely be cool. No matter how long I stared at the doorknob, the door was not going to open on its own.

The door opened.

Chapter Thirty-Seven

A boy, brown hair, brown eyes, maybe ten, stood in front of me. He was wearing only girl's pink panties. His face was expressionless. His eyes empty. His nose bled. He made no attempt to leave the room, nor did he turn around. He didn't even wipe the blood from his nose. He just stared at me. A vacant stare devoid of emotion.

I looked over his head and into the room.

Lynch had stopped laughing. A look of shock on his face. He was naked. Folds of skin hung from his midsection. Despite being in a wheelchair earlier, he was standing just fine. In one hand he held a long stick with two tines at the end. Probably a cattle prod. In the other, what looked to be a wired remote, with the wire going to a black box on the floor.

Two girls, somewhere around ten as well, leaned on Lynch's legs. They were also unclothed.

Various sex toys that I cannot bring myself to describe littered the floor.

Wires from the black box were clipped to different spots on the girls. One girl was smiling, though she had tears running down her face. The other had her eyes closed. She seemed so lifeless she might have been dead.

Searing. Hot. Fury. Erupted from my core. My eyes blurred. My fingernails gouged the skin on my palms. The desire—no, *need*—for violence overwhelmed me. I felt little chips of something in my mouth and realized I was grinding my teeth. Forcefully.

I wanted to beat that man. Torture him.

Kill him.

He was unbelievably strong. It would not be easy. I didn't care. And that wouldn't matter when he was dead.

I nearly gave into the hate, let go of the restraint, and surrender to the clarion call of sweet, vengeful violence… but I felt sharp needles dig into my right calf. Startled, I looked down and saw Winchester looking up at me.

The freaking cat bit me! I wanted to kick it down the hallway.

Then I heard, *Elijah, Elijah, come back. Listen to me. The black box shocks the girls. It can electrocute them. If you attack him, he will kill the girls.*

I stopped. I looked at the box, looked at the remote in the monster's hand. The cat was right. One of the girls might already be dead.

I tried to regain some semblance of control.

Winchester bit me to keep me from jumping off the cliff into full-on ferocity. In an embarrassed moment of brief clarity, I wondered if Someone else instructed Winchester to bite. I didn't understand what rules God had for intervening. Or not. I never would.

I also wondered where the goons or orderlies, or *anyone* were. I had planned on getting out and getting help. As much as I wanted to be a one-man search, rescue—and destroy—team, I couldn't.

This seemed too easy, too convenient to find Lynch, unprotected by his entourage. Was I being set up?

Lynch's look of shock turned into a wanton smile. "Little duck. I thought you were scheduled to be the new you tomorrow. You must be eager. The good doctor moved you ahead of schedule. Would you like to join us? We're having *so* much fun! Aren't we girls?"

144

The one smiling said in a broken voice, "Yes, His Grace." The slumped girl did not move or make a sound.

"Join us, little duck."

The boy moved to the side so I could enter.

I walked into the room.

Lynch's smile spread. He dropped the cattle prod and rubbed his hand over his chest and midsection, licking his lips. He still held the remote to the shock box in the other hand.

I was furiously trying to figure out how I could get the remote out of his hand before he again hurt the girls. My eyes glanced around at the objects on the floor, at the smiling but unhappy girl, at the unmoving girl.

I prayed she wasn't already dead.

A sudden but complete sadness washed over me. All of the pain, the humiliation, those girls and the boy had endured that night. And other nights. Other girls. Other boys. Countless.

Why would a man like Lynch be allowed to live? All of the evil, the agony he created.

And all of the other people like Lynch in the world, or even half as bad, a tenth. Why were they alive, allowed to hurt people time and time again? I didn't understand. Why didn't they drop dead from a heart attack? Why were so many innocent lives allowed to be corrupted… or snuffed out?

Hitler was before my time. Even with all of the suffering I have endured, that I have helplessly watched others endure, I cannot come close to fathoming what the *millions* of victims of concentration camps endured. The families, the children. And so I cannot do justice in trying to describe what they must have felt. Millions.

But I could imagine, all of them crying out, even as they exhaled that final, dying breath, *Stop him!*

Make him stop. Save the innocent. Protect them, for they cannot protect themselves.

We witness child abuse. Some witness it frequently. But we don't really *see*. Open forced-close eyes and *SEE*. Get involved. Protect. Be a safe haven. Even if it means stepping out of your comfort zone, putting yourself at risk. For you are more capable of defending yourself than a helpless child. Sacrifice.

If you have children, you know what I am saying. You know you would do anything to protect them, sacrificing yourself to do so.

Abused children do not have you, that hero, willing to sacrifice, willing to protect them. They need *your* protection. Inform authorities. Let justice take its course. We all know justice is not always perfect. But at least it provides those kids a chance, something they don't have without you.

I slowly stepped up to Lynch.

He looked at the girls and licked his lips some more. "Little treats. Sweet little treats. Would you like one?"

I nodded and held my left hand for the remote. I did not know if he would release control so easily, but it was worth trying. I did not speak, fearing my voice would betray the calm demeanor I faked.

He said, "Oh no, little duck, this is my favorite toy. Maybe someday you can try it. Want to see what happens to the—"

I stabbed Lynch in the neck with a syringe I'd removed from my pocket as I walked toward him, angling my body to hide the movement. He dropped the remote, staggered, and fell to a knee. Because of his immense bulk, the tranquilizer was not having an immediate, debilitating effect.

The smiling girl scrambled backwards. The limp girl just slid to the floor.

He reached for the dropped remote next to him. I quickly pulled out another syringe and stabbed him in the back. The needle broke before I could press the plunger. He yelled but kept reaching for the remote. "Little duck, watch the girl! Watch the girl *fry!*"

He was in between me and the remote, and there was no way I could reach it before he could.

I kicked him the face, snapping his head back, expecting him to fall down. He did not. I felt bone break from the impact. Blood gushed out of his nose.

I saw a blur of grey peripherally.

Winchester gingerly picked up the remote in his mouth and moved out of Lynch's range.

I took out a third syringe and again stabbed him in the neck, giving him the full shot.

He fell to his side, breathing heavily, still awake, but no longer able to move with authority.

I said, "Thank you, Winchester."

Lynch rolled his eyes up to look at the traitorous cat.

I wanted to see if the limp girl was alive, but first I needed to deal with the shock box. I'd never seen anything like it before. Allister's level of sophistication for torture peaked at baseball bats. Other abusive homes I'd lived in were a little more sophisticated, graduating to curling irons, yet still too barbaric in their methods of cruelty.

The box was not plugged into an outlet, so it must have had internal batteries of some kind. There was a tiny LED readout and a few buttons on top. I crouched to get a better look. I was afraid to touch it, not wanting to inadvertently send electric current to the girls.

The boy surprised me by kneeling next to me. He carefully grabbed each wire connecting the box and the girls and disconnected them from the box by pulling them. He did the same to the remote wire. He had experience with this box.

He then walked over to each of the girls and took off the clamps. There were six attached to each girl. He dropped the collected clamps in front of me.

I crawled over to the limp girl. I felt for a pulse, but did not find one. I put my ear to her mouth, trying to feel and listen for breathing, however faint.

I felt nothing.

For a second.

Then I felt rage.

I stood and stared down at Lynch. My shoulders rose and fell as I breathed deeply, seething.

Somehow he was still awake. He smiled.

I kicked his teeth in. I didn't say anything. I just kicked. I saw the cattle prod on the floor. It would do nothing to him. I started to kick him again. I was going to kick and kick and kick until his head caved in. Getting kicked in the head to death was too good for this worthless trash!

I moved to get into a better striking position—

Winchester bit my leg again.

"*Arg!*"

I turned on the cat, wanting to make a quick target of him.

He sat unphased, staring at me. *No Elijah. Not like this.*

146

Not like this...

Don't be like Allister. Don't be… a demon.

Lynch groaned behind me.

I turned back around and gave him the last of the four syringes I had. I wanted to save that shot in case I met anyone else. But I wanted even more to make sure Lynch was completely out.

And, who was I kidding, I still wanted to cave in his head.

But I didn't.

I looked at Winchester. For the second time in just a few minutes I thanked the cat.

I gathered one set of girl clothes and showed them to the smiling girl. "Are these yours?" She nodded meekly.

I took them to her.

She was still smiling, and her eyes were still crying.

I didn't know what Lynch had given her, nor how long her face would be frozen in a forced smile. The pain in her facial muscles had to be intense. Yet I am sure she had endured worse. Much worse.

I led her to a connecting bathroom so she could dress in private.

I pulled a small blanket from a bed and covered the dead girl. I looked at the still form underneath… then I fell to the floor.

And sobbed.

The end of a finger was exposed from under the blanket. I pushed the fabric back enough for me to hold the still warm hand.

This girl wasn't my Chloe. Nor was she my daughter, of course. I'd never seen her before. I didn't even know her name.

None of that mattered.

She was an innocent life, dying in torture, dying in vain.

If maybe I'd arrived a few minutes earlier…

I felt my body shaking with my sobs. I pressed my forehead to the floor. I didn't wail, beat my chest in anguish, or anything like that. I just sobbed. Defeated.

I knew it would do no good to ask why. But I did anyway. Repeatedly.

It's human nature. We were born to ask why, to try to understand things we never can. When someone dies unexpectedly, we want to know why. We do autopsies and investigations. I'm not saying those things are wrong. They're necessary. But they're born from our desire to know why. We want to know cause of death, in part, because that helps us deal a little with the why, why did this person have to die?

I felt a small hand on my back, and even a smaller voice said, "Amber."

I turned to see the boy squatting next to me. His face showed no compassion, but his actions spoke volumes. He had dressed. He was barely touching my back and seemed ready to bolt at any sudden movement. The courage it must have taken to approach me, to speak, was amazing. He removed his hand.

I was shocked at the simple act of kindness.

I wiped my eyes and face with my shirt with one hand, still holding onto Amber with the other. "Her name is Amber?"

He nodded.

We sat in communal silence for a while.

147

I didn't want to let go of Amber's hand, but I knew I had to. I could not hold on forever. Somehow, my mind said none of this was real as long as I held her hand. I guessed Reason had had enough and wasn't coming out.

I said, "What's your name?"

He said, "Tommy," so softly I could barely hear him.

"You're brave, Tommy."

"So are you."

The smiling girl returned, still smiling, still in pain.

We both looked up at her. I said, "Hi." I felt foolish, but I didn't know what else to say.

She looked at me without saying anything, then looked at my hand holding Amber's. She sat on the floor, drawing her knees up to her chest and wrapping her arms around them.

I said, "Is there anything I can do ease the strain on your face?"

She shook her head.

Tommy said, gaining a little confidence with me, "It wears off after an hour or so. His Grace brought us in here forty minutes ago. Amber's face smiled too until she got shocked too much."

I glanced at Lynch. Then closed my eyes, forcing back the rage. Again.

More communal silence.

I was worried one of the orderlies or someone would find us, but my scars did not burn.

I said, "What's your name?"

Tommy said, "She doesn't like to talk. Her name is Holly."

"Hi Holly. My name is Elijah." She didn't respond in any way. I looked at both of them. "Why is no one else here?"

Tommy said, "His Grace has everyone put to sleep each night except for the ones he wants to play with. Tonight was our turn."

"Where are the orderlies, or guards, or doctors?"

"They are asleep also. His Grace doesn't want any adult seeing him play. He likes to chase us. We run in the hallway, acting like we can't get away, which we can't, and he chases us. You can enter this part of the building but you can't leave except through a special door."

"Everyone is asleep?"

"Four people go around giving everyone shots that makes them sleep, to make sure no one can see His Grace. Then they give themselves a shot."

I raised my eyebrows. "Wow."

"It's true," said Tommy, defensively.

"I believe you, don't worry."

Communal silence.

"How long are you going to hold Amber's hand?"

I sighed. "I don't know. I wish I could forever."

"God will take care of her now."

That surprised me. "You think so?"

He nodded.

"You believe that after living... here?"

Tommy looked at the floor. "I have to believe in something."

I nodded.

Yes, God would take care of her.

I looked at the blanket covering Amber. It was time. I squeezed her hand lightly, said, "Goodnight, Amber, God bless you," and let go.

She reached for me.

Chapter Thirty-Eight

I admit it: I jumped. I didn't scream like a little girl, but I sure as hell jumped.

I'm not a doctor, nor have I ever had any medical training whatsoever. But I would swear Amber was dead. Or as Dickens wrote of poor Marley, 'dead as a doornail.' No doubt in my mind.

After she reached for me, she went still again.

I glanced at both Tommy and Holly. They both sat wide-eyed, staring at Amber's hand. Her body was still covered by the blanket.

Tommy said, "Is she a zombie?"

I said, "Zombies aren't real. But something definitely weird just happened."

We waited a little while longer to see if anything else weird would happen. Amber did not move. I wondered if it was some sort of fluke, a muscle spasm caused by the electricity that may have still been in her body.

I don't know, besides not being a doctor, I'm also not an electrician.

We waited.

Nothing happened. Nothing still happened.

Amber moved.

This time Holly screamed like a little girl, which was excusable since she was a little girl. Though it seemed ironic since she had to scream through the frozen smile.

Tommy scrambled to his feet and jumped back. I imagined if a shotgun were available, he'd be putting holes in the blanket.

Amber was naked under the blanket. Dead or alive, I loathed moving the blanket. Even if dead, she suffered such devastating, humiliating atrocities during life, she deserved to be treated with excess dignity.

Then she sat up.

Tommy fell down.

Holly crab-crawled backward.

I said, "Amber?"

She rubbed her eyes. "What?"

I fetched the remaining set of clothes and handed them to her.

She tried to stand, but couldn't. She didn't seem to be in pain, her muscles just weren't cooperating. The spots on her skin where the clamps touched were red, and there were burn marks.

I helped her stand, and Holly helped her get dressed. I carried her to a chair and gently sat her down.

Tommy was still on the floor. I was afraid he might really be in shock, but after Amber sat in the chair, he got up.

I said, not really knowing what else to say, "Are you all right?" I was still dumbfounded.

She said, "Can I have some water?"

What just happened? I mean, really.

I felt like I was in some freaky dream. What *did* just happen was impossible. She was dead. Now she's asking for water, like she only woke up from a nap or something.

I looked at Tommy and Holly for help. I had no idea where there might be water, outside of the bathroom sink.

Tommy disappeared into an adjacent room and returned with a chilled bottle of water.

Amber said, "Who are you?"

"Elijah."

Tommy said, "He saved us."

Amber seemed to consider me a moment, then said, "I'm all right. I feel kinda weird."

I waited for her to elaborate. She didn't, so I pressed a little. "In what way."

She started talking slowly, then words seemed to get easier for her. "I don't know. I remember hurting, hurting really really bad, more than I've ever hurt before. I wanted to die. And then I didn't hurt any more. And then I heard this voice, a man's voice that seemed to be coming from everywhere all at once. I looked around but didn't see him. No man has ever been that nice to me. They always want to do bad things. He said, 'Your pain is over now. You're safe here, Amber.' I didn't know how he knew my name. But I wasn't scared. He said, 'I want you to grow up and help children.' I said, 'How can I? I tried to escape once. I got beat up so bad it hurt to move for a week.' He said, 'The man who is holding your hand.' I looked at my hands, no one was holding either one. But then I saw a picture of me on like this giant TV, only I'm guessing it was a TV because there wasn't a box around it, and I'm guessing it was me, there was a blanket on me. And another man was holding my hand. Then the man talking to me said, 'His name is Elijah. You can trust him. He will help you.' And then I woke up. And now I'm thirsty." She took a drink of water.

Holly stopped smiling. She rubbed her face, massaging her cheeks.

Tommy got her a bottle of water. And me.

I sat down in a chair. I still didn't know what happened. It was beyond my ability to comprehend.

Then Tommy said what I couldn't put into words, and he said it well enough. "God did something."

Chapter Thirty-Nine

In the morning, evil orderlies found us. Lynch was still out on the floor. I had covered his body with blankets. It took three. Not to save his dignity, but so that we did not have to see him. There was a lot of blood on the floor by his face. I turned his head so he wouldn't choke.

One of the evil orderlies gave Lynch two more tranquilizers. Turns out he wasn't really evil after all, but that he was programmed in such a way that he was controlled by Lynch. Almost like mind control that was set up in advance. Lynch couldn't really control them. But they were altered so that they had no choice but to follow the routine that Lynch had programmed into them. Including the doctor Lynch referenced.

They were also programmed so that they could not lift a hand against Lynch. It just wasn't possible.

But Lynch did not have a failsafe in the event he died or simply fell unconscious. Not just asleep. He evidently assumed nothing would ever happen to him.

Word got around fast that Lynch was out. Electrical charges to the doorknobs were turned off. Doors imprisoning children were opened.

The Suit ran off. So did Boris. And Hecter the Lecter wannabe.

One of the orderlies found a cellphone belonging to Lynch. He called the police, and also gave descriptions of the Suit, whose name was Leslie Hillock, and also Boris, and Hecter.

He handed me the phone so that I could call Uncle Joe, who then called Ray and gave him my location. I realized I never received a phone call from Uncle Joe on the cell I set up. I couldn't even remember having the phone. I must have dropped it at the truck stop where I bought it. I'm an idiot.

I spent the rest of the day playing with the kids. The hospital was an awesome place to play hide and seek, and chase. Chase without any abuse associated. Chase just for the pure fun of chase. I don't think I'd ever run as much as I did then.

But some kids still couldn't bring themselves to play. I couldn't blame them. It would take a long time for many of them to recover. Some years. Some never.

And none would ever forget.

The next day, even though Christmas had passed a few days earlier, Ray came dressed as Santa Claus carrying more toys and games than you can shake a stick at. So many in fact, he had to have several elves (from the Network, not the North Pole, shhh) help out. No one cared that Ray was a black Santa. His smile was better than the real Santa's anyway.

Those kids not scared of Tyler loved all over him. And he loved them back. That is, until he saw Winchester and the other cats. Man it was great to see that dog again.

It was going to be an adjustment for both of us, but it just wouldn't be right if Tyler lived anywhere else but with me. Mr. Brox—Nick, would want it no other way.

Jenny was one of the elves. She looked amazing in an elf costume. I admit, I teared up a little when I saw her. Though I didn't cry like a little girl.

She gave me Perceptive Smile #9, push-walked me over to a semiprivate spot and kissed me, as in really kissed me. You know, the mouth-to-mouth kind, and there wasn't any resuscitating going on.

There were times when I wondered if I'd ever see her again. And now she was kissing me.

She didn't carry toys, though. She had a bag of Cheetos.

The way to show true love for that special someone in your life is to *cook* him/her Cheetos and rescue them from being brainwashed in the Upper Peninsula of Michigan.

Life is good.

Ray walked up while Jenny was, um, resuscitating me. "Pardon me," he said with a huge smile, "Are you interested in helping us hunt down the rest of the board members?"

Tyler said, *I'm in.*

I looked around for him, not knowing he was anywhere in the vicinity at the moment, and saw him standing a few feet behind me.

He said, *Yeah, sorry, I wasn't staring or anything. I was just making sure she wasn't a vampire the way she was slobbering on you. I got your back.*

I couldn't help it, I laughed. Which, of course, drew weird looks from Ray and Jenny. I chilled and looked at Jenny for her answer.

She nodded.

Ray extended his hand to shake.

I grasped it, and tried not whimper when he squeezed.

Tyler padded over, stood on his hind legs and placed a paw on top of our handshake.

Jenny put her hand on top.

I said, smiling, "Looks like we're all in, Santa."

Ray gave me a side hug fierce enough to lift me off the floor. "Brother Elijah, come home to the family!"

After he put me back down and I made sure my collarbones weren't broken, I said, "How did you and Jenny escape the office building? What happened to those two girls?"

Ray favored me with a big smile. "A miracle in itself, my brother. We don't know how the girls initially got away. But in doing so, they triggered an alarm at the security desk in the lobby. Two of the guards were already in the elevator on the way up to the 40th floor. The doors opened as we entered the hallway. The guards were not accustomed to the scene. One took off his jacket and covered the naked girl. They quickly took us back down. We returned to get you, but you were gone. The advertising office has been shut down. But there was no link from there to here. We thought you were in Florida somewhere."

Lynch was carted off in a different wheelchair. There were enough witnesses to his crimes that he would never ever feel freedom again.

I still say he deserves the death penalty. But, I'm not going to be the executioner.

Some of the Network were going to stay behind and call in favors with people to come out and/or donate to help turn the hospital into a real facility for children. Safe. And loving.

By the way, what number defines more things than you can shake a stick at?

153

Acknowledgements

There are several people I need to thank for bringing ELIJAH to life:
Sheri, Megan, and Corban, for bearing with me for ten years along this journey. Dad, Terry Redman, and Sandi Redman for their wonderful support in life and the Kickstarter. The beta reader's group: Bobby Cross, Brett Norris, Daniella Ojo, Diana Roca, Dyana Clement, Garth Brown, Glen Mora, Joe Wright, Josie Siler, Lynn Rush, Merle Gornick, Richard Page, Sandi Redman, Sara Smolarek, and Steve Hardin. Jason Christian for creating an über cool website. Tom Nynas for an amazing book cover. Dave Curlee for an incredible book trailer. Connor Torealba for his phenomenal acting. Richard and Dina Page for their undying support and direction. Pedram Kazemi for his brotherhood and enormous support. Tosca Lee and Erin Healy for direction. Cindy Conger for awesome memes. Lynn Rush, Claude Bouchard, Luke Romyn, and Erin Healy for their wonderful endorsements. Dr. Karen Fink and my Tumor Team for creating a treatment plan that has extended my life. Dean Koontz for his mentorship. Uncle John Foreman and "Uncle" Michael Fogassey, Rich Levinson, Ken and Martha Nichols, Garth and Alya Brown, Jason Christian, and Greg Devoll for their significant contributions. Everyone who backed the Kickstarter. All of my family and friends: I thank God for you.

A Note from the Author

If you are one of the estimated 42,000,000 sex abuse survivors in the US today, please know you are not alone, you are not doomed to be a victim, and God's grace can help you overcome your past.

Please reach out to Darkness to Light. https://www.d2l.org/

Call the helpline 1-866-FOR-LIGHT or text LIGHT to 741741 to have questions answered or chat with a trained crisis counselor, 24/7 at no charge. All conversations are confidential.

I believe all parents and individuals working with children or youth should take the two-hour sex abuse awareness training, Stewards of Children. https://d2l.csod.com/client/d2l/default.aspx

The Story of This Novel

I started writing the suspense novel, ELIJAH, in 2012 after my mentor, Dean Koontz, instructed me to bury my first novel in an unmarked grave somewhere in Antarctica where even the penguins couldn't read it.

ELIJAH is about inspiring hope in readers, about heightening awareness of sexual abuse and child prostitution, while also encouraging a smile here and there.

My hope is that you will think about your real life experiences, how you can have happiness in spite of hardships, and about how you could help save a child.

As Elijah states early in the story, "Happiness is a choice, not a circumstance."

Along the journey of writing ELIJAH, I was diagnosed with gliomatosis cerebri, an incredibly rare form of terminal brain cancer, in April 2013. I was given one year to live "if lucky." Yet God has blessed me, and I'm still here. After a year-and-a-half off to deal with brain surgery, radiation, chemo, and steroid treatments—and the fear of whether I'd be able to write again—I returned and finished the journey. The whole time, Elijah was speaking to me in my mind, urging me to let his voice be heard. He got his wish.

Many years ago, my wife and I worked for four years at a children's home. We saw firsthand how abuse—sexual, physical, verbal, neglect—can devastate a child. We know some of those children today as adults. They have overcome their past. They have completed their journeys and started new ones.

This is for them.

More information about my cancer is on the Gliomatosis Cerebri page at
www.inspirepublishing.guru
or www.frankredman.com

Please Like: https://www.facebook.com/InspirePublishingLLC/
And: https://www.facebook.com/RedmanReaders/

Reviews are incredibly important for an author and make a tremendous impact on the success of a novel. Please take a few moments to leave a review. And please tell others about ELIJAH.

Thank you!

About the Author

Frank Redman lives in Texas with his wife, Sheri, daughter, Megan, son, Corban, three rescued attack cats, and a rescued black Labrador, Shadow, who's Tyler's nephew.

Shadow even has his own Facebook page: https://www.facebook.com/ShadowDawg/

Frank is a four-year survivor of terminal brain cancer.

FIC REDMAN
Redman, Frank.
Elijah : a novel

08/23/18

CPSIA information can be obtained
at www.ICGtesting.com
Printed in the USA
LVHW03s1910150718
583826LV00003B/512/P

9 780997 934304